THE DARKNESS YOU FEAR

Ghosts of the Lost Blue Bucket Mine

(A Virginia Reed Adventure)

by

Duncan McGeary

Dedication and Acknowledgements

Dedicated to my wife, Linda, who I met in writer's group and who has always understood my need to write. She has been my amused, bemused muse from the beginning.

Table of Contents

THE DARKNESS YOU FEAR

Ghosts of the Lost Blue Bucket Mine
(A Virginia Reed Adventure)

Foreword

Virginia Reed Gerard, New York City, 1921

The journey west over the Oregon Trail was especially hard on women and children, who were uprooted, often against their wishes, from all that was familiar and comfortable and taken across the continent to a "Promised Land" that was in reality a raw and uncompromising frontier.

The Meek Cutoff wagon train is now a distant memory. There are few pioneers left who can retrace their lost meanderings. I have not told this story before now because gold fever forever stalks the souls of men. But perhaps it is finally safe to speak of the Lost Blue Bucket Mine, for there is little chance it will ever be found again.

If any are tempted to search for it, let this story be a warning.

Chapter One

<u>Walla Walla, Oregon Territory, June 1851</u>

Dearest Frank,

The land here reminds me of home. Everywhere I look, I see our ranch and I think of you. The high peaks and ponderosa pines, the sandy soil, the lava outcroppings, the quick mountain streams, even the scent of the air is comforting. It is dry on this side of the mountains. But once you cross the Walla Walla River, it becomes the Great Desert, which is familiar, but—even after the joyful time I have spent with you—triggers memories of my family's ordeal. No one here recognizes me. I am forever grateful to you for the blessing of your name.

Mr. McKinley has been very helpful, far beyond my expectations. I should be able to finish soon and return to you. Keep me in your thoughts and prayers, dear husband, for what I have learned has been disturbing, much too disturbing to put down on paper. I can almost hear your concern and worry, but I assure you, I am being careful, as promised. I seek only information, not confrontation.

Your loving wife,

Virginia

Virginia folded the letter and slipped it into an envelope. Kyle McKinley's foreman was heading south across the Columbia River in the next day or two and had promised to make sure the letter made it onto the mail route running between Portland and Sacramento.

How easy it is to lie to those I love, Virginia thought. She didn't question the wisdom of it, but regretted the necessity. It was, after all, for her loved ones' own safety and peace of mind. She was the Canowiki, and with that honor came both powers and responsibilities. She could never completely explain this to Frank, and she didn't try to anymore. She just told him a story and did what she had to do.

He probably suspected the truth of her activities, but he also knew that he'd be unable to dissuade her from them, so he tacitly accepted her explanations.

McKinley would be coming to get her at any moment. The head of the Hudson Bay Company post was uncomfortable in Virginia's presence, and she wasn't exactly sure why. Possibly he was unused to being in the company of unaccompanied females her age; he probably presumed she was available. She had lied from the beginning, giving him her maiden name. She wasn't exactly sure why. On the spur of the moment, she had decided that when doing the business of the Canowiki, she would remain the infamous Virginia Reed, toughened survivor of the Donner Party, rather than Mrs. Frank Whitford, the apparently demure wife of a prosperous rancher.

In her darkest moments, she suspected herself of using her feminine wiles on the coarse old fur trapper. Other times, she told herself she was pretending to be unattached only because she didn't want the creatures she was hunting to learn of her new home and husband.

McKinley's discomfort hadn't been because of her reputation, at least not at first. She could tell the moment he realized who she was. One night at dinner, he faltered while telling the story of a group of trappers who had been caught in the mountains the previous winter.

"It is said that they hae a wee bit of the long pig," he said to the other men at the table, winking at them as if believing that only the men would understand this phrase. Then he had blanched and cast a glance toward Virginia, who was unable to hide her understanding.

Since that moment of recognition, the old trapper had been avoiding her.

McKinley had an Indian mistress, Virginia knew. She didn't judge. The West was a vast place, and lonely, and most men saw few women of their own class and culture. The old man had been at the Hudson Bay outpost for many years, and for much of that time was one of the few white men in the territory.

There was a polite knock at the door. "Miss Reed?" The voice carried a heavy Scottish brogue and sounded reluctant.

"Enter," Virginia called out. She set the letter on the corner of the table. Like everything in the room, and indeed in the outpost, it was constructed of raw wood. The outsides of the buildings still had bark covering their planks in many places, and no thought had been given to finishing any room or piece of furniture. The long table in the dining room was one giant tree trunk cut down the middle and only roughly planed. Virginia had learned to avoid splinters by wearing her shoes from the moment she woke up in the morning until she was safely in bed at night.

It was a place constructed by and for men, and she was a woman, a stranger, and an inconvenience.

McKinley entered, bowing slightly. He was making an effort to look presentable, wearing a formal coat and a beaver hat. Virginia smiled at the irony of it. Beaver pelts were the reason that McKinley and the Hudson Bay Company were in the far West in the first place. Top hats made from beaver pelts were all the fashion back East, though few Westerners bothered with them. How strange that a hat should make the long return journey to sit perched ridiculously on the shaggy head of a grizzled trapper.

"Mr. Boyd will be leaving for Portland after lunch," he said.

"The letter is on the corner of the desk," Virginia replied.

McKinley walked over, snatched the letter, and turned to go.

"Mr. McKinley?"

He turned back reluctantly.

"Are you going to provide me with an escort, or must I go by myself?"

He stood at the doorway as if he wanted to leave, and it was clear that every part of him wanted to deny her request for an escort. But the request wasn't unreasonable; he couldn't seem to find a cause to deny it.

"I'll accompany ye," he said. "I cannae spare any of my men."

It was a lie. The trappers were spending more and more time in the outpost these days, as the market for beaver pelts was beginning to fail. The prices had dropped so low that it wasn't worth provisioning an expedition into the mountains. Nor was it safe, not since…

"The Whitman Mission is still standing?" Virginia asked.

"Aye, there be a few heathen converts still faithful to the Whitmans' memory," McKinley said. "They keep the place up."

Virginia hid the exultation she was feeling. She had feared she'd have to mount an expedition into Indian-held lands, but if the Indians were already there, at the place of the tragedy, she could pull them aside and question them.

"If they are converts, then they aren't heathens," she said, keeping up the pretense of a woman so pious that she had traveled hundreds of miles to be sure her deceased relatives were laid to rest with appropriate gravesite services.

"I cannae understand what ye want, missy," McKinley said. "There is naught there but a shell of a house and some graves."

"I promised my mother," Virginia said, using the same story she had used to convince her husband of the need for this trip: that Narcissa Whitman was her mother's cousin, and that her family wanted to see that the poor murdered woman's grave was properly cared for. Thankfully, Virginia's mother and husband never talked to each other, so they wouldn't discover yet another lie. Nor did McKinley have any reason to doubt her.

"They were buried right and proper, ye needn't worry," McKinley groused. "I saw to it myself. Bishop Blanchet came and said all the proper words."

"Catholic?" Virginia asked. She frowned as if she didn't approve. "Nevertheless. I promised."

"If ye must," McKinley said reluctantly. "We best leave if we want to be back by nightfall."

"I'm ready," she said.

McKinley had a buckboard ready. Virginia swallowed her objections. Riding a horse would be quicker and would give her the added advantage of not having to sit next to the trapper and try to carry on a conversation. But she'd seen how McKinley had frowned when she'd arrived astride a mount, as if it were improper behavior for a young woman.

The road was little more than a dirt track, and the wagon's wheels bounced over the rocks and shrubs on either side. The fort was on a large plateau above the Walla Walla River, and the few settlers who hadn't packed up and left after the massacre were in the valley below.

Virginia and McKinley maintained a strained silence for most of the journey. Virginia was surprised when the trapper finally spoke as they reached the edge of a steep crisscrossing path down to the valley.

"I met your father once, before I came west," he said. "At his store in Springfield."

"Oh?" Virginia didn't know what to say. It seemed so unlikely. Yet, now that he spoke of it, she remembered that Hudson Bay had a prominent supply outpost on the Sangamon River.

"He is a good man," McKinley continued, haltingly. "I understand that your family survived the ordeal in the Sierra Nevada without…without extreme measures?"

Extreme measures? Virginia wanted to laugh, but knew it would seem inappropriate. The man had no idea what she had endured, but he was coming uncomfortably close to the real reason she had come to this desolate place. She had sworn to track down the unnatural creatures who had tormented them that winter. It was her duty as the Canowiki to put an end to them.

She had to give the trapper credit for boldness. Most people couldn't even bring up the subject of the Donner Party around her. "Indeed," she said. "We took care of each other."

"Good," McKinley said, relaxing slightly as if hearing the truth in her words. They went the rest of the way in a silence that was, for some reason, less strained than before.

What would he say if he really knew the truth? she wondered.

Though it had been less than four years since the massacre, the Whitman mission building sagged to one side. There was smoke coming out of the chimney, so it was clearly occupied. Several Indians dressed in white man's clothing emerged to watch them: three old men, an old woman, and one younger woman about Virginia's age, eighteen or so. Virginia's heart skipped a beat. For a moment, she thought she was looking at her friend, Feather.

For her part, the Indian girl seemed equally surprised. She stared at Virginia until she was nudged by the old woman. The girl turned her eyes away, blushing.

McKinley hopped off the wagon and tied the horse to a post, then came around and helped Virginia down. She was dressed in a properly somber black dress with white trimmings, demure and a little old-fashioned. Virginia couldn't wait to leave this place and put on her trousers, shirt, and slouch hat and ride the trails free of encumbrances.

"This way, missy," McKinley said, pointing to the back of the mission. "Unless you need to stop and rest?"

"Thank you, Mr. McKinley," she said. "You go on. I'll be with you in a moment."

He didn't stick around, embarrassed that she was turning toward the outhouse on the other side of the mission. As soon as he was out of sight, Virginia strode toward the Indian converts.

The young woman backed up, her fist pressed against her mouth, her eyes wide. Her older companions surrounded her protectively.

"You recognize who I am, don't you?" Virginia said.

"You are the Canowiki," the girl said. Her voice was a whisper.

One of the male elders spoke to the girl sharply in their language, and she answered, and in among the foreign words, Virginia heard "Canowiki." After what she presumed was the girl's explanation, the older Indians stiffened and began eyeing Virginia more seriously than before.

"My father was Miwok," the girl said. "He told us about you before he brought our family here."

Virginia couldn't believe her luck. Not only did at least some of these Indians speak English, but they also understood who and what she was.

"Who did this? Who killed all these people?" she asked.

"It was the Skinwalkers," the older Indian woman spoke up. "But we cannot say that, because they will not believe us, and because…because we are Christian now."

"Where do I find them?" Virginia demanded.

The old man glared at her. He spoke in his own language, and the girl translated. "Grandfather says you should be knowing of this. They live among you, not among our kind."

Virginia was taken aback. She had talked to everyone at the Hudson Bay outpost. There had been no hint of anything unnatural.

The old man continued speaking and waved at the Blue Mountains to the east of where they were standing.

"The Skinwalkers are in the mountains now," the girl translated. "Killing everything. We dare not leave the mission."

Virginia nodded. She looked the old man in the eyes. "They will soon kill no longer," she said.

"Miss Reed?" McKinley came back around the front of the mission. "Are ye all right?"

"I'm fine, Mr. McKinley," Virginia said, reaching out and clasping the Indian girl's hands. "I was just blessing these fine people for all they have done."

McKinley eyed the Indians doubtfully. "Fine, fine. But we do need to get back to the fort as soon as possible, so…" He motioned vaguely toward the graveyard.

***

They returned to the Hudson Bay outpost in even deeper silence than before. McKinley had watched as Virginia said prayers over the graves. The prayers were heartfelt, if perhaps not "proper," because she had no idea what she was doing. She had been a good Methodist before leaving Springfield, which meant saying her nightly prayers and going to church and going through the motions. But she hadn't been back to church since arriving in California.

The somber silence was appropriate, however. Thirteen people had died at the Whitman Mission, and others had been captured and held by the Cayuse. Some had not survived that ordeal.

The Indians were blamed, of course. When they were attacked, the tribes had retaliated, which only seemed to confirm their guilt.

But Virginia now knew better.

She left the outpost early the next morning, alone, over McKinley's strenuous objections. The old man had finally warmed up to her, apparently.

"Ye cannae go alone, missy," he said. "The Indians are still riled up."

"I'll be fine," she said. She wasn't trying to keep up her ladylike pretense any longer. She'd emerged from her quarters in trousers and boots, her blonde hair tied back under her slouch hat, wearing a long coat that fell to her knees. She'd resisted the urge to put on her sidearm as well, but kept it ready in one of her saddlebags.

McKinley watched her ride out the gate, his mouth open in surprise. She waved at him cheerily. As soon as she was out of sight, she turned toward the Blue Mountains.

There were three of them. They were drifting in and out of human form, drunk and naked one moment, hairy and snarling the next.

Good, Virginia thought, watching from the shadows. *Werewolves can't handle their liquor. Let them get good and drunk.* The creatures couldn't see her or smell her, as they would have any other human. She was the Canowiki.

The camp smelled of decayed flesh, and parts of animals big and small were strewn about the clearing. There was no campfire. The werewolves didn't need fire for warmth or protection.

Virginia should have been cold, and she should have been night blind, just as she should have been frightened. But she was none of these things. When she finally started a fire, it was not for warmth or vision, but as a weapon.

The branch she was holding in the fire flared. She threw it into the middle of the drunken trio. They rose up, snarling, unable to see her through the fire's sudden glare. She was among them before they knew it.

She fired her pistol, and it blew the largest creature's jaw off. He was twice as tall as her, and his long arms swiped out at her, his claws barely missing her. She dropped the expended weapon and charged him. She drove her bowie knife into his chest and shoved it upward into his heart.

He fell before the others could even react. Virginia's knife was wrenched out of her hands, stuck between two of his ribs.

Claws dug into her back, and she cried out despite herself. The cry seemed to give the creatures courage, for they howled in triumph and closed in on her.

She lunged through the gap between them, an opening so small that any other human would have missed it or been too slow to make it through before it closed. Then she was behind one of the monsters. She jumped onto his shoulders, put an arm across his throat, and began to squeeze.

The creature's thrashing kept his fellow werewolf from approaching. He heaved and twisted, but she held on and squeezed ever tighter until he stood unmoving, gurgling, and then toppled over. His head struck a rock and cracked open.

Virginia leaped off the body and whirled around just as the remaining monster rammed into her, his fangs cutting into her arm and shoulder. He was trying to get his jaws down on her, to inject her with his unnatural blood, to turn her into one of them.

She reached out for the still-burning branch and shoved it into the creature's huge red eyes, and he howled. As he exposed his neck, she grabbed the same rock that had cracked the other werewolf's skull and slammed it into the monster's throat. His throat crushed, the monster rolled away, turning human, his hands grasping at his neck as if to open a passage for air.

"You!" he gasped.

She recognized him: Peter Graves, who had been a young boy when the Donner Party was trapped. He'd not been a werewolf then, but had been turned in the meantime. No matter. He had slaughtered the Whitman missionaries and was as guilty as any.

Virginia stood over him until his thrashing slowed and his eyes dimmed.

After a time, she realized she was still holding the rock, which she looked at curiously, coming back to herself. She was suddenly immensely tired.

She was Virginia Reed Whitford again, not the Canowiki, and she could barely stand. She stumbled over to the first werewolf and grabbed the handle of her bowie knife. With both booted feet pressed against the creature's unmoving chest, she finally pulled the knife out.

She reached for her pistol and almost fell over.

Her horse was used to the smell of blood by now. He let her approach without shying away. She managed to get into the saddle. She rode back down into the valley. In the distance, she could see the lights of the mission.

Should I tell them? she wondered as she dismounted. She made a hasty camp and lay down to rest for the night. It would be another half a day's travel to the mission, and she wanted to go home.

She fell asleep still pondering the question.

Chapter Two

<u>Portland, Oregon Territory, July 1851</u>

Dearest Frank,

By the time you read this, I will be home, at your side. These thoughts and feelings will be a part of the past by then, but I want you to understand what is happening at this very moment.

You will discover that I was wounded while I was on this journey. I will try to hide it from you, but you've always been good at seeing through me. My only justification is that I have an obligation, as the Canowiki, to fight these creatures. It is not only revenge that motivates me. I must defend humanity from the monsters of the world or I am derelict in my duties.

I will not lie to you again. I thought perhaps I could keep these incidents to myself, but it is becoming harder and harder to hide my actions. I have no choice but to continue, wherever and whenever my road leads me, unless and until another Canowiki comes to take my place—and I fear that will only happen when I have been defeated. I should never have brought you into this, but I was weak.

Pray forgive me, dear husband.

Love,

Virginia

After finishing her letter to Frank, Virginia wrote a quick note to her parents in San Francisco to inform them that though she would be passing through the city on her way to Sacramento. She would not have time to visit them and that she would see them at Christmas.

Virginia sent the letters off with the steamship company; the same company on whose ship she was about to embark. The letters would probably sit in purser's office for days, if not weeks, if experience was any guide.

I am a coward, she thought. She should tell Frank about her adventures to his face, but she preferred to put it in writing, hoping, perhaps, he would read the letter before she returned. Hoping, perhaps, the letter would be lost. Hoping, perhaps, that by the time he read it, things would have changed.

She didn't deserve him. He was decent and forbearing, tolerant of her eccentricities. She tried to fit in with the other ranch wives, and sometimes she even succeeded in forgetting, for just one meal or for just one dance, who and what she was. Then the festivities would recede before her eyes, and she would see among the celebrants the husband who was planning to beat his wife that night for flirting, the wife who was stealing kisses with the foreman, the rancher who was stealing his neighbor's cattle and rebranding them.

None of it was her business, but she couldn't help but see it.

Her friend Feather had given her a name. The Indians called the possessor of these abilities a Canowiki.

Virginia had known she was different from the moment her family was caught in the snows of the Sierra Nevada with the Donner Party. She had protected her family and her friends from those who preyed on them. The Reed family had survived, and they had not resorted to "extreme measures." But Virginia never felt normal again after that ordeal. She was no longer just an ordinary young woman, no matter how she tried to be a dutiful wife and good neighbor.

She checked out of the hotel, the proprietor raising his eyebrows at her formal dress and stylish hat. She had arrived late the previous night, dusty from the trail, having sold her horse to the local stable for half of what it was worth. In the dim light of the front office, the clerk had called her "mister." She had laughed, taking off her hat and shaking loose her blonde hair. Instead of being embarrassed by his mistake, the clerk had frowned at her brazen behavior.

Now, as she walked through the streets, her saddlebags traded for a proper carpetbag, she sensed men watching her. There were few other women on the street, and men accompanied those few. She hadn't gone very far before she received her first offer to carry her bag. She smiled brightly and turned down the help. The bag was too heavy for most men to carry, filled with gold as well as her guns and ammunition.

Portland was a vibrant town; the bounty of the sea and of the wilderness lined its docks and streets. Virginia could hear shouts from the fish market, whose tables were overflowing with salmon. Raw lumber was piled in every vacant lot, and next to almost every vacant lot, a structure was under construction. The stumps of the trees from which the lumber had been harvested still lined the streets. Before she had left Illinois, she had heard this place was called Stumptown. Few people wanted to live here then, preferring the more civilized Oregon City.

Virginia looked at the forested hills, at the Willamette River, and thought that Portland would soon overtake Oregon City.

As she neared the steamship's gangplank, a dockworker all but wrenched the carpetbag from her hands, thinking to help her across the divide. The bag slammed to the ground with a clank, and the man backed away, wide-eyed.

"Thank you, sir," Virginia said, picking up her bag. "But I wish to carry my own things."

The man opened his mouth to say something, then looked around at the other dockworkers. "Sorry, miss," he muttered. "It slipped out of my hands."

She smiled brightly and walked up the plank and onto the deck. She stowed the carpetbag in her room, then went back up on deck to watch the ship's departure. It was starting to drizzle even though the skies were blue. Virginia had heard grumbling about the clouds and rain in Portland, but to her, it was a refreshing change.

As she watched the town recede into the mist, she felt a sudden longing to live there. How many times during that terrible winter in the snows had she wished they had stayed on the path to Oregon instead of taking the disastrous detours, the "shortcuts" that Lansford Hastings and Jim Bridger had promised, that had led them to the slaughter in the Sierra Nevada?

But if they had gone to Oregon, she never would have met Frank Whitcomb. She closed her eyes and imagined him standing next to her.

Virginia spent almost no time in her cabin that first night, instead wrapping a blanket around herself and sitting on one of the deck chairs. By the second night, men were once again approaching her, but now she was Mrs. Frank Whitcomb. She was wearing her large gold wedding ring, and she politely declined their company.

They arrived in San Francisco late on the third day.

To Virginia's surprise and delight, her parents were waiting for her on the dock.

"How did you know I was coming?" she exclaimed.

"Your letter arrived this morning," her father said smugly. "There is a new mail ship that is faster than any ship before. We weren't going to let you pass through San Francisco without seeing us."

"Of course I'm happy to see you," she said, feeling guilty. "It's just that I've neglected Frank for so long…I'm sure you understand. And I knew we would be seeing each other soon."

Her mother was staring at her dolefully. Virginia didn't know what to say, so she clasped her mother in an embrace. Margret Reed stiffened for a moment, then melted into her daughter's arms. Unlike Virginia's father, her mother had seen Virginia using her abilities, and though she had never said anything, she had been slightly uncomfortable around her daughter ever since then.

James Reed understood only that Virginia had shown remarkable courage and resilience in the face of adversity. Or so he pretended. But she'd seem him staring at her speculatively more than once. He too had seen the monsters. He must have suspected that for Virginia to have fought them off, it had taken more than mere courage.

Virginia stayed the night with her parents. James Reed had done well for himself. They lived in one of the new homes constructed on the hills above the wharf. He insisted on paying for the stagecoach and saw her off early the next morning.

He hugged her and whispered in her ear, "Be careful, daughter. You are not invincible."

"Hardly," she whispered back. "But I do what I must."

He held her at arm's length and stared into her eyes, and he must have seen the resoluteness there, for he shook his head ruefully. "I don't know why I worry about you. You're more capable than any of us, including me."

"Oh, Father, you're being silly."

He laughed. "Perhaps."

The stagecoach didn't stop when evening fell, and Virginia fell asleep to the back-and-forth swaying, waking only when she heard the drivers' shouts. They arrived at the station just as the sun was rising.

She wasn't surprised to find Frank waiting for her. Things were changing fast on the western edge of America. Gold was bringing money and people and industry, and transportation and communications were improving with every day. Soon the West would be settled, at least the parts on and closest to the coast. Soon the West would be indistinguishable from the East.

Virginia looked forward to that day, for she sensed that when the wilderness was gone, the creatures who infested the wilds would be gone as well.

She smiled at Frank, who looked away, frowning.

Oh, dear, she thought. *I never should have written that letter.*

Frank wasn't his usual easygoing self on the way back to the ranch. Even though they were sitting right next to each other on the buckboard, he didn't say anything beyond vague pleasantries until they reached home. But the second the door closed behind them, he confronted her.

"Why didn't you tell me?" he shouted. "You could have disappeared; you could've died. I would never have known what happened to you!"

Virginia stood near the door, frozen. She remained silent.

"What must you think of me?" Frank demanded. "That I can't help you? Have you no respect for me at all?"

She let him shout himself out. He could never stay angry for long. It simply wasn't his nature. He stomped about the room, and then, in the middle of his tirade, stopped abruptly and sat down on the divan, putting his head down into his hands. Virginia sat next to him, pulled one of his hands away, took hold of his chin, and turned his head toward her. He wouldn't look her in the eye at first. When he finally did, what she saw in his face wasn't anger, but fear.

Few men wanted to believe their women were emotionally stronger than them, though many might know it in their hearts. Fewer still wanted to believe the fairer sex to be mentally stronger than them, though a few of the smarter men might suspect it. But no man wanted to believe his wife to be physically stronger than him, to be better in a fight, to be the protector, not the one who needed protecting.

Virginia admired Frank for understanding that she was all these things and accepting it. But she didn't like to rub his nose in it.

"It is something I must do," she said softly. "You know this."

He nodded. He was staring at the opposite wall, but his eyes were unfocused, as if he was far away.

"I thought I could accept it," he said. "But I feel so useless…"

"Frank," she said. "Without you, I can't do any of it. *You* are my strength. I am merely the tool that God is using."

He took both of her hands in his. "Never again, you hear? Don't you dare leave without me. Wherever you go, I go with you."

"Who will take care of the ranch, Frank?" she said.

"You have gold," he said. "Don't deny it. I've seen it. We can hire caretakers."

Beneath the back shed, Virginia had buried enough gold to last them a lifetime, and she knew where to go to get enough to last a hundred lifetimes. After confronting the Ts'emekwes, she had returned to their cave. The giant creatures whom she had once feared she would have to fight to the death were gone. She hoped they had taken her advice and moved far away from civilization. She'd heard few reports of the Skoocooms since, and the giant ape-like creatures were quickly passing into legend. Perhaps, in time, they would be forgotten. She hoped so.

The cave was buried under a landslide, but because Virginia knew where to look, it hadn't taken much digging for her to uncover the cavern with its walls of solid gold. She didn't tell Frank, who was working hard—but happily—to keep the ranch.

"You don't love this land for the money it brings, Frank," she said. "You love it because it is your home; it is in your blood. It was the land your father cleared, that your mother and brothers lived on. I would never take you away from this."

He didn't answer, because he knew she was right. "We can hire a foreman, a crew," he insisted. "I don't have to be here every moment. I love the land, but I love you more."

"Perhaps we *could* do that," she said. *But you would never be happy.*

She stood up. "We can talk about it tomorrow. I need to sleep, dear husband. I've missed you. I want to hold you."

Virginia changed into the heavy flannel nightgown that she saved for the coldest nights. When the lights were out, Frank put his hand on her stomach questioningly. She raised the gown, and they made love, slowly at first, but then feverishly, and she felt the wounds in her back opening from the friction.

In the middle of the night, Virginia awoke, feeling moistness beneath her. She waited for hours for Frank to awaken. She pretended to be asleep when he finally got out of bed, and then waited until she heard the door slam before getting out of bed herself. The back of her gown and the bedding were drenched in blood. She took off the nightgown and quickly gathered up the bedding, took them into the laundry room, and hid them. She had told Frank in her letter that she was wounded, but telling and seeing were two different things.

She cleaned herself up as best she could. She was already healing. She was the Canowiki.

Frank would want to make love to her again that night, but she would coax him to being gentler, and the threat would pass.

He must never believe I am truly in danger, she thought.

Virginia was cooking eggs and bacon when Frank returned from milking the cows. He was his usual cheerful self. Neither mentioned the drama of the previous day.

"By the way," he said after breakfast, "there's a letter for you in the study. It's from Oregon City."

"Oregon City? Who's it from?"

"Someone named Mary. I couldn't make out the last name."

Mary? Virginia wondered. The name sounded vaguely familiar. She closed her eyes and tried to remember where she had heard it before. *Mary…of the green eyes and freckles?*

"Could it be Mary Perkins?" she asked as he began to hand the letter to her.

He squinted at the return address. "I think that might be it. Who's Mary Perkins?"

She sat down at the table and Frank sat across from her, as if sensing there was a story in the offing.

"I don't know if I've told you this," she said. "My father took me on a trip to Independence in the spring of 1845."

Frank immediately interrupted. "1845? Didn't you cross over in 1846?"

Virginia frowned at him, making it clear that she didn't want to be interrupted.

He smiled at her. "So you would have been thirteen years old?"

"It was supposed to be a business trip, but in hindsight, it is clear that my father was investigating the possibility of joining the exodus," she continued. "He'd promised my mother that we would stay in Springfield, but that couldn't stop him from wanting to see what was happening.

"When he asked me to join him, I was as happy as I've ever been. It might have been the last carefree spring of my life. It was the first time since my early years that I had time alone with Father: two weeks without chores, and without competition from my brothers and sisters. I loved every minute of it.

"Independence was a magical place. London, or Paris, or New York wouldn't have been more exciting to me—though now that I look back, it was no more than a dusty pioneer town. My father left me alone while he conducted his business. We were perhaps a little bit small-town naïve, but nothing untoward happened to me.

"Perhaps because I was alone so much of the time, everything looked big and prosperous. Those who were getting ready to set out West were eager, and it was impossible not to pick up that feeling of excitement in the air. I wandered about the shops. They were so much bigger than our store back home, and they were always crowded.

"It was in one such store that I met Mary." She fell silent, and Frank waited patiently for her to continue.

"I saw her slip an apple into the folds of her dress. I didn't say anything, just watched out of the corner of my eye. I noticed that the storekeeper had seen what she'd done and was waiting for her to leave before pouncing on her.

"I walked over to her. 'You'd rather have an apple than candy?' I asked. She was a red-haired girl with pale skin, but if possible, she paled even more at my words. I remember the freckles on her nose standing out against the whiteness.

"I said, 'Let me buy it for you, dear cousin.' Without waiting for a response, I picked up another apple and paid for both. As we walked out, I bit into the apple, and it was soft inside. I spit it out.

"'I hear that Oregon has the best apples in the world,'" Mary said. She was walking by my side. She was taller than me by about six inches, and I guessed her to be about seventeen. Over the next ten days, I grew to believe she was the most worldly person I'd ever met, though I know now that she was probably only a scared girl trying to act confident.

"Mary lifted her chin. 'I am not a thief,' she declared. 'I was just so hungry. I would have paid him back, I swear.'

"It turned out that Mary's father was a teamster who was joining one of the wagon trains. Mary herself was planning to be a stowaway.

"'I'm supposed to go back to Mother,' she said. 'But I won't do it. If Father won't take me, I'll go with someone else.'"

"That night, the two of us ended up sitting on the bluffs above the Mississippi. The lights of the campgrounds lit up the sky on both sides of the river, and there were more lights blinking on the boats passing by, and off in the distance was the glow of the fires from the wagon trains that were only a day into their journey. It was as if the heavens had descended onto the Earth.

"We spoke of what we'd find out West, and for some reason, Mary focused on the vast apple orchards she was sure would be there. 'The weather is perfect for the fruit,' she said, as if enamored.

"It was so exciting, and even Mary's rebellion seemed to be part of that excitement. I realized later that my friend was hinting, asking if I could somehow hide her away. But I was too naïve then to pick up on the allusions. Only days later, well onto the trail, did I awaken in the middle of the night and realize that Mary—in spite of her spirited nature—had been desperate not to be left behind."

Virginia stared down at the worn letter. It looked as if it had been bent a hundred times, it had strange brown stains on it, and the paper was yellowed. Across the top, the word "Lost" was handwritten in pencil. There was also a date: "1849."

She felt a tingling premonition.

I don't have to open it. Whatever news it contains will be two years out of date. There is probably nothing I can do.

But her hand went the flap without volition, and she opened the letter. There were several thin pages of cramped writing, some of which was blurred by water stains. Before reading the text of the letter, Virginia's eyes scrolled down to the signature.

Mary Perkins.

She gazed down at the soiled letter, suddenly certain that her friend was equally battered and soiled and that whatever the letter contained, it was not good news.

It was a cloudy day, and Virginia squinted at the cramped writing. She got up, lit a lamp, sat back down and spread the sheets of paper on the table.

Taking a deep breath, she started reading.

Chapter Three

<u>Oregon City, Oregon Territory, September 23, 1849</u>

Dear Virginia,

I don't know if you will remember me. I must be a dim memory by now, after all you have gone through. I was so frightened for you when I learned of what happened. I wished I could sprout wings and fly to you. As bad as things have been for me, I cannot but imagine what you went through. If I could have taken your place, I would have…though perhaps that would not have been for the best, for while your ordeal is over, mine continues.

I remember you well, Virginia, for you were kind to me, befriending me when I was alone, making me laugh, giving me hope that there was a life beyond the misery that I was feeling.

I didn't tell you everything. You were so happy and innocent in Independence that I didn't wish to darken your thoughts. My father intended to leave me behind with my mother, but I had no intention of staying. My father is a strict man, and his way of admonishing me was often rough. But my mother…I will not tell you about her, save to say that she was a monster. I would rather have died than stay behind with her.

When I slipped into the back of a wagon, I expected to die on the trail. I didn't know who owned the wagon; I had no money, no food, only the clothes on my back. I would offer to work, to be a slave if need be, as long as someone along the trail took me in.

This was a week after you went back to Springfield. It was a miserable time. I was alone. My father didn't speak to me before he left, sensing, I suppose, that I intended to disobey him. He departed without a goodbye.

So I was abandoned there, and I had to steal my food and find shelter wherever I could find it. When I saw the open flap of a wagon, I climbed in on an impulse. I covered myself with sacks of flour. Their weight upon me, and being hidden away, was somehow comforting, and I fell asleep.

I awoke to the sounds of the muleskinners shouting out to the beasts pulling the wagon and a lurch as the wheels were released. The four sacks of flour tumbled off me, and a box from above landed on my head, cutting my scalp, making me bleed all over my soiled dress.

I managed to stay out of sight for three days, long enough, I hoped, that they would not try to send me back. Fortunately, the family whose wagon I invaded were so excited to be underway that they spent most of their time outside, walking beside the wagon, venturing inside only to get supplies for meals. They were predictable in their routines, and I succeeded in keeping out of their way.

I felt guilty about stealing the family's food, but I had chosen what seemed to be the most prosperous of the wagons lined up to leave that day. I hoped that I was not putting them in jeopardy. Soon I would leave the safety of the flour bags and venture out alone, and I resolved to steal only from those who could afford the loss.

It was thirst that finally compelled me to come out of hiding. I had found an open bottle of milk in the wagon that one of the family members had forgotten, and that was enough for a day or two, but by the third evening, I could think of nothing but my thirst. My mouth was so dry it seemed to be swelling, my tongue was like sandpaper, and my teeth felt as if they were cutting into my cheeks. I couldn't stand it any longer.

I crawled out of the wagon. I suppose I intended to remain a ghost, to trail the wagons from a distance and sneak up at night to steal enough food to survive—no more than that, for while I am many things, and I have done far worse things since, at that time I was not yet a thief in my mind.

I poked my head out from under the wagon's back flap. The family's campfire was near the front of the wagon, and while I could see a few yards in the flickering light, I doubted that anyone could see me once I was away from that small, dim circle.

As I crawled out, I met the wide brown eyes of a child, age seven or so. She stared at me as if I was a monster from the deep and ran screaming to her mother and father. My legs didn't want to cooperate with my panic, and I stumbled upon hitting the ground and managed only a few steps before Augustus Catledge came around the back, gun in hand.

"Hold it right there, young woman," he said.

I froze, for there was no mistaking the menace in his tone.

"Please, sir, I mean you no harm," I said.

"Have you been hiding in the back of our wagon?" he asked.

"I have only taken a small portion of food, sir. Let me go and I will bother you no longer."

"A small portion?" he muttered. He lowered his gun and shook his head. "I can believe that."

I couldn't look him in the eye, but stared at the ground in shame. I could sense him examining me and raised my head. I was ashamed, but I still had some of my pride in those days. I have only done what I need to do to survive.

He looked me up and down, and his stern expression began to soften. "Come with me, young lady."

I looked out into the darkness. Even as weak as I was, I could have escaped. I could have hidden so they never found me. But what then? Wait until the next wagon train passed and hope that I could somehow attach myself to it? I looked down. My dress was torn and soiled. I put my hand to my head and felt matted blood and tangled hair. I must have looked a horror.

There was something in Mr. Catledge's face that reassured me, for to my own astonishment, I followed him.

The campfire was between three wagons, which were in a rough circle. Three families were congregated there, and it was these people who held my fate in their hands.

Abigail Catledge met her husband with a worried look on her face, not seeing me at first. She hugged him in relief, her head barely reaching his chest. She was short and round, while he was tall and lanky. He must have been older than his wife by a decade or more, for his face was lined and craggy, and her face was round and smooth. She looked even younger than she was.

Their young daughter, Becky, was a combination of the two: tall for her age, and also plump. She possessed her father's serious demeanor along with her mother's sweet nature. Of all the people who could have discovered me, I could not have found anyone nicer and more sympathetic to my plight. She was fourteen, and sometimes acted the child and sometimes the young woman.

They were, perhaps, too nice for their own good.

Abigail finally noticed me, and her eyes widened. "Who's this?" she asked.

"We've a stowaway," Gus answered. "A starving sparrow."

Abigail motioned to the log she'd been sitting on near the fire. I could smell the beans cooking over the flames, and despite how thirsty I was, my mouth watered. The moisture was sopped up by the dryness in my mouth, and I started to choke.

"Quickly, husband," Abigail exclaimed. "She needs water."

Gus walked in long strides to the water barrel strapped to the side of the wagon and brought a dipper to me.

There has never been anything before or since that tasted as wonderful as that water. I closed my eyes, and tears sprouted underneath my eyelids and squeezed out, dripping down my cheeks.

"Sit, girl," Abigail said, taking me gently by the arm.

Dizzy, I sat there for a moment, sensing that I was surrounded. I opened my eyes to see everyone staring at me.

To my right was the Parsons family, Bartholomew and Karrie, a young couple with two children, as well as Karrie's elderly mother. They looked disapproving, but eventually accepted me, especially eleven-year-old Cager and ten-year-old Allie, who were soon to fall under my supervision.

To my left was Jonathan Meredith and his poor wife, Ellen, and their brood of children. Jed was oldest, at fifteen, and thirteen-year-old Edwin did everything his brother told him to. Sitting on the ground was a young girl who looked a hundred years old. A blanket hid her legs, and I later learned that she was crippled, her legs not growing like the rest of her body. Sarah could move around on crutches, but she needed help for most things. The Merediths had two younger, healthy girls too, Mattie and Nan, eight and six years old, respectively.

By now, Virginia, you must be wondering why I am telling you all this. Why is it necessary that you know about these people? What is the purpose of this letter?

I ask that you bear with me, for all these people are important to my story, and they are the reason I am writing you. For it was what happened to these children, and my suspicions of who did it and why, that compels me to write you.

I will not linger on what happened over the next few months. Suffice to say that because of the Catledges, I was accepted among the pioneers and given the duty of watching over the children. Abigail gave me a castoff dress, which draped about me like a tent and only reached my shins, to wear until my own dress was cleaned and mended.

The Parsons family accepted me readily enough, happy not to have to watch their children every second. Jonathan Meredith accepted me only begrudgingly (I do not know what Ellen thought, and it doesn't matter, since Mr. Meredith decided everything), but he soon realized that he benefited most of all, for his children were my main duty, and he was free to do as he pleased.

So now I come to the events that necessitated this letter.

The trip was long and arduous, which I needn't tell you, and things happened that even today I'm loath to talk about. You will learn of these things if you come here to Oregon City, for they are detailed in the journals of which I have come into possession.

Our situations were similar, Virginia, though your ordeal in the mountains was far worse than anything I experienced.

Nevertheless, we were both led astray by frauds and suffered because of it.

Stephen Meek, the brother of the famous mountain man Joe Meek, led our wagon train. He assured us that we could take a shortcut across the High Desert of Eastern Oregon and avoid the Blue Mountains.

Over a thousand souls followed this benighted man into the desert, and many lost their lives.

Our own group, at the insistence of Jonathan Meredith, split off from the main party and became even more lost.

One day, as we camped beside a small creek, the children wandered away. For once, I was not with them. Perhaps if I had been doing my duty, none of this would have happened. Perhaps I would have known to hide my discovery, and all the tragedy that followed could have been avoided.

But on that day, Abigail was feeling poorly, and I felt it more important to take care of her than the children, who by then were accustomed to the trail and knew what to do and what not to do. Or so I thought.

"Be careful," was all I said to them. "Don't wander far."

They took the blue buckets from the backs of all three wagons, for it was our habit to fill them whenever possible with dry twigs and moss so that the fires would be easier to start in the evenings.

Mr. Catledge and Mr. Parsons insisted on traveling north in hopes of finding the main party, while Mr. Meredith insisted on pressing on westward. For once, Jonathan Meredith was overruled, probably because Gus was worried about Abigail and Bart by then loathed Meredith. (By then, we all knew how he treated his family, and we couldn't wait for the journey to end and to be away from that awful man. I will not speak of my experience with him, for I have tried hard to forget it. Little did I know, until I received Ellen's journals, how bad it really was for the others.)

The children were gone longer than they should have been, and after they returned, when I had time to think about it, I realized they were more subdued than normal. Even as desperate as things were, the children always seemed in high spirits.

They had put shiny rocks into the buckets instead of dry tinder, and I almost mentioned my dismay, then simply shook my head in exasperation and began to dump the rocks out.

"Please, Miss Mary, can't we keep them?" Becky pleaded.

I looked around, snatched one of the empty flour bags out of the back of the Meredith wagon, and poured the rocks into it. Ellen and Jonathan Meredith came around the corner of the wagon at that moment. Jonathan frowned. He turned to his wife. "Won't you be needing that cloth?" he asked.

"We are almost to Oregon City," Ellen said. "If we need it, we will dump out the rocks then."

"To what purpose?" he asked. He reached over, picked up one of the rocks, and examined it curiously. His face didn't betray a thing. "Still, I don't suppose it will hurt anything. The wagon is nearly empty, and old Clyde and Peter can pull a little extra weight a few extra miles." Clyde and Peter were the Merediths' poor, abused mules.

It was only a few days later that tragedy struck.

We woke up on a cold morning. Fall was approaching, and we were almost to our destination. As lost as we were, we were still many miles farther west, closer to our goal. We were hopeful.

And then all our hopes were dashed. The Parsons family usually woke up later than the rest of us, so we were already eating breakfast when their children were discovered missing.

Allie and Cager were always the noisiest of my rabble. I never worried about them the way I worried about the quieter Meredith children or brave, adventurous Becky.

We searched for days. We never found any sign of them.

I was blamed, though it was not my fault. If it had been my fault, I couldn't have borne the burden. The children left in the middle of the night when the adults were asleep. In the nighttime, the children were their parents' responsibility. Yet somehow, I was blamed for their disappearance.

And I accepted the censure, because I felt the children were my responsibility. I did not try to defend myself.

When we finally reached Oregon City, even the dear Catledges abandoned me. I was left as I began, without any resources to my name. I have survived, but I am too ashamed to speak here of how I did so.

My burden is not the reason for this letter. If there is one good thing I have done in my life, it was to care for those children: dear Becky, precious Allie and Cager, little Nan and Mattie, and even Jed and Edwin, as mischievous as they often were.

Further tragedy struck when we reached Oregon City. The two Meredith daughters, Nan and Mattie, died of typhoid fever. Within a few months, Ellen Meredith, who had survived the long trip to Oregon City, was also gone. She too died of a disease, it was said. Jed and Edwin disappeared, no doubt eager to be away from home now that their mother was gone. Jed was an adult by then, and Edwin nearly so.

Not long after, I found a package on my doorstep. To this day, I don't know who delivered it. I opened it up and found Ellen Meredith's journals. I had often seen her writing in them and wondered what she was saying.

When I started to read them, my memories of the journey west returned, but now they were colored by new information. It is the contents of these journals that made me write you.

You are the most capable person I know, Virginia. I have heard stories of how you survived the Donner Party. People speak of you in awe, and I have often nodded and said, "Yes, I know Virginia Reed. She is every bit as brave and resourceful as you have heard."

I have nowhere else to turn, dear Virginia. I am hoping you will come to Oregon City and read the journals and tell me what to do.

It is a lot to ask, I know. If you can't do it, please write back and tell me so, and I will find another way. For something must be done. There is still one witness to the events on the Oregon Trail, and she is the most precious of all people to me: Becky Catledge, who is growing into a beautiful young woman.

Virginia, there is one more thing I must tell you, which you may have already guessed. When I heard about the discovery of gold in California, I had a sudden suspicion. Before leaving the wagon train for the last time, I had grabbed, as a keepsake, one of the shiny rocks the children picked up while we were lost.

I took it to an assayer, and my suspicions were confirmed. It was pure gold.

It all seems amazing to me now that we didn't know. But none of us had ever heard of gold in the West. It was not even conceivable in the summer of 1845. All we had seen was white quartz with shiny streaks in it.

I have lived off that gold nugget for the last few months, and it has bought the paper and pen and postage with which I now communicate with you. But the money will run out soon.

I have heard that Jonathan Meredith is looking for me. I have changed my name and gone into hiding. If you decide to find me, I have left a message at this address:

Please let me know if you can come. If not, I understand. This is not your problem, dear Virginia, and the situation may well be dangerous. But I have nowhere else to turn.

Yours truly,
Mary Perkins

Chapter Four

Oregon Territory, July 4, 1851

I can only guess what day it is. That is an irony, for on this day I will be free of my pain at last. I will be free of all thought and all worry.

I write this in the last light of the dying fire. I have no more wood, no more matches. Soon the ghosts will come for me, and I will no doubt join them, to become as aggrieved as they are, for I sense that they too were taken unfairly.

Let this serve as my Last Will and Testament, though I have nothing to leave but this diary, scribbled in the dark. I am writing this last message at the front of my small book. What follows is my account before my fall, leading to this last day. Be warned.

***

June 28, 1851

"You can take off your blindfolds now." Our employer's voice was loud, as if he thought that in our blindness, we couldn't hear him.

I reached up hesitantly and pulled the cloth away. The sunlight stabbed into my eyes, and I was forced to close them tight. The red afterglow shone on the insides of my eyelids. When the glow dimmed, I dared squint open my eyes.

Desert—the same desert that had been there before I was blindfolded; the same expanse of red and yellow rock, sandy soil, and occasional scrub brush. In this desolate terrain, a tree was a landmark; the hills all looked the same, piles of boulders and weathered columns of lava, as if sculpted by a colony of lost Greeks.

If my employer had told me then that we hadn't gone anywhere at all, I'd have believed it, except that I'd just spent most of a day being led around by a rope. We had climbed hills, forded streams, and slid down embankments. Twice, we were led onto a boat and crossed a river, though the second time, I had the sense that the boat had turned around in midstream.

It didn't matter. I was completely lost. Hell, I'd stopped trying to keep track in the first half hour.

When we'd first left Vale, five other heavily armed men had accompanied us. I am accustomed to hard men, but these men were of a different breed: not brawlers, like I am used to, but men who were quick with a gun.

We reached the banks of a small creek. There, on the other side, were three Indian braves. One of them rode across the creek and stopped only a few feet away.

"You may not pass through this land," the Indian said. "It is sacred to us. This is where the First People came from out of the earth and taught us to live on the land. No one is allowed here, not even my own people."

"You speak English very well," Meredith said.

"I was schooled at the Whitman Mission," the Indian said. "I speak for my people now. We have noticed you in our lands before, but we have not stopped you. But now more white men come. They let their pigs run wild, and the pigs eat the acorns from which we make our bread. They stop the creeks with mud so the salmon cannot pass. They stop us from burning our fields so that the blackberries will ripen. They hunt the deer and the elk. We can no longer let you pass."

Meredith turned to his companions. "Well, boys. This is why I pay you. Make sure none of these savages escape."

The Indian in front of us didn't move, as if he couldn't believe what was happening. He was shot down before he could draw a weapon. The two Indians across the creek whirled their horses about, but they were both shot in the back before they had gone more than a few yards. One of them was still alive. Meredith strode across the creek. The water reached his thighs, no higher. He pulled out his pistol, stood over the wounded Indian, and put a bullet in his head.

I turned to Jake and Virgil, who both had their mouths open. I think we all realized at that moment that we were at the mercy of a madman.

Meredith came back, reloading his gun as he walked up to us. He reached into his coat pocket and brought out three bandannas. "I'm going to tie these over your eyes," he said. "I can't let you know where the mine is."

"What about them?" Virgil asked, waving at the armed men.

"They're here to make sure we aren't followed," Meredith said. "They'll be guarding the perimeter, so don't get any ideas."

***

After what felt like almost a full day of walking, we reached our destination and took off our blindfolds.

Virgil and Jake were beside me, blinking, obviously just as lost as I was.

Jonathan Meredith stood in front of us, grinning. He is a big man, but his bulk is mostly muscle, not fat. His black beard reaches his stomach. He looks like a dockworker, except his boots and coat are of a higher quality, and he carries himself like a boss.

"We're here, boys," he said. "Wait till you see this!"

Gold. The idea drove away any other thought. We'd been promised gold, as much as we could carry. When we set out, I had the notion that I'd fill all my pockets as well as the largest rucksack I could find.

It was immediately clear that I would need to reconsider this idea. I was already exhausted from stumbling around, even with empty pockets and a nearly empty rucksack. If we are blindfolded going back—and I am certain Meredith will insist on that—it will be nearly impossible to carry such a load.

I looked up gold prices before leaving Portland, and calculated that I needed only to fill the pack halfway and I'd be set for years. Maybe I'd even start that little hardware store that Libbie always talked about.

I looked around. There was nothing to be seen; no gold mine, only a rubble-strewn hillside that looked like every other rubble-strewn hillside.

"What are we doing here?" Virgil asked. "I thought we were working a mine."

"Working a mine?" Meredith said. "Well, sure, but first we have to uncover it. It's right behind you, boys, under all the slag. Well hidden, I made sure of that. See that red cloth? Start under there."

In midsentence, he turned to the mule and starting unpacking the pickaxes and shovels, handing them over his shoulder to the three of us without even looking at us.

"We gonna work in this heat, we need water," Jake grumbled.

"Of course," Meredith said. He untied the water bag from the mule and handed it over. "Drink up. There's a stream at the bottom of the cave, so the sooner you uncover the entrance, the sooner we get more."

We found the entrance pretty quickly. Problem was, every time we tried to open the hole, more scree came tumbling down. There was a hillside of rocks above us.

We were still digging when nightfall came.

After working all day yesterday, we retreated to the base of the hill at nightfall and started a fire. At the last moment, I had thought to pack a blanket, and for that I was grateful. Though I'd figured we'd have the shelter of the mine, I brought a few supplies as well, just in case it was more than a one-day's journey back to Vale. I had planned to jettison it all to make room for the gold, but I was glad I'd planned ahead.

Beside me, Jake was shivering, while Virgil was already snoring, lying on his back without any covering at all. Meredith extracted a heavy coat from one of the packs on the mule and wrapped himself in it, then sat staring into the fire. He looked up to catch me staring at him. His eyes hardened, challenging me.

I averted my eyes with a grunt. I'd heard stories about Meredith. The man owns the biggest lumberyard in Portland. He pays well, but he still has a large turnover in manpower because of his rough manner toward his workers, men who are willing to work hard but aren't willing to take being shouted at.

Yet the man had been nothing but cordial to me since I'd met him a few days ago. He wasn't exactly friendly, but then, I don't expect my bosses to be friendly, only fair. At that point, I had no complaints.

As we started digging this morning, the sun rose behind us, and with every hour, it got hotter.

Meanwhile, Meredith sat in the small patch of shade the mule provided, waterskin in hand, sipping. I didn't think anything of it. Bosses are always like that—that's why they're bosses.

Finally, Virgil took command, and we started rolling some of the bigger boulders to each side of the entrance. Jake scrambled down to the base of the hill and came back with a few sagebrush trunks, which we used to bridge the divide. The scree kept sliding, but the branches stopped it, finally.

We were going to need to get on our hands and knees to get in, but the entrance was stable enough. As long as no one did anything foolish, it ought to hold.

We stood back, waiting for our boss to enter first, but Meredith waved us on. "Go on in, boys," he urged. "I'll be right behind you."

Virgil went into the darkness first, then Jake. Meredith had gone back to the mule. I looked over my shoulder right before entering the mine and saw the man taking a rifle out of its holster.

What does he need a rifle for? I thought. I felt a sudden chill. *Is there something in the cave?*

I fear the darkness; always have. But I wanted gold even more.

I followed my friends, squeezing through the entrance. There was a broad cavern beyond. Virgil was lighting a lantern just as I stood up. The cave was suddenly riddled with points of light, covering the walls and ceiling. I walked over to one of the shiny reflections and tapped at it. A rock dislodged and fell at my feet. I picked it up. It was unexpectedly heavy.

It was gold—it had to be.

"Enough gold to fill all your pockets and not even make a dent," Meredith said behind us. The man had the wide-barreled shotgun pointed at us and a pistol in his belt. I started backing up immediately, thinking to make a run for it, while Virgil and Jake simply stood there, uncomprehending.

"Don't worry, boys." Meredith lowered the shotgun, his point made. "I just want you to understand that I can't allow you to leave until all the bags the burros can carry are filled. Then you can grab all you want for all I care."

He left the cave, and in the short time he was gone, the three of us talked in whispers.

"He's gonna kill us," Jake said, "just as soon as we've done what he wants."

"Why would he do that?" Virgil asked. "Like he said, there's enough gold here for a dozen men—hell, a hundred men. We don't know where we are. That's why he blindfolded us."

"Look around, Virgil," I said. "Other men have worked this mine already. There are tool marks everywhere. So…where are they? Why did Meredith need to hire a new crew?"

"We've got no choice," Jake said. "We'll just have to look for our chance to get away."

"What are we going to do?" Virgil said. "He's got the guns."

Virgil had been my foreman on the docks of Portland. A tough man, he always carries a big bowie knife. I don't know Jake as well, but he has a reputation as a brawler. I'm a runt compared to them, and because of that, I carry a tiny single-shot pistol in my pocket, what women call a muff gun. I've never shown it to anyone, and even then, when it might have given us an advantage, I was too embarrassed to reveal it.

Meredith returned, and he looked at us as if he knew we'd been talking about him and didn't care. He threw the bundle of pickaxes and shovels onto the floor of the cave. "Get to work. The sooner you finish, the sooner we can get out of here."

Virgil grabbed one of the pickaxes and started toward one of the shining walls.

"Not here," Meredith said. "The easy pickings have already been taken from the front chamber. Farther down the shaft, the gold is easier to get to. Hell, you can almost just shovel it into the bags."

That's what he told us, but when we returned with our bags filled, he poured them out onto the floor, picked up a few nuggets, and pushed the rest away with his boot. "This is crap," he said. "We want the nuggets, not the quartz. Someday we'll come for the rest, but for now, let's take only the nuggets. *Comprende?*"

He was right, of course. We had known it even as we were digging, but we'd been in a hurry to get out of there. Once, the lamp went out while we were working, and there was a blackness deeper than I've ever experienced. The darkness surrounded me like the fear.

I was greatly relieved when Virgil got the lamp lit again. Earlier tonight, back in the front cavern, I filled a pocket with matches when no one was looking. I'm not going to be left in the darkness again.

June 30, 1851

There are two natural tunnels leading off from the mine's entrance, both of which have been widened by tools. When we approached the left-hand tunnel, Meredith stopped us.

"That tunnel has been played out," he said. "Take the middle one."

A few hundred feet farther on, the right-hand tunnel narrowed, filled with rubble. It was here that Meredith told us to work. Our employer retreated back to the entrance, where he sat in the light shining in from the outside, his shotgun in his lap. Sometimes he leaves the cavern altogether, I know not where or why, since there is only the hot sun and desert outside, but it is clear to me that he is nervous in the darkness of the cave.

I have decided that the next time I am alone, I will check out the left-hand tunnel, for I am certain that Meredith is hiding something.

It was late in the afternoon when we heard the boom. Jake must have had the same thought as me, for we started running for the entrance. I was certain that Meredith had sealed the cave, taking the gold we'd already excavated.

Instead, he was standing near the entrance, holding an enormous rat by the tail. "Little buggers infest this place," he said. "Tried to get into our food. God knows what they feed on when we aren't around."

<u>July 1, 1851</u>

After lunch today, Meredith left us alone. I waited until Virgil and Jake disappeared down the middle tunnel before lighting the extra lamp and venturing into the left-hand tunnel. It was narrower than the one we've been working in, as if work there had only begun before it was abandoned.

There was plentiful gold, however, the most I had yet seen.

Why aren't we working on these veins? I wondered. I saw something white glowing on the floor of the cave a little farther ahead. I walked over to it and kicked it curiously with the toe of my boot.

It looked like a thighbone. I reached down and pried it from the ground. At first, I couldn't comprehend what I was seeing. An Indian burial, perhaps?

It was a small skeleton. As I bent down, I saw that another small skeleton was next to it. This skeleton wore the remains of a yellow dress. To my horror, I realized it was two children, dressed in white man's clothing.

I shouted, I'm not sure to whom—to my friends, to Meredith, to God, to anyone who would listen. Then I turned, intending to run back and tell the others.

A faint figure stood in the middle of the tunnel.

It was a small girl, hovering above the floor, stock still. Her eyes were missing, and there was only blackness where they had been, and her head was misshapen, as if part of it was also missing. She seemed to glow from within. I stared, my mouth open in shock, and another figure blinked into view beside her, a boy only slightly bigger than the girl. His legs appeared uneven, and he leaned to one side.

He reached out a skeletal hand.

I don't know what happened then. I just started running.

Somewhere along the way, I must have dropped the lamp, for I was running in darkness, tripping over the uneven footing, slamming against unseen walls. Too late, I realized I was running deeper into the cave.

Then there was nothing under my feet, and I was falling. I landed on my back. The shock knocked the air out of me. I rolled over and something struck my face. There was a bright flash of light. I was certain that a bullet had split my skull.

Then I was certain of nothing, only vaguely aware that I was still plummeting down a steep slope.

I was unconscious before I hit the bottom.

Chapter Five

<u>Sacramento, California, July 10, 1851</u>

Dearest Frank,

You will find this letter after I have left. When you stopped speaking to me last night, I knew that I had lost the argument. But it won't change what I must do. I don't want to endanger you, dear husband, nor do I want you to worry about my safety. I am the Canowiki, and I can take care of myself.

There is no choice. I know you understand this in your heart, but it is too painful to face. So do not worry that I went away without our reconciling, because I know that by the time you read this letter, you will already regret your words.

I heard you leave this morning but pretended to sleep still, because I knew that you didn't want to continue our argument. I will be staying at the Washington Hotel in Oregon City if you wish to send me a letter. I will write to you regardless, as often as possible. I love you, Frank, never doubt that. But I cannot be who I am if I do not do my duty. I know you realize this, and it is your steadfast love that gives me the strength to go on. It is likely that I am too late to do anything, but I feel I must at least try to help Mary Perkins.

I will return as soon as possible.

Love,

Virginia

Virginia left the letter on Frank's pillow and grabbed the carpetbag from the foot of the bed. It was slightly lighter than the last time she'd packed it. She'd discovered she didn't need to bring much gold with her; that indeed, it was a danger and an inconvenience. She intended to turn it into dollars when she reached San Francisco, no matter what the going rate of exchange was.

She wasn't sure what she could do to help Mary Perkins. The events in the letter had happened long ago, nearly as long ago as her own ordeal in the mountains. Whatever had happened to the children was in the past and couldn't be changed. It was only her concern for Mary that compelled her to return to the Oregon Territory so soon after leaving it.

She returned to Portland by the same route she had taken before. The same steamship was waiting at the docks, with the same men loading it, and the same captain and first mate, who stared at her curiously.

The ocean was stormy. The captain informed his passengers that it would take an extra day to reach Portland. Most of the passengers stayed in their cabins, many of them seasick from the constant rolling, but

Virginia was unaffected, apparently yet another advantage of being the Canowiki.

The ocean scared her more than any beast she had ever confronted. Huge and pitiless, it didn't care that she was the Canowiki; it would drown her with all the rest. The crew didn't seem worried, however, and so she walked the small promenade, keeping her balance in the pitching waves. It was a particularly severe tipping of the ship that alerted her to her shadow as he slammed against the railing behind her. She glanced back and saw him glaring at her, as if it was her fault. Then he looked away and ignored her as if she wasn't there.

He was small man, with quick, furtive movements. His head bobbed as if he couldn't keep still. He was holding onto the railing for dear life, not looking at the ocean but resolutely at the deck. He was wearing a kind of hat she had never seen, but sensed was the latest fashion back East— the type of haberdashery that was taking the place of beaver felt hats. It was short and round, with an inch-wide brim.

Virginia turned to approach him, but he immediately bolted in the opposite direction. She let him go, but after that, she was on alert. He wasn't unnatural; she would have sensed him sooner if he was. Whoever he was, he was human.

He came for her in the middle of the night. She heard his footsteps outside her door and was instantly awake, slipping out of the bed and tiptoeing across the room, bowie knife in hand. There were scratching sounds, and then the lock sprang and the door opened. He poked his head in. Virginia recognized the shape of his hat in the dim moonlight. She hooked a hand around the back of his neck and dragged him the rest of the way into the room, tossing him to the floor.

He didn't cry out as he rolled and rose, facing her in a crouch. She had planned to jump on top of him and put the blade to his throat, but he was surprisingly quick and agile. She squared off against him; then, suddenly, he straightened up and spread out his hands.

"Listen, miss, I mean you no harm," he said.

"You broke into my room," Virginia observed. "And you have already shown hostile intentions."

"Not hostile, simply careful," the man said. "I figured you saw me and thought it was time we met. Besides, I didn't want *them* to see me."

"Them?" she said.

"You know, the creatures…*them*." His voice rose until the last word was both a whisper and a shout.

"Quiet…you'll wake up everyone," she said. *And why not?* she asked herself. *I'm the innocent party here.*

Yet something about the man was unthreatening. There was more going on here than simple thievery or assault.

"There are only humans on this ship," Virginia said.

"Well, now," he said, his voice becoming smoother, more confident. "You'd be knowing that, not me. But I'm glad to hear it. Mr. Reed was sure you were being followed."

"Apparently I was," she said.

He grinned at her.

"Sit down, sir." She waved to the divan across the room. "You need to tell me what you're doing here and what my father has to do with it."

He turned his back to her and strode to the sofa, but before sitting, he turned around and said in a pleading voice, "I was sent to watch over you, Miss Reed."

"Mrs. Frank Whitford," she corrected him.

"Ah," he said. "But I was given to understand that when you travel, you take your maiden name."

How does he know that?

He was still standing, not yet willing to sit down. He hesitated and then extended a hand. "Name's Porter," he said. "Angus Porter."

Virginia didn't even glance at his hand, nor did she lower the bowie knife. "Go on. You were about to tell me why you're here."

Porter dropped his hand. He didn't seem insulted. "Well, I've been hired by your father to watch over you, miss. Which I intend to do."

"I don't need your help," she said. What was true of her husband was true of any human who tried to help her—they would only be in her way. She'd be concerned for their welfare as well as her own. They'd only end up being a distraction, perhaps at the most crucial moment.

"I beg to differ," he said. "I've seen you at work, miss, and I admit you can take care of yourself. But you can't watch every direction all the time, nor can you avoid sleep. Sometimes, I dare say, you need to relax, if only for a moment. You need someone to guard you. I can perform that service for you. Believe me, I've had experience."

"Sit down," Virginia repeated, this time with a commanding tone. Porter looked surprised, but he plopped down on the sofa. She went to the lamp on the desk and lit it, and then brought it over and stood over him.

"Tell me from the beginning," she said. "How do you know who I am, and how did my father come to hire you?"

"No need to use your witchcraft on me, Miss Reed. I was going to tell you just as soon as you calmed down."

"I'm calm," she said, then laughed at the deadly serious tone of her own voice. "All right, *now* I'm calm. I don't think you mean me harm, and I sense you are telling the truth—but not all the truth, so out with it."

Porter straightened his collar, which had become askew when he tumbled to the floor. He was dressed in some of the latest fashions, most of which hadn't yet reached even San Francisco. His hat was still ensconced on his head.

"What kind of hat is that?" Virginia asked abruptly. She'd been wondering since she had first seen it, and the question just popped out.

He brightened up at her enquiry. "It's a bowler, Miss Reed. All the finest Englishmen wear it."

"Is that so?" she asked. She examined him. Though his clothes were stylish, they were somewhat tattered. *A dandy,* she thought. *A dandy who spends what little money he has on clothing.* It wasn't reassuring, nor was his physical appearance.

Porter seemed to read her thoughts. "I know I don't look like much, Miss. I'm five foot three inches tall, as I'm sure you'll want to know. I'm nearing old age—I'm fifty years old—but I'm still vigorous. But despite my looks, I assure you, I know how to take care of myself. I've spent most of my life serving in armies in Europe, fighting for whoever needed me. I fought with the Duke of Wellington at Waterloo when I was but a lad. I've been serving in one army or another ever since."

"You're English?"

"No, miss. I'm American, like you. My father was a sailor. I barely knew him, but when I was thirteen, he came to me and asked if I'd like to sign on as a cabin boy. By the time we reached England, I knew that I never wanted to be a sailor again. I'm no good at it—as you saw yesterday, I can't get my sea legs. So I stayed in England, mostly. I crossed to the Continent when I needed to, but I never wanted to cross the Atlantic again…until…"

"Until?" Virginia prompted.

"Until I met *them.* You of all people know of whom I speak."

Virginia didn't say anything, simply waited for him to continue.

"I got a letter from my father. He'd gone back to his family's farm in Pennsylvania after his seafaring days. My sister and her children were living there. For the first time, I learned that I had three nephews and two nieces. Some wild creature was attacking them, and they didn't know what to do.

"I made the long journey across the ocean, swearing it would be my last time on the water. I arrived to find that my sister and three nephews were dead. At first I suspected my father, who could be a right bastard when he was drinking, but he was a shriveled husk of a man, too frightened to leave the house. My two nieces were keeping the place up as best they could; little ten-year-old Sophie and fourteen-year-old Molly, who is a resourceful girl. Reminds me of you, actually."

"Go on," Virginia said.

"Whatever the beast was, it only attacked at night. So I went about setting a trap, certain of my abilities, for I had fought in many a battle. I am a hardened and seasoned soldier, but nothing prepared me for what came that night. I shot it point blank in the chest, and it didn't even seem to feel it."

Virginia broke in. "I've found that bullets will kill the bastards when you can hit them."

Porter gave her a rueful grin. "As you have discovered, Miss Reed, there is more than one kind of creature out there. This was a were-animal, but not the kind you're used to. It was some kind of hybrid, part man, part bear. Its fur was so thick that my bullet couldn't penetrate it. But beneath that fur there was a beating heart, and my saber was sharp, and when I lunged at it, I got lucky, for it was charging at the same moment. The blade went straight to its heart, and the last thing I remember hearing was an awful roar.

"I awoke to Molly and Sophie trying to push the huge carcass off me. They succeeded enough to let me breathe, thankfully, or I wouldn't be talking to you today. My arm was broken, but I was otherwise unharmed.

"I stayed with my nieces until Molly married a neighbor boy a couple of years later. My father died not long after. After that, I wasn't welcome there—I was too strange for them, nor was I a farmer—so I set out to offer my services to whoever could pay me.

"I don't know why, but each of my cases since has had a bit of the weird about them. The unnatural attracts me, I guess. In short, I know what you do, Miss Reed, and I'm impressed by your courage and abilities."

By then, Virginia had sheathed her knife. She was pacing back and forth in front of the sofa, listening to the man's story. It had the ring of truth.

"You still haven't answered my question," she said. "How did you come to find my father, and why did he hire you?"

"As to why, naturally, he's worried, as is your husband."

"Frank knows about this?"

"Yes. I've been keeping him up to date for some time now. In fact, as wealthy as your father is, my services aren't cheap. I…uh…pointed out your stash of gold to your husband and told him how much of it I needed to do my job."

Now it was Virginia's turn to be impressed. If Porter had been following her for months and she hadn't realized it, he was talented indeed.

"I heard about your experience in the mountains, Miss Reed. The moment I started reading accounts of the Donner Party, I knew that something else had happened, and that you were at the center of it.

"By the time I tracked down your father, you were off on one of your adventures. I didn't find you until you returned to Sacramento and married Frank Whitford. I waited until you were gone on one of your mysterious trips before approaching your husband. He contacted your father, and between the two of them, I was hired."

I'm going to kill them, Virginia thought. *Both of them.*

Then she felt a strange sense of relief. This man was a hired mercenary whom she wouldn't need to feel guilty about leading into danger. Maybe it wasn't such a bad idea after all.

Porter must have sensed her hesitation. "I will be following you with or without your permission, Miss Reed," he said. "But it would be better if we worked together."

She put her hand out. "If we are going to work together, call me Virginia."

He took her hand, but at the same time, he was shaking his head. "No, miss. That is not how I do things. I work for you. I am not your friend: I am your bodyguard. A little formality will remind me of that. I am well aware of the danger. If it was only for gold, well…I'd probably take the money and run. But there is more to it than that. Just like you, I feel that I have a calling. I may not be a Cano…Cona…"

"Canowiki," she said.

"Yeah, I may not be that, but serving you seems a good way to spend the rest of my life, however long I have left."

"Very well, your services are accepted." The moment she said the words, Virginia felt herself relax.

Porter stood up, a big grin on his rat-like face. "So…what beasties are we going after this time?"

***

They debarked in Portland, then caught the afternoon coach to
Oregon City. Virginia was pleased to find that Angus—Mr. Porter, she
reminded herself—was a quiet companion, only speaking when spoken to.
There was something so comfortable about him that she couldn't help but
think of him as Angus. Sometimes she could almost forget he was there.
He often stayed to one side, or behind her, and most of the time, if an
observer didn't know they were together, he or she might well not realize
it.

It was a smart strategy. It would give them the element of surprise.

They found a coach outside the station, gave the driver directions to
the Washington Hotel, and told the man to wait while they stored their
luggage inside. Then they gave the coachman the address that Mary
Perkins had given in her letter. It was getting dark out, and the man gave
Angus and Virginia a suspicious look.

"I'm sorry, sir," he said, addressing Angus and ignoring Virginia. "I
won't go into that part of town after dark."

"Nonsense, good fellow," Angus said. He pulled a twenty-dollar gold
coin out of his pocket, more money than the man probably earned in a
month. "We'll make it worth your while."

"Can't spend it if I'm dead," the man said. "I'll take you to the street,
but no farther."

"Carry on," Angus said, slapping the side of the coach.

The coach set off toward the wharf. Angus sat back and closed his
eyes, and Virginia was certain that he fell asleep during the twenty-minute
journey, despite the intense rattling of the wheels on cobblestones.

When they finally stopped, it was completely dark. Virginia peered
out. There were houses and other buildings on the street, but none of
them had their lamps on except for one building at the very end, right
where the street made a sharp turn. It was brightly lit. There was the
distant sound of laughter and music.

"That's the place you're looking for," the coachman said. He looked
from Angus to Virginia and back again. "If your companion is a lady, she
won't want to be going there. If she's not a lady, she should still stay away.
It's the last stop for their kind, and your friend is still much too pretty."

"The lady is not 'mine,' and she is indeed a lady," Angus said, handing
the coachman the promised gold piece.

"No offense, sir," the man said, snatching the coin as if he was afraid
it would be withdrawn. He tipped his hat. "I could wait a few minutes."

"We won't need you," Angus said. "Take your gold piece and be gone
with your insults."

The man cursed and whipped his poor, bedraggled horse. He quickly disappeared in the night.

"Was that wise?" Virginia asked. "Won't we need a ride back?"

"See, now, I'm already earning my keep," Angus said. "A man like that you don't want hanging around. He's liable to think there are more gold coins in my pocket and to try to figure out how to get them all. Better he be gone from here and unable to do mischief."

Virginia nodded. She followed Angus toward the brightly lit building. Men were leaning up against the walls outside, smoking. They catcalled Virginia, but she ignored them. One of them broke off from the others and faced Angus at the door.

"You've delivered her, little man," he said, leering. "Now leave her to me."

Angus didn't say anything, just stared up into the man's face. There must have been a message there that only the bigger man could see, because he blanched and moved to one side. "You'll not be coming back out again," he muttered. "You'll see."

"How do they ever make any money?" Angus asked into the air. "Driving away customers like this?"

Virginia followed Angus into the building, trying to seem demure and decorous—why, she wasn't sure. Inside, she was tensing up. She sensed nothing supernatural here, only the aura of men who bought and sold women for their own pleasure. But she had never felt more in danger.

Angus appeared unperturbed. Despite his stature, he radiated something that kept other men from approaching them. There were four or five men for every woman, sitting at round tables, some of them eating or playing cards, most of them drinking. The volume of noise didn't drop when Angus and Virginia entered, and it wasn't as if everyone in the place turned to watch them. But all of the patrons took a peek at them at some point on their journey across the floor.

They think I'm his, Virginia suddenly realized. *It's the only thing keeping them away.*

Angus's aura worked all the way to the back of the place, where there was a room with a Dutch door where a heavily bosomed and made-up woman watched them approach, frowning.

"It'll cost you a buck to come in," she said.

Angus produced a one-dollar gold piece and tossed it into the woman's cleavage.

Virginia held her breath, but the action seemed to break the ice. The woman threw back her head and laughed loudly, her fat jiggling. "What

will be your pleasure?" the madam asked. "Perhaps your little woman
wants to join in?"

Virginia blushed, aware that now all eyes were on her.

"I'm looking for a Mary Perkins," Angus said.

The woman showed no sign of recognizing the name. "Listen, honey,
whatever name you knew her by, she ain't that now. We got Roses and
Gingers and Angels and Kittys, but we got no Marys."

"She's got red hair and green eyes and freckles," Virginia said.

The woman opened her mouth and then hesitated. "What did you say
your name was?"

"I didn't," Virginia said. "Virginia Reed."

All expression dropped from the big woman's face. She stepped back,
opened the half door, and ushered them in. They went into a back room
that was surprisingly staid and bourgeois. There were pictures on the wall
of straight-laced men and women who bore a resemblance to the madam.
Virginia had the sudden insight that no woman started out her life this
way.

She'd seen it along the trail. Without a man, a woman was vulnerable.
The lucky ones quickly remarried or had family to shelter them. A few
strong-willed women were able to start businesses that it was acceptable
for women to run, laundries or restaurants or hotels…or brothels. But
most depended on the mercy of men, and sometimes there was little of
that.

"Ginger…that is, Mary wanted me to give you these," the woman
said, bringing a stack of journals out of the back room. "It was the least I
could do for her."

"Where is she?" Virginia asked, her heart sinking.

"I don't know," the madam said. "She saved up her money, and she
left. She's the only girl to do that in all the time I've been here. But if you
ask me, I'd look for her in the brothels in Portland or Eugene, because I
doubt she'll escape her past so easily. But then…maybe if she had
friends…" She looked Virginia straight in the eye, and there was no
challenge there, only genuine concern.

"She has friends," Virginia said. "I would like to see her again, and I'm
in a position to help her."

"Well, God bless," the madam said. "I hope you find her. But if that is
everything, I've discharged my duty to Mary. My advice is to get away
from here, the both of you. You don't belong."

Angus was already heading for the door. He opened it a crack and
peered out. Then he motioned for Virginia to hurry. She picked up the

journals and started out, then at the last moment turned back to the madam. "I wish…I hope…"

"Go, girl. It's too late for me and every other woman here. Live your life, and try not to judge us too much."

Virginia nodded. She slipped her hand into Angus's coat and drew out his small bag of coins. She tossed it to the madam without a word and left the room.

"I hope we don't need that money to get out of here," Angus said as they walked through the crowded room. They were ignored. Apparently being taken into the back had made them acceptable.

They left the bright lights of the brothel and walked in the general direction of their hotel.

"Maybe we should have asked the coachman to wait," Virginia said, though she didn't really mind walking in the cool night air. It would take a couple of hours to reach their hotel on foot, but that was a small distance compared to most Virginia had had to travel.

"Why?" Angus said. "We have no money to pay the man."

Virginia laughed. She reached out and hooked her arm through his. "I think I'm going to like you, Mr. Angus Porter. And I don't care how formal you intend to be, I'm calling you Angus from now on."

"Whatever you wish, Miss Reed," Angus answered. He patted her hand, and they walked together down the darkened street.

Chapter Six

Dearest Frank,

As I feared, Mary has fallen onto hard times. She was not at the address given, but I still hope to find her and help her if I can.

I thank the Lord every day that you came into my life when you did. I was sure I was destined to be alone, for my virtues are not something that would attract most men. But you are not most men, Frank, and I cannot express my gratitude enough.

Mary left Ellen Meredith's journals for me to read, and I have decided that, whether or not I find Mary, I will honor her request and investigate what happened on that fateful journey. The parents deserve to know what happened to their children. And I suspect, though I cannot yet prove the need for it, that the children deserve justice.

I will return home as soon as possible, dear husband. Keep me in your prayers.

Love,

Virginia

Virginia set aside the letter and picked up Ellen's first journal. There were three books in total. The early pages were neat and tidy, but by the end of the third book, words were simply scrawled across the pages without regard for clarity or space. Most of the entries were simple recordkeeping, the miles traveled and the day-to-day activities. These passages Virginia merely skimmed.

She turned up the lamp so she could make out the small, crabbed lettering of the first entries. No doubt she'd have to pay the hotel more money for the profligate use of oil.

She had chosen the same hotel to stay in as on her last visit to Portland. The same supercilious clerk was behind the counter. However, he obviously remembered the generous gratuity Virginia had left and managed not to wrinkle his nose at her traveling attire. Also, Angus affected a posh English accent, which obviously impressed the clerk and got them two nice rooms on the first floor.

"I shall meet you for breakfast in the dining room, Angus," Virginia said at the door of her room.

"Aye, I'll be there unless I'm sleeping," he said.

Just the mention of sleep was enough to make Virginia sleepy, but after writing her daily missive to Frank—a practice she was determined to continue—she forced herself to sit and read through the account of the first few days of Ellen Meredith's journal. She closed the book with a yawn and lay down, fully clothed, to rest her eyes.

A premonition of tragedy suffused the narrative, perhaps unwittingly. Certainly, Virginia recognized Jonathan Meredith as a monster, but whether he was a human monster or the other kind, she couldn't yet tell.

She could learn so much more if she could find Mary and question her. As informative as Mary's letter was, it seemed to Virginia that her words had only hinted at the tensions that had arisen among the travelers. From her own long journey across the continent, Virginia understood the rivalries, the resentments, the friendships made and broken on the long trip. But most women would never say anything about it. They were taught to accept whatever the men in their lives wanted.

Virginia had the impression that Ellen had seldom spoken her own thoughts aloud, instead saving her true feelings for her journals. But it was clear that the terrible events at the end of the journey were presaged by those early days.

Virginia closed her eyes, and it was as if she could see the children clearly, though she had never met them. She fell asleep to their playful laughter in her mind, and a sense of sadness followed her into her dreams.

***

Angus was already eating when Virginia came into the dining room early the next morning. His bowler hat was on the seat next to him, and his thinning hair was neatly combed. He stood up, blushing. "I'm sorry, miss. I couldn't help myself. I had very little to eat yesterday, if you remember."

"It is for me to apologize to you, Angus," Virginia said as she realized that they had skipped meals the previous day, as was her habit when she was on the hunt. *I'll have to remember to be more thoughtful from now on if I'm to have a fellow traveler,* she told herself.

She ordered a big breakfast, and Angus watched her with bemusement. "Thank God you have an appetite," he said. "I was beginning to wonder if you were one of those women who are concerned about their shape and eat like birds."

Virginia chomped on a piece of bacon and laughed. "Hardly. I eat as much as I please, but it never seems enough."

Angus sat sipping his coffee, waiting for her to finish. When she dabbed her lips with her napkin and set it down, he asked, "What now, Miss Reed?"

"I would like to find Mary Perkins, if possible," she said. "But I have no idea where to start."

"I believe the madam of the…uh, establishment we visited yesterday was correct," Angus said. "Miss Perkins will be someplace that is unsuitable for a lady such as yourself, no matter how brave. Let me do some searching of the likely spots. They'll be easy enough for a man like me to find. You stay here and read those journals—yes, I saw your lamplight burning late into the night, miss."

"Are you sure you won't need my help?" she asked.

"Your presence would be a distraction," Angus insisted. "I'd have to spend all my time defending your honor instead of searching."

Virginia nodded, knowing he was right. It hurt her to think that Mary was in one of those places, and she wanted nothing more than to lead the poor girl out of her purgatory the instant she was found. But it was a man's world; some women were little more than chattel. It wouldn't be as easy as that, and Virginia would probably have to expend part of her gold just to secure the girl's release, much less find her a secure home and position.

And so she remained at the hotel while her new companion investigated the wharfs and side streets of Portland.

Angus returned that night, unsuccessful. They met again in the hotel dining room.

"I do not believe she stayed in this town. Not one of these unfortunate women have heard of her," he said.

Virginia eyed him. His hair was no longer neatly groomed; his clothing was askew. *It is not for me to judge*, she told herself.

"Perhaps she went back to Oregon City?" Virginia said.

"Not if she wanted to remain hidden. My guess is that she has moved on—gone someplace where she can lose herself. To Seattle, perhaps, or even San Francisco."

"It would be unfortunate as well as ironic if we have come all this way only to find she is where we began." Virginia felt her hopes start to fade. She'd known it was a gamble, but as a Canowiki, she had become accustomed to such long shots paying off. On the other hand, she wasn't dealing with the supernatural here, but with a woman's degradation

"If you are willing to wait another few days," Angus offered, "I will travel to Salem, the next big town hereabouts. Perhaps I'll catch wind of her there."

"It will take me some time to finish Ellen's journals," Virginia said. "There is more there to read and understand than I expected. So I expect to stay here for another few days at any rate."

"It is decided, then," Angus said. "I will travel by coach tomorrow and return the next day. You can decide what further steps to take at that time." He hesitated. Then he lowered his voice and said, "Have you noticed that the men at the table behind you are staring at you?"

Virginia resisted the urge to turn around to check them out. "Tell me about them," she said calmly.

"Three men, rough looking," Angus said in a low but conversational voice. He wasn't looking behind her, so he had obviously been studying them before he spoke. "They feel dangerous to me," he added. "I've learned to trust those feelings."

How could I have missed them? Virginia wondered. *Am I already depending on Angus too much?*

"I must visit the ladies' room," she said, getting up. "I'll be right back."

The three men were sitting at a corner table, and Virginia dared a single long glance at them, memorizing their faces. She didn't recognize any of them, but they were all staring back at her, appraising her brazenly.

Angus was right. There was something peculiar about them—and yet, they didn't seem to be setting off the Canowiki in her, just the part of her that was a woman. When she reemerged, she still hadn't decided what to do, and so was surprised to find herself walking over to them.

"Gentlemen," she said, looking down on them. They looked surprised but not threatened, but then she saw them tense and she sensed that Angus was approaching. "I feel that you have been staring at me."

"Beg your pardon, miss." The speaker was nondescript: average in height and looks, with a short beard. He was older than the others, and she assumed at first that he was in charge. He was dressed in workman's clothes, but they were of fine quality and they fit him well. A workingman with money, a rare combination. "If we stared at you, it was only because of your beauty."

Virginia blushed despite herself. She rarely got compliments, though she knew that men found her attractive. She wasn't sure whether she should be flattered or insulted. The men hadn't done anything blatantly improper.

"Would you care to join us?" the man sitting in the center of the trio asked. He was unshaven, his hair unruly, but he seemed to have the best manners, for he stood up and motioned to the chair opposite him.

The third man was the biggest, clean-shaven, which was unusual in this town, and it appeared he had shaved his head as well. He had on a funny little bowtie, which his Adam's apple weighed down. His neck seemed as wide as his head, and his shoulders threatened to burst through his shirt. Virginia almost dismissed him as mere muscle, and then caught the canny look in his eyes. He was the leader, she decided, though he hadn't spoken.

"Do you have business with me?" she asked him bluntly.

The two other men turned to their leader, who nodded and finally spoke. "Indeed we do, Miss Reed," he said. "Excuse us for not approaching you directly, but we weren't sure if you were the right woman. Nor did we wish to alarm you."

He stood up, and the other men joined him. "I'm sorry we've been so rude," he said, bowing slightly. "My name is Terrance Drake." He pulled the fourth chair out from the table for her, but she continued to stand. "These are my friends, John Sims," he pointed to the man with the unruly hair, and then to man in workman's clothing, "and Martin Franklin."

"What do you want of me?" Virginia asked.

"We've been sent by Mrs. Oliver Hoskins. She didn't tell us for what purpose, Miss Reed. She said only that we were to follow you and bring you into her presence."

Angus spoke up. "Follow her from where?"

Drake hesitated, as if looking for the proper words. "From where you have been searching."

"Why would we come with you?" Angus demanded.

"Mrs. Hoskins told me to give you a message," Drake said. "She said, 'The apples in Oregon are even sweeter than we imagined.'"

Beside her, Angus scowled and began to speak, but Virginia reached out and lightly touched his arm. "We are ready to accompany you gentlemen," she said. "If you have finished your meal?"

"Yes, Miss Reed. Right away," Drake said.

Chapter Seven

<u>Diary of Ellen Meredith</u>

<u>The Oregon Trail, April 29, 1845</u>

The great adventure begins! There is a general uplifting of all our spirits. Our small party of God-fearing folk has joined a larger group, the largest, we are told, of the season. There are over a thousand souls and more than two hundred wagons of all shapes and sizes. Such numbers give us all a sense of safety as we travel into the wilds.

Because we arrived late, we were at the tail end of the exodus. While Jonathan prepared the wagon, the children and I climbed the high bluffs on the western side of the Missouri River and watched the first of the overlander wagons as they wound their way along the broad horseshoe bends. The white canvas coverings look like the sails of boats. It is easy to see why they are called prairie schooners. It was a glorious sight.

The harness chains make a musical sound, and the wheels drum upon the road in accompaniment. The drivers call out to the mules and oxen, "Get up!" or "Whoa, now," and to my ears it sounds like a song.

We have started late, but God willing, we will make good time. To our surprise, as we set out from Independence, the citizens of the town, who had seemed so intent on selling us shoddy goods at ruinous prices, came to cheer our departure. After we are gone, the town will sleep until the next season, or so I have been informed.

I must admit here, for I intend to make these journals an honest accounting of our journey, that I have misgivings. I did not wish to leave the small homestead to which my first husband and I dedicated our lives. I married Cullum when I was but a girl, with no experience of the wider world, but for a long time, that didn't matter. I was happy with Cullum. When Jed and Edwin were born, good strong boys, my life was complete.

But Cullum was not a physically strong man. He suffered trying to keep the farm intact, and over time, he was forced to sell some of the better pasturelands to our neighbor, Jonathan Meredith. I admit that I was aware of Jonathan's glances even then, and I was flattered, though I never acknowledged them.

I loved Cullum, but the life of a farmer's wife is not an easy one, and I could not help but look upon Jonathan's more prosperous lands and feel envy. Jonathan was married to a nag. I'm sorry, but it must be said. Eliza was cruel to him in speech and manner. They had a daughter named Sarah, and whenever I had doubts about Jonathan, I simply watched him around her, for it is clear that she is the center of his existence.

Then came word that Eliza and Sarah had been in a wagon accident. Eliza was killed, and Sarah gravely injured. When she recovered, it became clear that her legs will never function again, and while the rest of her body grows, her legs remain sticklike and small.

It was shortly after this tragic event that Jonathan's attentions toward me became more obvious and direct. God forgive me, I did not completely reject them.

I thank God every day that Cullum never knew how I felt, for bless the man, he tried hard to be a good husband. The boys, who, if Cullum had lived, might have helped relieve his burden, only added to his worry when they were young. The responsibility wore him down, so that when he came home at night, he was but a shadow of himself.

Jonathan helped us as best he could, paying Cullum for his help with the spring roundups and the fall harvests. Perhaps we would not have survived at all without Jonathan's aid. I could not help but notice how powerful a presence Jonathan was. When he was around, Cullum seemed to fade away.

I was a loyal wife, and I never strayed in so much as a glance, but…it was impossible not to notice the differences in their demeanors.

Then came the awful day when dear Cullum did not return. I waited a full day, sending the boys out to milk the cows and do those chores that were Cullum's to do. Then I set out the next morning with Perty, our old, broken-down nag of a horse, harnessed to our buckboard. We had but one good horse left, which we called Goldie and which Cullum rode. I arrived at Jonathan's farmhouse in time to see the search party returning with Cullum's body.

No one ever knew what happened. He was found on the trail with a broken neck, and his horse was missing. People from throughout the county came to the funeral, and I learned that Cullum had been highly regarded, which surprised and pleased me. I was given small gifts of money, and in my desperation, I accepted them. I noticed when the funeral was over that Cullum's horse, Goldie, was in the barn.

"Found him this morning," Jonathan said when he caught me looking. "Meant to tell you when the funeral was over."

"Thank you for taking care of him, Mr. Meredith," I said.

Jonathan was so kind over the next few months as I grieved poor Cullum's loss. I allowed myself to smile at my neighbor when he was gallant, no matter how unseemly it might have appeared. How could I not? Jed and Edwin and I were helpless without him.

When Jonathan proposed after the proper mourning period had passed, I immediately accepted.

I now speak of matters that, as a good wife, I should not. But I have sworn to be honest in these journals, and it must be said. I have never seen Jonathan read anything but contracts, or write anything but his name, so I have faith that he will never read these journals. He will not be interested in the nattering of his empty-headed wife—or so he thinks me. And for all his faults, Jonathan has boundaries he does not cross, and I believe reading someone's diary is one of them, strange as it sounds.

By the time our first daughter, Nan, was born, I knew Jonathan was not the man I had thought him to be. I was so used to gentle Cullum, who never raised his voice, who never cast aspersions, who, if he said anything at all, was supportive.

Jonathan was quite the opposite, always speaking in a loud voice and unhappy with everything I did. I could have endured this without complaint, even in these journals, if he didn't also go after Jed and Edwin, who never measure up to their stepfather's standards.

It broke my heart when Jonathan told the boys that their father had been "worthless."

I was used to being let alone, for Cullum was so exhausted at night that he would fall asleep immediately. Jonathan still had energy, but no interest in marital relations except to have his own son. As soon as I was with child, he ignored me.

When Mattie was born, I could see the anger in his face. I saw Jonathan looking at other women, and could sense him measuring them, wondering if they would bear him a boy.

No doubt he had thought he had a sure thing with me, as I have already borne two sons.

It is inalterably sad to me that he cannot take into his heart the two boys he already has. Jed looks up to him and does everything he can to please his stepfather, but nothing he does pleases Jonathan. Edwin stays out of the way and is never in the same room as Jonathan, though Jonathan doesn't even seem to notice.

There is no doubt that he loves his own daughter, Sarah. It gives me hope to see them together, Jonathan so tender with her, helping her up the steps, teaching her to ride a pony.

So it surprised me when he announced that he had sold the farm and that we were moving to Oregon. I fear that the fragile girl will suffer on this long journey, unlike my daughters Nan and Mattie, who are excited by the prospect.

"I'm doing it for Sarah," he said. "This farm will never provide more than a hardscrabble existence. We need to go someplace where I can take care of her."

"Then let us go home," I said. "My parents will help us, and you told me that you inherited your grandparents' place in Maryland."

He snorted. "A field of rocks. No, we must go westward. That is where the future is; that is where I can make enough money to help Sarah…to help all of us."

I said no more. It is not a woman's place to tell her husband where the best opportunities lie. But it is because of Sarah's crippled legs that I fear for this trip.

<u>May 5, 1845</u>

I have decided not to erase the previous entry, though it is unfair to Jonathan, who, after all, is doing what he thinks is best for his family. If he believes that going to Oregon is what is best for us, I must not question it. Sarah seems happy, though she constantly apologizes for how we must help her. She is a sweet girl, and no one minds.

I do not wish to start this journey in complaint, and I shall endeavor to write of only the good things that happen along the way. As we set out on our long adventure, I cannot but hope that it shall give us all a fresh start.

<u>May 10, 1845</u>

The weather is tolerable, if confounding. The sun beats down until we remove the covering over the wagon seat, only to have wind blow and sprinkles of rain fall on us moments later.

The road is so rutted that our wheels must follow the path of others, no matter how we might wish otherwise. The rain softens the tracks but makes them harder to travel, and Jonathan becomes enraged, whipping the horses, including poor Goldie, who is of advanced age. Goldie is the last reminder, other than Jed and Edwin, that I have of Cullum, and I hate to see him treated so.

"Can we not move to the side of the road?" I asked, for I had seen others do that, and they seemed to be making better progress than us. By this time in the season, there are many different roads, and few are following the earliest paths, even if they appear to be straighter. Indeed, we have fallen behind the others. There is a small group of us at the rear of the train who have banded together, pulling our wagons close at night.

There are the Catledges, Augustus and Abigail. Gus seems much older than Abigail, but despite the discrepancy in age, they have begot a daughter, Becky, who is about the same age as my Edwin. They have taken under their wings a young stowaway, Mary, who has been put in charge of the children—all but Jed, who insists at staying at his stepfather's side.

There are the Parsonses, Bart and Karrie, with a son and daughter, Cager and Allie. I am thankful for their company, and that my children have companions of their own ages to play with.

When I made the suggestion that we try a different path, I spoke without thinking, for I was happy. Our small group had banded together the night before to eat a deer that Gus had shot, and Bart had brought out some whiskey, and in a moment of weakness, I drank some of the foul liquor. It did not take much to make me tipsy. I was not sorry, for I was still in a good mood the next day, despite my headache.

Jonathan glared at me, for I rarely make suggestions, and he treats all such advice as unwanted. He might have done as the others, finding a new path, if not for my interference. Sarah suffers in the back of the wagon, and he simply doesn't see it because he is riding ahead.

I could see Jed also glaring at me, as if he agreed with his stepfather, but I understand this behavior, and I forgive him no matter what, while his stepfather sees fault in everything he does. Instead of rebelling, my eldest son hews ever closer to his demanding stepfather. My youngest son, Edwin, stays close to my side, and sometimes when I look at him, I see gentle Cullum as I first saw him, kind and handsome and still hopeful about life.

And so we stayed on that dreadful, rutted road. After a few hours, Sarah, in some discomfort despite being cushioned by as many blankets as I could find, begged to be allowed to ride Goldie. I hesitated, for she had never ridden without Jonathan accompanying her alongside, but the poor girl was suffering, so I agreed.

In midafternoon, Goldie collapsed without warning, and Sarah was trapped beneath him. Jed and Edwin tried to move the dying creature, but couldn't. Jonathan came riding up, and with the strength of a father, whose daughter is threatened, managed to lift Goldie's hindquarters enough for Jed to pull Sarah free.

Jonathan marched to the back of the wagon and pulled out his rifle.

"No, Jonathan," I implored him.

He ignored me, put the barrel to Goldie's head, and pulled the trigger.

We spent another hour trying to get the harness and tack off the dead horse. We probably should have stored his meat, but we were falling farther and farther behind the others. The Catledges and the Parsonses moved off the main trail, forced off by our blockage, and when we finally started up again, we too moved to the side, as I had suggested all along.

Sarah was again ensconced in the back in her blankets. "I'm sorry, Father," she said in a little girl voice.

Jonathan's face softened, and he reached out with his huge, rough hand and stroked her cheek gently. "It is not your fault, daughter," he said.

He turned away from her and glared at me, and I was suddenly certain whose fault he thought it was.

I shall always remember the sight, looking back on poor Goldie's yellow mane glowing in the last light of day.

It was at that moment that I knew we had left our past lives behind forever.

Chapter Eight

The Oregon Trail, May 15, 1845

I love the mornings on the trail, the bright dew still fresh on the green plains. The smell of bacon and coffee and the bustle of the overlanders around me make me hopeful that all will be well.

The land is flat, and in the distance stretch patches of wildflowers whose myriad colors make me wonder if we shouldn't stop here and stake our claim. The land must be fertile for such profusion to exist. But the men, as ever, have their hearts set on Oregon.

Our journey thus far has been uneventful. The trail is well blazed, with few surprises. There is the weather to contend with, as always. The wind blows steadily in our faces, a warm wind on most days, though if the heavy clouds roll over us, the breeze can have a bite.

The other thing we have to contend with is our fellow overlanders. There are so many types of people: immigrants who don't even speak English, down-on-their-luck bluebloods, adventurers, and those of us, like me, who were reluctant to come but are loyal to their loved ones. The huge wagon train has broken into groups who travel, camp, and cook together.

Our small group is congenial to each other. The only visible strain is between my husband and the other men. Jonathan has a tendency to boss them around, as if only he knows what to do. Their wives do not hold it against me, fortunately. Meanwhile, the children are enjoying the travel, seeing it not as hardship but as an adventure. I try my best to emulate their example.

The younger ones are oblivious to the tensions between the adults, though I have seen Jed cast worried looks toward his stepfather when he gets loud.

In our homestead, Jonathan never drank. But both Mr. Parsons and Mr. Catledge are fond of a few sips of whiskey after everyone else has gone to bed, and he has been joining them. Jonathan comes to my side late at night, and he is more affectionate than I am accustomed to. I have tried to accommodate him, though I fear getting with child on this long journey.

When I dared to say something, he grew angry. "You'll give me a son," he grunted into my ear. "I want a son."

There is little privacy in our nightly campsite, for we are huddled together for safety, but everyone pretends not to hear certain things. I am ashamed that it is happening where Jed and Edwin can hear, but I cannot refuse my husband.

<u>May 18, 1845</u>

We followed the Platt River for several days, and it was only when we left that flat, well-traveled terrain that we ran into difficulties. Each group has to decide which path to travel, and some drivers seemed to have a knack for determining which way is easier, which is faster, and which has the most fuel along the way. The farther one goes from the established trails, the more wood can be found for the campfire, but the more dangerously isolated we become.

I had thought to bring everything our family might need in Oregon, but I've realized that we must lighten the load. I carefully stacked the extra set of dishes alongside the trail. I suspect that more belongings will be discarded over the coming days.

If we should have need of anything, we can find what we need in the discarded piles of other travelers as they also take pity on their poor oxen and mules.

<u>May 21, 1845</u>

We are entering Indian country. Though we haven't heard of any attacks this season, there are always raids, and if any cow or horse wanders out of sight, it often cannot be found the next day.

The men speak excitedly at night around the campfire about how they will deal with the savages if they dare attack. Their voices get louder as the whiskey flows. But in the morning, as the men sleep in a little longer than usual, we women tend to speak of the opportunities that such an encounter with the Indians might provide.

The young servant girl, Mary Perkins, seems to have to most knowledge of the Indians. "We can trade with them," she said. "Everyone says so. They will give you an entire deer or buffalo for a few shiny beads, or a knife, or even a hat."

We are all wishing for fresh meat. Everything that is left in our wagons is canned or salted, or hardtack, or dried vegetables and fruits. Everything is becoming stale or moldy, and when we stumble across fresh game, even if it is merely a rabbit, it tastes wonderful.

As the days passed, I began to look forward to meeting some of these Indians, whom I have previously only seen on the streets of Independence, well-groomed and wearing white man's clothing (and looking terribly unhappy).

This morning, we finally came across a small encampment of Indians. The Indian braves stayed back and watched as their women approached us. I was able to get a haunch of buffalo in exchange for a spare blanket, and I was well satisfied with the deal.

Our men stayed back as well, staring suspiciously at their counterparts.

I looked into these Indian women's eyes, and they looked no different than those of my fellow travelers. The delight the maiden took in my humble blanket, which I had knitted myself, was the same as my own daughters' was when I first showed it to them.

The trading was conducted peacefully and amicably, with both sides satisfied, and I look forward to our next meeting.

<u>June 1, 1845</u>

The rain and wind are unrelenting. Even when the sun is shining, we can't be sure the weather won't turn against us within minutes. Before leaving Missouri, I worried whether we would find enough water along the way. Never did I imagine there would be too much.

The three men in our group take turns choosing the path to follow. Mr. Catledge most often stays close to the central trails, which are rutted but direct, but which offer very little in the way of fodder. My husband always chooses the most outlying route. Though it takes a little longer for us to catch up to the rest of the wagon train, there is plentiful fuel and clean water, and sometimes we even see wildlife that hasn't yet been hunted or scared away. Mr. Parsons most often chooses a path somewhere in between.

This matches the personalities of the three men as I have observed them. We have learned to stock up on food and wood when following my husband's lead and to enjoy an early night when we follow Mr. Catledge's lead. It has worked out strangely well, and after some initial grumbling, we have fallen into a comfortable pattern.

There is another advantage to following my husband's path. We do not encounter nearly as many graves as when following the old trails. There are hundreds of these graves along the trail, but most were dug in the early years. By now, there are fewer natural hazards, except disease, which is the most dangerous thing of all. The more of us who travel this route, the more cholera and other human-caused diseases plague us.

<u>June 4, 1845</u>

I have spoken too soon. Yesterday we came across a fresh grave, and I anxiously read the name of the person carved on the wooden cross, hoping I would not recognize it. I had another reason to examine the gravesite. I wished to learn the cause of death, whether accident or disease or one of the natural tragedies of life.

The grave gave no clue, but I choose to believe that this woman's passing came from natural causes. As hard as it is to follow the less-traveled trails that my husband leads us on, I have come to prefer it. The water is less fouled, the air less dusty. I believe it is a healthier, if harder, route.

But there is a reason that most of us choose to stick to the tried and true trails. The Indians tend to stay away from them, for they understand the dangers of disease and nervous men.

When next it was Jonathan's turn to lead, he took us father away from the others than ever before. At first I was glad for it, for the land was flat and without ruts, and there was plenty of food for the animals. The children ran alongside the wagon and piled wood into the back. When we came to a stream, it was unspoiled. No cattle had trampled away the bank; the water was clear and fresh, and tasted like ambrosia.

Jonathan was driving the lead wagon, and I was walking beside him, thankful that we were not eating the dust of the other wagons. There was a flicker of movement on the rocky hillside to the left and the flash of a white-tailed deer.

"Jed!" Jonathan cried, pointing at the retreating animal.

Jed appeared from the other side of the wagon, unslinging his rifle. Without hesitation, he took aim and fired.

The deer tumbled end over end, slammed into a large boulder, and lay there unmoving. "Woo-hoo!" Jed cried.

Jonathan was laughing, a welcome sound. We had stopped moving forward, and Gus Catledge and Bart Parsons joined us and slapped Jed on the back. Jonathan jumped off our wagon, handing the reins to me. Then the men went toward the deer, with Jed proudly at the center of the group. After a moment, Edwin followed. But when Cager and Becky—who are always together now—tried to join them, they were waved back.

Jonathan was just reaching the deer's side when three Indians came around the boulder. Both parties looked surprised. The men of our group reacted first. Only Jonathan and Bart were armed. Jed still carried his rifle, but he had not reloaded. Jonathan and Bart raised their rifles while two of the Indians retreated behind the rocks, but the third stood with his hands stretched outward.

He pointed to the dead deer and then back to himself. Jonathan was shaking his head vigorously. It appeared that Gus was trying to calm him. I saw Edwin glance back at me, and I waved to him furiously to return. But he was looking to his older brother, who was standing stalwartly at his stepfather's side.

Jonathan suddenly raised his rifle and shot into the air.

It shocked everyone. The Indian bolted into the maze of boulders on the hillside. Jed furiously began to reload his rifle. Gus and Bart looked ready to run back to the wagons. Jonathan shouted at them, and they took hold of the deer's legs, lifted it, and stumbled back to us.

They hoisted the carcass into the back of our wagon, and by unspoken agreement, we went on, out of sight of the small hills we had been traveling through, until we reached a wide, flat spot between the curves of the river, so that we were surrounded on three sides by water. We circled the wagons on the unprotected side and brought all the animals inside the circle.

"Keep an eye out, Edwin," Jonathan said as he pulled the deer onto the ground and dragged it to the lone tree within our enclosure big enough to hang it from. I almost said something, and my husband saw it, so he added, "Stay inside the circle of wagons, but keep a watch."

Later, the men started a fire, and we gathered around it. I looked back at the deer, hanging there in the tree. There was a wound in its neck, but there was also one in its hindquarters. Jonathan had jerked the arrow out of the neck wound, but not before I'd seen it.

Jed had hit the deer in the rump, but the Indians had struck the killing blow. By rights, the deer was theirs. Not only that, but I had noticed that all three Indians had been emaciated, with jutting ribs.

But I did not say anything then.

The men were jubilant now that the danger was past, even Gus Catledge, who was normally the most peaceful of men. Jed and Edwin were so excited that they could barely contain themselves. The women were quieter, and I sensed that I was not the only one troubled by the unfairness of what we had done.

The whiskey flowed freely that night, and it was left to Jed and Edwin to keep watch. I went to bed early. When Jonathan finally joined me, he was too drunk to be amorous for once, for which I was thankful. I waited until he was quiet before I spoke.

"Jonathan," I whispered. "Don't you think we could have shared?"

"What are you talking about?" he grumbled. I should have heard the warning in his voice.

"I think those poor savages were starving," I said.

He rose up on one elbow. His free hand shot out and took me by the throat, and he squeezed until I could barely breathe. He put his face just inches from mine, his foul breath flowing down on me. "Don't you question me, woman," he growled. "I know what you're thinking. You're sorry you married me. You wish you still had that worthless husband of yours who kept you in rags."

He shoved me away. I fell backward, and my head struck the tent post. I felt the blood flowing from where I bit my tongue and cut my lip.

"You aren't the only one with regrets," he said. "You seem capable of only producing girls and boys who might as well be girls, for all the good they do. Now leave me alone. Be glad I'm here to protect you."

He rolled over and went to sleep immediately, snoring loudly, as he usually did when he was drinking. But I didn't sleep at all that night. My mind searched for an escape, but there has never been a woman more at the mercy of her man than I, so far from civilization. I have nowhere to run, no one to protect me. The other families will stay out of it; it isn't their business. Jed would probably blame me rather than his stepfather. Edwin might be tempted to try to save me, and I fear what Jonathan would do to him.

For this reason, I have decided that I must never tell anyone.

<u>June 5, 1845</u>

This morning, it was as if Jonathan couldn't remember what he had done. He stumbled out of the tent and didn't come back to my side until darkness had fallen. As we cooked breakfast, the other women were quiet, and I saw them looking at my cut lip. I told them I had stumbled into the tent post upon rising in the night, but I could tell they didn't believe me.

As we set out on today's journey, the Catledges realized that they were missing the small pony that Becky sometimes rode. The little creature had been inside our protective circle along with the other animals—along with us.

Edwin and Jed said they hadn't seen anything, but they looked abashed. I suspect that they fell asleep while on watch.

I thank God that the Indians did not seek retribution, but only what was fair.

June 7, 1845

I know not how to speak of this, but I must. Sarah has gone to her heavenly reward. May God give her the happiness she never found here on Earth. A fever overcame her in the night. It was quick, so quick that it still hasn't sunk in. Jonathan is silent, brooding. The others in our party try to comfort him, but it is as if he doesn't know they are there. I tried to comfort him as well, but he shook me off angrily, staying by Sarah's side to the end.

She spoke in a fever, but what she said chilled me. "Where's Mama?" she asked.

Jonathan tried to shush her, to put his gnarled fingers against her lips. "Rest, daughter," he murmured.

"Papa?" Her little voice rose. "Where's Mama? Why do you hurt her?"

Jonathan froze for a moment, then said, "Mama is at peace, Sarah. She is waiting for you."

The others had given us privacy. No one else overheard Sarah's words.

I turned away, tears in my eyes. But beneath the sorrow, I felt a strange foreboding come over me. *Why do you hurt her?*

Sarah didn't speak again, but simply stopped breathing. We will bury her in the morning. Jed is by the campfire, carving her name into a wooden cross. Edwin has gone to the Catledge camp, led there by Becky. Nan and Mattie are silent.

I fear that things will change now. Jonathan always showed kindness to Sarah. He was always careful not to upset her.

Now I fear that there is no one he cares about.

June 9, 1845

Jonathan refuses to bury his daughter. He has wrapped her in canvas and commanded that I sew it tight.

"But, Jonathan," I began, but he glared at me with such venom that I fell silent. I set to work. He placed her gently in the back of the wagon.

The others of the company are watching in disbelief, but thus far no one has said anything.

June 11, 1845

Gus Catledge and Bart Parsons have confronted my husband about Sarah. The odor has become unbearable. The weather is unseasonably warm, and her canvas shroud is not keeping foul-smelling liquid from escaping. I fear our wagon will be unusable before long.

"It's unclean!" Bart shouted when Jonathan turned his back on him.

Jonathan whirled, his voice low and mean. "I promised Sarah I would take her to Oregon, and I'm going to fulfill that promise."

"That's crazy talk," Gus said.

Jonathan wouldn't listen. He climbed into the back of the wagon and closed the flap, and no one dared follow.

June 12, 1845

Jonathan is in a rage. I'm afraid he will hurt someone.

In the night, someone took Sarah's body away. No one will confess to the deed, and everyone is avoiding Jonathan, so in his eyes, we are all guilty. I noticed—and thankfully Jonathan did not—that Becky returned his gaze defiantly. I also noticed that the small marker that Edwin had carved Sarah's name into is missing from the back of the wagon.

I am secretly relieved that she is gone, though I don't dare say so to Jonathan.

Chapter Nine

I do not know what day this is. I write this in darkness, filling the pages copiously, for there is no need to save blank pages for the future. Here at the end, I've found a strange peace, an acceptance of my fate. I'm calm enough to actually think about these horrible events without fear.

I will write this down as if it is happening now, for my memory is clear, here at the end. The pain and the fear are still in my mind, but I find I can write about them dispassionately. I will relive the last day of my life.

***

The scribble-scrabble of tiny feet on bare rock wakes me up. Something licks my cheek. I try to slap away the rough tongue, but it moves to my other cheek and then down my neck. Small, sharp teeth gnaw into my skin.

My guttural cry echoes down long corridors of blackness.

Awareness of who I am and where I am finally comes to me.

Gold. I am in the Blue Bucket Mine, and my friends are somewhere up above. Surely they heard me fall and are coming to rescue me.

Or are they? The doubt grows, and suddenly I am certain they aren't coming. Without me, there is more gold for each of them. They will tell themselves it isn't their fault. They will make the convenient assumption that the fall has killed me.

"Help!" I shout as loud as I can.

The sound seems to bounce right back, unlike the scrabbling sounds of the small animal, which echoed for a long distance. Strange. It is as if someone is holding a blanket overhead, muffling my voice.

"Help!" I try to cry again.

This, time no sound emerges at all. I feel my throat, and there is a hole where my voice box should be. It is big enough to put a finger into and rough around the edges. I cough at the sensation, and a fear that is greater than the pain takes over my consciousness.

No one is going to save me. I am going to have to save myself.

I try to rise, but one leg has no feeling in it at all, and I tumble onto my face. I reach down and touch the jagged shard jutting out of my thigh. There is no pain at first, only a numb sensation of something wrong, as if this is happening to someone else. As I run my fingers over the shard, a dim realization comes to me that it is my bone.

Then the pain strikes, a jolt running up my leg and into my chest, exploding into my head. I don't think after that, I just scream.

Again I wake to tiny feet. They are walking up my chest. Liquid is flowing down my neck and over my shoulders. The pain in my leg is now a heavy throb, as if my leg is buried under rock. When I try sitting up, the leg is jarred and the pain jolts me again, and I scream but somehow remain conscious. My fear of the creature eating me is greater than the pain.

I grab at the small weight on my chest, but it moves too quickly. The scribbling sound moves away and behind me. After a time, I hear it approach again.

I lay back, waiting, feeling helpless.

A light appears above me, and at first I am certain my mind is creating it out of fear and pain. Then the face of a young man appears, deep eyes staring down at me impassively. It is the same ghost I saw in the corridor above, the one who startled me, who sent me tumbling down the rocky slope.

The rat scurries away at the sight of the ghostly light. Other lights appear, floating up out of the darkness, until there are three apparitions. This time I can't see their faces, but I can see the outlines of arms and legs, and something makes me believe they don't mean me harm, that they are sad for me. There is a small boy and a small girl. The first ghost is bigger than the others. He floats above me protectively.

I'm sure I'm imagining them, but their presence comforts me, so I choose to believe they are real. Their concern only intensifies the guilt that overcomes me at this moment. I have been a fool. I have left the woman I love for a fool's errand.

Why did I let Virgil talk me into this? I was happy enough back in Portland. I had a good job at the docks; I had friends. Most of all, I had Jenny. I was in love with her, and I was pretty sure she was falling in love with me. The future seemed bright.

A deep feeling of loss comes over me. I look up and see the girl ghost staring down at me again, I sense out of pity. If only I'd stayed with Jenny instead of running off with my friends. Even while I was courting Jenny, I'd spent many a night drinking until the wee hours with Jake and Virgil. Now I regret every moment away from her.

It was the gold. From the moment I heard of the gold strikes in California, I wanted to board a boat headed south. But something, I didn't know what, kept me from making the final decision for a long time.

I now understand what it was that kept me back.

Fear.

I'm not a brave man, never have been. I've always been willing to settle for what I can get without striving or risking too much. Just surviving is good enough for me.

But when Virgil challenged me, when he implied I was a coward for not wanting to go along, it was easier just to join him. I didn't figure we'd actually find any gold. It was going to be a little adventure with friendly companions, perhaps the only real adventure in my life. I thought I'd return to Jenny and probably never leave the docks again until they carried my cold, lifeless body away.

It would have been good enough for me.

The remorse I feel at this moment is stronger even than the pain. I will try to get back to Jenny, no matter the cost.

I tug at my belt, sliding it off. I reach down gingerly; I feel the bone. I wonder if I have the courage to reset it. I loop the belt around my leg and bone, every small motion sending waves of pain up my body. Before I can question my course of action, I pull the belt tight. My leg feels as if it is falling away, and my vision disappears into the pain. A muffled scream bursts from my ragged throat. I lose consciousness again.

***

I awake to claws scratching at my forehead and tugging at my hair as the creature leverages its tiny body to bite into my cheek. I try to slap the animal away. My fingers brush something round and soft lying on my cheek. My mind goes blank in gibbering horror at the realization of what it is. I reach up and touch the edge of the hole where my eye is supposed to be.

In the darkness, I can't tell I am blind. The pain in my head is dull compared to my broken leg, but the thought of my detached eyeball is even more horrifying. I gurgle my protest, a primal, gibbering stutter of breath.

Where are my protective spirits? Why have they abandoned me?

I push the eyeball back into its socket, knowing it is useless but unable to endure the thought of it gone. I breathe deep breaths, and slowly my thoughts come back to me.

The knowledge that I am a dead man lodges in my chest, and yet my mind still rebels against the thought. I reach down tentatively to feel my leg. Miraculously, the bone has slid into place. I push myself up, the pain in my neck and leg sharpening, and stars appear in the darkness where my vision should be. Perhaps I have reached some kind of limit, for I don't pass out.

My fall was a tumbling one, not a straight drop. If I can crawl upward, if I can reach the corridor above, it will be but a short distance to the mine's entrance. If my friends see or hear me, they will have to help me or acknowledge their guilt. Jake and Virgil are greedy men, but I don't believe they are murderers.

The scrabbling sound returns, but this time, there is more than one rat. They come boldly to within inches of me. I strike out, and the little feet patter away, then come back. "Help!" I try to shout, but it comes out as a croak. I search the darkness for the ghosts, for I realize now that the rats run away each time one of the ghostly figures appears.

"Little bastards," I try to say, not sure if I mean the ghosts or the rats.

All that comes out of my throat is a squishy sound. I see colors in the darkness, as if my brain is trying to supply vision: the red of a dull throb, the white stars of the sharper pains when I move abruptly, a kind of blue color that is my weariness.

I've lost a lot of blood, and I am weak. I reach over my shoulder, and amazingly, my pack is still there. I manage to slide it off. I reach in, feel for the waterskin, and bring it to my lips. The water enters my mouth, flows down my throat, and emerges from the hole in my neck, splashing over my chest. But a small amount reaches my stomach, and within minutes, I am feeling slightly more alert.

With the alertness comes a sharper awareness of the pain. It is the price I pay for consciousness. I almost long for oblivion. It would be so much easier to simply lie back and let it happen. It won't take long. The loss of blood, the lack of water, and my own despair will take me quickly. I won't be awake when the rats come.

Strangely, it is the thought of the little beasts feeding on my corpse that motivates me to try to save myself. I reach into my pack again and find the matches.

Almost afraid of what I'll see, I strike a match against the rock.

The light flares, but only to one side. My other eye is dead. My surviving eye struggles to compensate, to take in the full scope of my predicament.

I see something scurry away from the light. I can't get a good look at the rat, but it is bigger than I expected. The match goes out.

In the darkness, I catch a glimpse of the ghostly children glowing in the shadows. I can't make out their expressions, but it seems to me that they are sad. If they are haunting me, they are gentle in their persecution.

It makes no sense. The entrance to the cave had been covered by a rockfall until we cleared it away. Why are there children in here? What could have happened to them?

It has to be an illusion, I tell myself. *I am filling the darkness with my fear.*

I shake my head, and my pain redoubles with the motion. *I don't have time to waste*, I think.

In the darkness, I count the matches carefully, one by one. There are twenty-four of them. But I don't need them for most of what I need to do. I know the direction I want to go. I simply need to turn around and start climbing.

I start crawling into the darkness, hands outstretched, feeling my way.

***

It is impossible to move. My leg is useless; I'm too weak to haul myself upward by my arms alone. My hands feel like unfeeling lumps of flesh. My heart is pounding so hard it is as if it is trying to escape my chest.

I light a match and nearly sob at the sight it reveals. Only a few feet down is the smeared puddle of blood where I lay before. I let the match go out, barely noticing it burning my fingers.

I see the ghostly children above me. Soon I will join them. Once again, despair and guilt overcome me. I see Jenny's smiling face as if it is before me. *Why did I leave her?*

In the darkness, I reach out and grab a rock and pull myself up another few inches.

***

Sharp teeth tear into the open wound on my leg. There is downward pressure, as if the teeth are trying to grab ahold of my flesh and drag me backward. I slap at the rats and hit my broken bone instead. I scream, but the sound is only inside my head. Outwardly, only a wheezing sound emerges.

I am tugged downward, as impossible as it seems. I am dragged slowly over the sharp rocks, each inch sending waves of pain through my body, helpless, wordless pain.

I reach into my pocket, bringing out the little muff gun. I bought it at a cigar store in Portland, a small gun, made to fit in a woman's muff, as the name implies, or her handbag. I thought it simply an extra precaution, carrying it loosely in my pocket.

The weapon has only a single bullet in it, but there are more than one of the creatures. I hold the gun in my hand. *I will save that single round for the end.*

My leg has stopped hurting. I reach down and feel the wound. My hands feel something sticky, and I lift my fingers to my nose and smell the odor of decay. It is my own rotting blood.

The rats continue to drag me downward. I light another match, and the rats move off a short distance but don't hide. I see their glittering eyes and white teeth.

I am back where I started. I barely feel the match burning into my thumb before it blinks out.

Now it feels as if teeth are biting into every part of my exposed flesh. Something is burrowing under my clothes, and a fresh pain erupts in my stomach, as if the creature is eating its way into my body.

I fumble for the last match. I still want to live. Fire will drive the beasts away, if only for a moment. I light the match, and my one blurry eye sees nothing but lumps under my clothing, and where each bulge squirms, I feel teeth ripping into me.

The ghostlights approach again. The children illuminate the darkness, and the rats scurry away. Remorse at my wasted life fills me again. The children bring guilt and shame with their presence, and I realize that I am indeed being haunted. The children are no longer blurry, but seem as real as my own existence. I know that they will stay with me to the last. I pull out this journal and start writing.

***

My mind is slowing to a crawl, and a peaceful lassitude is washing over me. I can barely hold the pen. I have the muff gun in my other hand, and with the last of my strength, I will bring the muzzle to my temple, and I will put an end to this existence.

Strangely, it is the ghosts of the children who give me peace, for if they exist, so too must an afterlife of some kind. I search my heart and believe I have been a good man in this life. I feel sorry for my little ghost companions, for I sense that something terrible must have happened for them to be here. I am now certain I will not linger on here as a ghost, nor will I sink down into the fires below. I am strangely at peace.

I'll just lie here for a while. I don't really need to move. Here is good enough.

Chapter Ten

Diary of Ellen Meredith

The Oregon Trail, June 19, 1851

Over the last week, Jonathan has rejoined our company—in mind and body, at least, if not in spirit. After Sarah's body was taken, he stalked off into the open plains by himself, taking no supplies, not so much as a canteen of water. He returned a day later, but would speak to no one. Then, yesterday morning, he joined the daily discussion at breakfast.

I believe that he knows that Sarah is better off now, and that it needed to be done. Yet I don't believe that he has forgiven any of us. His eyes are cold now, and he never smiles.

Our map informs us of landmarks along the trail, names like Chimney Rock and Scott's Bluff and Devil's Gate, but these marks on paper do not prepare us for the splendid beauty of these places. They seem placed at our convenience, for as soon as we leave one landmark behind, we spy the next on the horizon, and it beckons us forward, giving us a goal where we can happily end our day, having reached our destination.

While these places no doubt will become happy memories for most of my fellow overlanders, for me, each of them represents an argument or a fight, or their aftermath, the bitter, silent recriminations.

Jonathan did not strike me again for some time. Indeed, he seemed contrite, and for a time he was mindful of my needs. But as the trip has gone on and the frustrations have built, he has begun to lash out again. He never speaks of Sarah, but I know that with every angry outburst, he is thinking of his poor daughter.

The other couples are starting to keep their distance, though to their credit, they haven't abandoned my children and me. They keep quiet when Jonathan is around, for he can be withering in his scorn.

He is certain he knows best in all things. If one of the others suffers a mishap—ties a knot incorrectly so that a horse gets loose, or fails to secure a load on a river crossing, or suffers a broken wheel—according to Jonathan, it is their fault and they should have known better. He will help, but only because he knows it is expected of him. He does not hide his scorn.

Yet if the same thing happens to us, it is simple bad luck—or worse, someone else's fault. Jonathan does not handle adversity well, for he always had his way at his ranch, always had others in his employ to do his bidding. One of those who were under his orders was my own dear Cullum. I have begun to question the story, told to me by Jonathan (for Cullum never complained), that it was he who had kept Cullum from failure. I wonder, rather, if it wasn't Jonathan's inheritance that bought him success. I wonder, even, if it wasn't Cullum who kept Jonathan's ranch going.

Such thoughts are strangely comforting; to know that once I loved such a man, and such a man loved me. Life is hard; this I know. But I experienced those few short years of happiness with Cullum, and for that, I will always be grateful.

My younger children spend most of their time with the other children under the care of Mary Perkins, and while my mother's heart mourns the loss of their company, I know it keeps them safe, away from Jonathan's harsh words and glowering disapproval.

June 28, 1845

We will soon leave the plains, and in the distance, the Rocky Mountains are looming. They look impassable, but our maps—and the many trekkers before us—assure us there is a way over them.

"We shouldn't always trust the map," Gus said one night around the campfire as we inspected the route. "There are hucksters selling their own routes for their own reasons."

"Aye, but perhaps we are blindly following the blind," Bart said. "If a better way is found, are we to distrust it without even chancing it?"

"We left Independence late in the season," Jonathan said. "It will be a close thing if we do not find a way to shorten our journey."

In the end, it was decided that we would to continue to follow the well-worn ruts and avoid the dotted marks of paths unproven. Though my husband didn't see it, it was his urging to try the shortcuts that decided the matter, for whatever he suggests, the other men reject, though of course they don't say so out loud.

It adds to my husband's frustration, however, and it is slowly, inexorably turning into rage. The others don't see the coming storm. But at night when we are alone, with deep, urgent tones, especially after he's been drinking with the other men, he insists that we are being fools; that we are missing our chance to get to Oregon faster.

I have learned to stay silent as he slowly winds himself into a rage the longer he talks. His whispers become louder until I am certain that everyone can hear him. Still, there is nothing he can do without our lone wagon striking out on our own, and even he is not so foolish as to do that.

At night, Jonathan thrashes so violently from his nightmares that I must move to the wagon and sleep as best I can on the wooden floor. He cries out "Sarah! Sarah!" over and over again, and it breaks my heart.

<u>July 14, 1845</u>

We have reached the South Pass of the Rockies, which is far less strenuous than any of us expected. By now, so many have crossed this way that the trail is clearly marked, and there are helpful signs along the way, scratched into the sides of boulders, carved into tree trunks, telling us where to find water, where there is plentiful fodder for the livestock, and where we can find firewood already cut and dried.

I, for one, am glad to be leaving the flat, dry plains, which are intolerably dusty one day and as windy and rainy as a hurricane the next.

Both of my boys are enamored of Becky Catledge. The other children already follow her, and I sometimes wonder if Mary Perkins is in charge of Becky or if Becky is in charge of Mary, for the younger girl seems more mature.

One day, as we reached a high meadow surrounded by stands of ponderosa pines, we decided to end our travels early, glad for the brook that burbled through the grasses. The women set about cleaning clothes, and the men took the opportunity to relax and do minor repairs.

The boys went hunting, with Becky trailing along. Jed has been given a rifle, and Jonathan sometimes lets Edwin carry his if he doesn't think he needs it.

They came rushing back a few hours later.

"Becky shot an elk!" Edwin cried out the moment they entered the camp.

"An elk!" Bart cried, springing to his feet. "Are you certain?"

None of us had yet seen an elk. We'd seen buffalo herds in the distance, but we were told to leave them be if we didn't want confrontations with Indians. Since we were still well provisioned on the Great Plains, we obeyed this stricture. Once, I saw some lean, tan creatures leaping high in the air as they fled from us, and I understood them to be antelope. Deer are plentiful, but not so easy to kill as one might think. Gus is a good hunter, Bart sometimes gets lucky, and Jonathan has had to be satisfied with one giant buck he stumbled upon, but which was, in truth, the biggest of the prizes.

I wasn't sure I even knew what an elk looked like. A big deer, I supposed.

"You left it untended?" Jonathan asked.

"It is so big, Father," Jed started to say. "We couldn't…"

Gus interrupted before it could become an argument. "How far?"

"Just over the ridge," Becky said. "Come on!" She went running up the hill. Edwin ran after her. The rest of us followed more slowly, either through fear or the infirmities of age.

As we neared the crest of the hill, we saw Edwin and Becky standing stock still, and when the clearing came into view, the rest of us saw the reason.

The elk was huge indeed, its rack of antlers as big as a small deer. It was lying on a slope, its belly and head slanted up at an ungainly angle. But sitting above the huge animal was a creature that was even bigger.

It was a bear, but unlike any bear I've ever seen, not like the smaller black bears that sometimes ventured near the farm looking for scraps and who ran away at the first smell, sight, or sound of humans.

This bear was a light tan color, with long, shaggy hair, and an enormous head. It looked up as we reached the top of the hill and grumbled warningly. For a moment, none of knew what to do. In hindsight, we should have simply retreated and let the bear have its prize.

In their rush, neither Bart nor Gus had thought to bring their rifles. Both Jed and Edwin were still carrying theirs. Without a word, before any of us could raise an objection, Jonathan grabbed the rifle out of Edwin's hands and raised it.

There was single loud click. Jonathan's arms dropped, and he looked at the rifle in shock, his face white. Then he turned to Edwin, who avoided his glance. The boy had forgotten to reload the rifle.

The click succeeded only in alerting the grizzly to our intentions. It rose up on its hindquarters and roared, and I swear that the hair on my head stood straight up and my blood froze in my veins. Jed was fumbling to unsling his rifle and take aim, but I had my doubts that a single bullet was going to stop this monster from reaching us. Beside me, I saw Gus pull his bowie knife, and I nearly began to laugh hysterically.

And then Becky rushed toward the bear, waving her arms and screaming at the top of her lungs. Moments later, Edwin joined her.

I couldn't take it in. It didn't seem possible—this slight blonde girl charging such a beast, and my own youngest son following her. But the bear seemed to hesitate, and when the rest of us saw that, we joined in, raising our voices, swirling our arms about frantically.

Becky Catledge was too much for that bear. It turned slowly and loped away, looking over its shoulder in alarm.

It took us the rest of the day to drag the elk carcass to the camp. We slung ropes around its antlers and dragged it downhill. It was so enormous, we gutted it right there on the ground, and then quartered it so that we could deal with the smaller portions. We built a large fire and made sure all our weapons were ready in case of a return visit from the bear.

That night, Edwin sat beside me by the fire while the elk meat cooked. He was staring at Becky, who was sitting with the younger children, laughing as if nothing unusual had happened.

My twelve-year-old son turned to me and said, "I'm going to marry Becky Catledge."

I didn't laugh. I considered it. He is such a dear, sweet boy, and I see Cullum in his manner and in his looks. I said, "I think that would be a fine idea, Edwin. A fine idea."

Jed was cleaning his rifle a few yards away. Though he wasn't staring at Becky quite as obviously as his younger brother was, he was sneaking glances whenever he could. Jed doesn't have the smiling, happy presence of Edwin—instead, he has taken on some of Jonathan's anger and scorn. I think he will be a formidable man someday. I saw the resolute look in his eyes as he took aim at the grizzly.

It is clear that Edwin has a rival suitor for Becky's affections, and as much as I love Edwin, I think he will be fine without the help of a good woman. But Jed could use a woman's tempering touch.

Becky looked up at last, and her gaze went to Jed, not Edwin. Jed looked down at his gun as if he didn't notice, but Edwin did, and it broke my heart to see the look of dismay on his face.

Chapter Eleven

<u>Portland, Oregon Territory, August 1851</u>

Dearest Frank,

I know that you do not approve of me taking the Skoocoom gold, regarding it as unseemly wealth, but if you accompanied me to Portland or on my other travels (an entirely unfair statement, since you have begged to come with me), you would see how important wealth can be. How much gold we possess may not matter so much at our ranch—gold does not feed the horses, plant the crops, or milk the cows—but here among the crowds of the city, wealth can be everything.

I have seen the hotel clerk trying to decide whether to grant me a room; I have noticed waiters arguing among themselves about who would serve me; I have had hansom cabs pass me by though I am hailing them. But people's attitude changes completely when I pay them, and it makes things much easier from then on.

Gold is a tool, nothing more.

Love,

Virginia

Virginia and Angus followed Terrance Drake to the front of the hotel, where a magnificent carriage awaited them. It was the kind of carriage that Virginia had seen only at a distance, on promenades where she wasn't welcome. She caught Angus ogling the coat of arms on the door of the coach, as if trying to figure out which noble family awaited them. As Drake opened the door for Virginia, she noticed the hotel clerk staring at them, his eyes wide in amazement that such a vehicle would be calling for the likes of her.

She smiled to herself. *He won't be looking down on me again soon.*

Drake got in and sat across from her, while Sims and Franklin took up seats in the driver's box.

Angus sat next to Virginia. "I must say, Miss Reed, I think being your companion is going to be an interesting experience," he observed.

The carriage moved quickly through the crowded streets. It was as if the other coaches and pedestrians made way for it. They climbed into the hills until the city and the river was a panorama below them. The houses grew larger the higher they went, until at last they entered a long, winding driveway that led to an enormous house on the crest of the hill. In Europe, the structure would have been deemed a castle, but Americans called it a mansion.

The coach went around the wide steps facing a magnificent rose garden and turned down a dirt path that wound around the mansion. It stopped at a carriage house. Not far away was a smaller home, from which a small man emerged. In truth, he was even smaller than he looked, for he stood extremely upright, his chin in the air.

"I'm John Lee," he announced. "I've been instructed to ask if you are hungry or thirsty. Mrs. Hoskins may not be ready to receive you for some time."

"See here, my good man," Angus intoned, laying the English accent on thickly. "Is there some reason we can't simply walk through the front door?"

Lee appeared shocked that anyone would question Mrs. Hoskins's wishes. "No slight was intended, sir," he said. "The front entrance is being newly tiled; I assure you that is the only reason."

"Of course," Angus said. "Naturally."

"I could use a drink of water," Virginia said.

"Come into my parlor, miss," Lee said. "I'll fetch you a glass."

Angus followed them into a small sitting room. "Do you have anything with a bit of spirit to it?" he asked.

"Certainly not," Lee said, looking affronted. "Would you like water, sir?"

"Yes," Angus said drily. "That would be lovely." To Virginia, he whispered loudly enough for Lee to hear, "I thought I left all this phony folderol back in England."

Lee returned with two tall, narrow glasses that clinked while he walked. He handed one to Virginia, who almost dropped it, for it was unexpectedly cold. "We have ice shipped in weekly," Lee said.

Angus took a deep drink and looked up with a grin. "Almost as good as spirits. Jolly good."

Virginia rolled her eyes. When Angus was speaking to her, his English accent all but disappeared. It seemed he could put it on or take it off depending on circumstances.

"Sit down and join us," Angus said as he sat down in a large, overstuffed armchair. The appointments and furnishings in this butler's house were more luxurious than those in Angus's own home.

Lee stiffened, as if the request was inappropriate. "I'm honored, sir. But I have my duties to attend to." He turned to leave the room.

"How did Mr. Hoskins make his fortune?" Virginia asked abruptly.

"I'm sure I don't know, miss," Lee said archly, turning around. "It is none of my business."

Angus laughed. "Come now, you don't expect us to believe that. What was it? Gold, lumber, wheat?"

"Well," Lee ventured, "Mr. Hoskins has extensive holdings in timberlands. Among other investments." He hurried out of the room before he could be asked any more questions.

"Interesting," Angus said. "Do you know this Mrs. Hoskins, Virginia? Are we to presume she is the lady in question?"

"I would assume so," Virginia said. "I can't imagine who else it would be."

Mr. Lee never returned, instead sending in a young Irish girl in a maid's uniform who took their empty glasses and asked if they wanted more water. From her tone of voice, she was hoping the answer would be no, and both Angus and Virginia declined. Then they sat awaiting the pleasure of her ladyship for the next hour.

Finally, the maid came and got them, and led them up a narrow path to a door on the lower level of the mansion. There was a laundry room beyond, and then a hallway with servant's quarters to either side. They were ushered up a flight of stairs that were so narrow and winding that when they emerged into a large ballroom, it was as if they were being set free from a cage.

Virginia saw a red-haired woman gazing out the window at the far end of the room. The maid curtsied and disappeared back into the warren of rooms below. The woman turned around.

"Virginia!" she exclaimed. "I'm so happy to see you!"

As Virginia stood motionless, shocked at the change in her friend, Mary rushed forward to take her hands.

Mary, who had been but a wisp of a girl when Virginia had first met her, had grown into a full-figured woman, though Virginia couldn't quite tell where Mary's body began and where the regalia she was wearing ended. It was a style at least ten years out of date, even in the backwoods of California, but she looked stunning in the ensemble, a dress of black and white layers, frilled and soft-looking, and a large black hat sweeping over her red hair. Her freckles were hidden under face powder, and her green eyes stood out in bright contrast to her pale skin.

She took off her hat, patting her curls into place.

Angus was certainly impressed. He bowed to her and said, "Angus Porter, at your service."

"Pleased to meet you, Mr. Porter," Mary Hoskins said. Her voice was low and deep, unlike the high, girlish voice Virginia remembered. Then it was as if all the starch went out of her, and she threw open her arms and embraced Virginia. "Oh, how I've missed you!" she exclaimed, and Virginia was surprised by the fervor of her hug.

Mary broke away and swept an arm toward the pure white couches at the center of the room. "Please, sit. I'll have Jane bring us some water." She lifted up a bell sitting on a table and rang it. "We have ice, can you believe it?"

"We've already partaken, Mrs. Hoskins," Angus said as they settled onto one of the couches. "While we were waiting."

"Waiting?" Mary looked confused. "You were waiting?"

"Below, in Mr. Lee's cottage," Virginia said.

Mary's skin was so white that when she flushed, it was startling, as if a fire had been lit just below the surface. "I gave strict instructions that you were to be brought to me as soon as you arrived."

Jane had reentered the room and was standing by the door. "Mr. Hoskins's orders, ma'am," she said quietly. "He wanted to meet the guests. He is on his way."

"Thank you, Jane, that will be all," Mary said in an imperious voice. The second the maid left the room, Mary whirled around and sat down in the chair across from them.

"I thought we'd have more time," she said. "Virginia, I didn't think you would come, but just in case, I left a message with Flora—or Rosie, or whatever she calls herself now. She saw you go into the madam's chambers and sent me a message."

"Are you all right?" Virginia asked.

Mary hesitated, then nodded. "I had no right to expect such a life as this," she said. "I'm very fortunate."

Which doesn't answer the question, Virginia thought.

"Much of what I know, I already told you in the letter," Mary said. "If you have Mrs. Meredith's journals, you know nearly as much as I do. But a few things have happened since I sent the letter. I'm now convinced that Jonathan Meredith murdered his wife and his two eldest sons, but I have no proof."

"You want to bring him to justice?" Virginia asked.

"I want nothing more," Mary said. "But if it were only that, I'd ask you to leave off now. It is too dangerous, and what is done is done. But..." She stood up and started pacing, her mind somewhere else. "I've gotten word that Becky is missing, too."

She stopped in front of Virginia, who felt compelled to stand up and take her shaking hands. "I can't bear the thought that something has happened to her, or if she is still alive, that she is in danger." Mary closed her eyes. "I tried not to have favorites, but I couldn't help it. Becky is such a brave, resourceful girl. She…she reminds me of you, Virginia."

"Me?"

"Yes," Mary said. "I've heard stories about you, Virginia. And when my husband found out I knew you, he investigated you. He was quite excited to think that he might meet you someday."

Angus had been turning his head from one woman to the other to follow their conversation. Now he broke in. "Your husband investigated Virginia?"

Mary looked surprised by his question, then smiled shyly. "Yes, Mr. Porter. My husband always investigates the people in my life. And yes, my husband knows of my past. It doesn't seem to bother him. In fact…" She shuddered slightly, but didn't finish the thought.

The door of the ballroom burst open and, as if summoned by their mention of him, a tall, elegant man strode across the room with a big smile. He wasn't as old as Virginia had expected, perhaps only a decade older than Mary. His black hair and closely trimmed beard had streaks of gray in them, but his face was unlined. He too was dressed in clothing that was a little out of date, but on him, as with his wife, it looked fashionable. It was a statement, Virginia realized, that he could afford the best but didn't care what others thought.

"I'm sorry I'm late, dear," he said to Mary. "I would have come sooner if I'd known we had guests." He turned to Virginia and bowed. "Mr. Lee has told me who you are, and I must say, I am delighted to meet you."

She nodded, not quite sure what to say.

He turned to Angus, who had gotten to his feet. "Mr. Porter, delighted to have you visit. I hope you've been offered a drink. No? Well, Mr. Lee doesn't approve, so I'll have to do the honors."

"We aren't staying," Virginia said. She looked over at Angus and shook her head almost imperceptibly.

"Sadly, Virginia is right," Angus said smoothly. "We have to meet the cattle buyers early in the morning, and we need a fresh start."

"Are you certain?" Hoskins asked. "I have the finest single malt whiskey from Scotland. I save it for just such occasions. I understand you are a world traveler of some renown, Angus…if I may call you Angus."

"I've been here and there…Oliver," Angus said.

Virginia caught his eye and motioned her head toward the door. Angus continued, "And one thing is the same the world over. Business can't wait."

"Yes, I know that well," Hoskins said ruefully. He was standing behind the chair his wife sat in. Mary seemed to have melted, as if her bones were softening. She was staring at her feet. Her husband reached out and put his hand on her shoulder. She jumped, so slightly that it would have been easy to miss.

"I really must insist you stay a while longer," Hoskins said. "Mary has so been looking forward to seeing you."

Angus had started to get up, but he shot a glance at Virginia, and since she wasn't joining him, he sat back down.

"That's better," Hoskins said, in the tone of man who was accustomed to getting his way. "You have certainly traveled a long way for something as humdrum as buying cattle."

"We are looking for fresh stock," Virginia said.

"I'm given to understand that you are married, Miss Reed," Hoskins said. "Or should I say, Mrs. Whitford. I find it odd that you would travel under your maiden name."

"My husband is a famous cattle rancher," Virginia said. "I find that I can make better deals if I'm am poor helpless Miss Reed."

"Helpless?" Hoskins laughed. "Surely anything but that. But I've been told that the gold fields are not far from your ranch. Aren't you tempted to search your own lands for gold?"

Virginia tried not to show her surprise. It couldn't be a coincidence that Hoskins was bringing up the subject of gold.

"I have no interest in gold," she said.

Hoskins's eyes grew cold at her answer, as if he was enraged by her evasiveness. For a moment, his face shimmered, as if it was an illusion. Beneath the sophisticated exterior, Virginia glimpsed the face of a brute, with thick eyebrows and a jutting jaw, and huge eyes and ears. His body appeared to grow, his shoulders taking up twice the space as they had before, his arms seeming to extend to the floor.

And then the image blinked away, and Hoskins was speaking to her in a mild voice. "And yet I'm given to understand you pay for everything with gold nuggets."

Virginia looked around the room, but it was clear that no one else had seen what she had seen, except perhaps Mary, who appeared to have been pushed down even more firmly into her chair by the thick hands on her shoulders.

"It is the currency where I come from," Virginia said. She rose briskly and turned to Angus, who also stood up. "I've enjoyed this visit, but I really must be going."

"Pity," Hoskins said. "Well, perhaps on your next visit you can stay longer. I'll call Lee and have him see you out."

"Jane can do it," Virginia said. Jane was standing near the door, so quiet it was easy to forget she was there. Virginia started for the door before Hoskins could object. "We'll be on our way."

The front entrance of the house was tiled nicely. It didn't look as if any repair work had been done recently. Virginia and Angus walked down the broad steps, waiting for the carriage to be brought around.

"Seems like an intriguing fellow," Angus ventured.

"He is a monster," Virginia replied.

Chapter Twelve

Diary of Ellen Meredith

July 16, 1845

We have reached the western side of the Rocky Mountains. We have caught up with the main body of the wagon train and are no longer the laggards. This is due mostly to Bart's insistence that we start early each day and travel till nearly full dark. We are weary, but the joy of finding the others has helped revive our spirits.

The larger group has already been camped here for several days, resting for the final push across the last of the Great Desert. We are only weeks away from the borders of the Promised Land.

But even in this restful place, there is disagreement. Jonathan wants to take the cutoff south to Fort Bridger and then on to California, where the weather is said to be milder than the wet Northwest. But those in the wagon train who wished to go that way already left a few days before our arrival at this camp. Thus, if Jonathan cannot talk our small group and a few others into going along, we would be alone in the endeavor.

I fear that Jonathan is so stubborn that he will take this path with only his family, a single wagon in the wilderness. I have not said anything, hoping he will change his mind. But if I must, I will speak up for the sake of the children, though I fear what his reaction will be.

I feel safe among this vast congregation of wagons, stretching as far as the eye can see. Campfires flicker through the trees, as if the stars of heaven have fallen upon the Earth and are still shining. Because we have so many companions, I have not worried about the children, nor have I had to pay as much attention to my husband, who seems as eager for company other than me as I am for company other than him.

I wandered off on my own, ostensibly to find firewood, but in truth, I was happy just to be in these verdant pastures and tall trees. *Why can't we stay here?* I wanted to ask, but I knew the answer. When winter comes, these foothills will be covered with snow, which might be fine for the mountain men who came before us but won't do us farmers much good. No, we must push on to the valleys of Oregon or California.

I still have my heart set on the Willamette Valley. I know it cannot possibly be as fertile as the stories tell us, but I do not doubt it will be better than the rocky Missouri valleys we left behind.

I picked up an armload of firewood and, with a heavy sigh, began to return to our camp. Darkness was falling, but I had no fear of becoming lost, for I could still see the trail in the dimming light, and in the distance, I saw the campfires. When I heard familiar voices, I knew that I was almost home.

"We can't leave them," I heard someone say from up ahead. It was Becky Catledge, her voice more stress-filled than I had ever heard. She was a sunny girl, and little seemed to bother her.

"We aren't leaving them," Kerrie Parsons answered. "There are a thousand other souls in this wagon train. Let them join one of the other groups."

"But the others don't know them like we do!" Becky objected. "They won't know how Jed and Edwin are treated; they won't care."

"It isn't our business," Kerrie said. "They are not kin of ours."

"Is that how you feel about us?" Gus Catledge said. "Will you abandon us when we become inconvenient?"

"I didn't say that," Kerrie said. "You are friends and have been nothing but supportive and helpful. You don't quarrel, you don't—as far as I know—beat your wife."

There was a deep silence after this. I felt my face flushing in the darkness and wondered if I could back away without them seeing or hearing me. I stood stock still, hoping the darkness would deepen so they would not see my shame.

"My wife is right," Bart Parsons said, finally. "It is none of our business. What matters is that we get our families safely to Oregon. And Jonathan Meredith is a threat to that."

"How is he a threat?" Abigail Catledge asked. "We have outvoted him at every turn. He must follow us or go it alone."

"Yes," Kerrie said, "and he becomes angrier each time he is thwarted. I fear someday he will forget himself and strike someone other than his own family. I don't trust him, and I don't like him."

"But what of Ellen?" Abigail asked. "What of the children?"

Again there was a long silence. I was so riveted by the conversation that I didn't notice the firewood beginning to escape my grip. When the branches fell, they dropped to the ground with a clatter. I closed my eyes, wishing I were invisible.

"Ellen?" I heard Abigail's kindly voice ask. "Is that you?"

No, I devotedly wished I could say. *It is not me.* But in speaking, I would, of course, reveal myself.

It was too late. I felt someone take my arm, and I was led into the firelight. I opened my eyes. Becky was at my side. Everyone was looking at me, even the children, and I was so mortified that I could not speak.

"You heard us?" Bart asked.

"Of course she heard us," Abigail retorted. "We should never have been speaking thus in the first place. If you can't say something to someone's face, you shouldn't say it at all."

"I'd say it's decided," Gus said. "We stay with Mrs. Meredith, with Jed and Edwin, and with the girls. There will be no more such talk."

No one contradicted him. A few hundred feet away, I saw the familiar outline of our wagon, so like a hundred other wagons and yet different— damaged where a branch had fallen on it and bent one of the staves, and on the back, the outline of the extra barrel with its distinctive lid. There were small, quick shadows in the firelight: the girls playing some game; the slower, larger shadows of the boys; and biggest of all, unmoving in the firelight, as if he was listening, the outline of my husband.

"The main group is leaving tomorrow," Gus said. "But the forward movement will not reach us until the next day. What do you say we go on one last hunting trip, Parsons? Lord knows, after seeing that grizzly, I'm never going into the woods alone again."

"I'll join you," Bart said. "Gladly."

As they began to discuss their plans, I stood up, hoping to slip away without anyone noticing. I saw sad smiles on Abigail and Karrie's faces, but it was the servant girl, Mary Perkins, who came over to me and kissed me softly on the cheek.

I was astonished at her familiarity, and yet it was strangely comforting. *When was the last time I felt a kindly kiss?* I wondered.

She accompanied me without a word to my campsite, but left me before entering the circle of light. Jonathan glanced up at me curiously, but didn't say anything.

July 17, 1845

The men have gone hunting. Jonathan saw their preparations and joined them. The other women are solicitous toward me, and no one has brought up the events of last night. I'd almost rather they didn't treat me with such kindness, for it makes me feel as if I am an invalid. Becky stayed near our wagon all day, talking to the boys, playing with the girls, and every once in a while casting a worried glance my way.

<u>July 18, 1845</u>

Last night, the men returned with a couple of braces of rabbits. We fixed a stew. We will be leaving at first light, the last of the wagons once again. As the men passed the whiskey jug around, they got louder, especially Jonathan, who brought up the detour to Fort Bridger again.

"We can replenish our supplies there," he insisted. "You don't have to make a decision on California until we are there."

"No, Jonathan," Gus said. "We are close to our goal. I will not waver now."

"Nor I," Bart said.

Jonathan looked ready to push the issue, and I saw the other wives exchanging glances.

"Enough, Jonathan," I said. I barely believed it was my own voice, for was firm and steady.

He looked around as if he couldn't figure out where the voice had come from. Then his eyes flashed, and I knew that he was filling with rage. He rose, seeming to expand like the grizzly bear, raising his fists.

"Don't you touch her!" Becky Catledge was suddenly standing between my husband and me. She was in a defiant stance, hands on her hips and her chin jutted out as if daring him to strike her, a slight fourteen-year-old girl half my husband's size.

"Becky Martha Catledge, you get over here right now," her mother said sternly.

"No, Mama, I will not," Becky retorted. "Why won't any of you do anything? Why do you let him get away with this?"

"Becky," I said. Everyone fell silent at the sound of my soft voice. "I am quite capable of taking care of myself. Please…go to your mother."

Becky stared at me, then glared at my husband, who was standing there with his mouth open, as if he couldn't believe what he was seeing and hearing. Becky gave him a last warning glance and then went and sat by her mother.

I stared into the fire as if nothing unusual had happened. I heard rather than saw my husband leave.

That night, I lay under my blankets, waiting for Jonathan to return. I was at peace. Whatever happened, I would accept. He might beat me, but I would never be silent about his bullying again.

He came to the wagon late and crawled in beside me, stinking of whiskey. He turned his back to me and went to sleep.

Chapter Thirteen

<u>Portland, Oregon Territory, August 1851</u>

Dearest Frank,

I received your letter at the hotel, which was a wonderful surprise. The mail routes seem to be getting more reliable all the time! I have found that everywhere I go on the Pacific Coast, communication and transportation are becoming faster. Soon we will be as cultured as the East Coast, and certainly more settled than the Midwest. Strange to travel so far over such wild territory and find civilization once again on the farthest side.

I was greatly surprised at your news that Feather visited the ranch. The last time I saw her, she was very reticent about where she was living and what she was up to. But she seemed happy, so I did not question her closely. You hint that she has news? Do you not trust the mail? I will be home soon, I hope; however, I believe I may have to travel into Eastern Oregon—back into the wilds. I will continue to write to you, but if you do not hear from me for a few weeks, it is because I could find no place from which to mail my messages.

Your loving wife,
Virginia

As the carriage pulled up in front of the Hoskins mansion, the door opened from the inside. Terrance Drake was sitting there, waiting. He handed Virginia an envelope as soon as she got in.

"Mr. Drake, I'm sure we don't require your company," Virginia said. "We can find our way back to the hotel."

"Read the note, miss," he said tersely.

The stationery was thick and pink, and it felt so luxurious to the touch that Virginia wanted to run her fingers across it. It gave off a faint smell of perfume, the same scent she'd smelled on Mary.

Dear Virginia,

I'm writing this with Mr. Hoskins in the next room, so I must be quick. I have told Mr. Drake most of what I know, which he is to communicate to you upon your bidding. I believe Mr. Drake to be loyal to me, and his men loyal to him, so I think we are safe. However, in the end, it is my husband who pays Mr. Drake, so I can't be completely certain. Everything depends on it, however. There is no choice. Mr. Hoskins will not soon let me out of his sight again. These circumstances have nothing to do with the matter at hand, I assure you. It is something that is happening between my husband and me.

Virginia looked up at Terrance Drake, who was watching her. She handed the letter to Angus, who immediately started reading it.

"It appears that I am to trust you, Mr. Drake," Virginia said.

"Yes, ma'am," he said.

"Can I trust you, Mr. Drake? Or will you tell Mr. Hoskins what has happened here today?"

"I will, of course, tell my employer anything he wishes to know…should he ask," Drake said.

"Then perhaps we had best be going," Angus said, handing Virginia back the letter, "and he can ask after we're finished with our business."

"I think that might be for the best," Drake said. He slapped the top of the cab, and the carriage started moving.

"Very well, Mr. Drake," Virginia said once they were underway. "Please tell me what Mary wished me to know."

Drake looked over at Angus and then back at Virginia. "I am supposed to tell you and no one else," he said.

"Mr. Porter is as trusted by me as you are trusted by Mrs. Hoskins."

He gave her a thin smile. "I hope Angus is as grateful as I am for that trust," he said.

Virginia didn't say anything, but she couldn't help but wonder what the true relationship was between this man and Mary. He was a big, handsome fellow, certainly, and he had a certain brusque sympathy that Mary probably craved. Mr. Hoskins was outwardly friendly, but there was coldness beneath his exterior that he couldn't hide, and Virginia had glimpsed his true nature.

"Get on with it, man," Angus growled.

"Very well," Drake said, his smile dropping away. "I was tasked by Mary…by Mrs. Hoskins to find the Catledges. She was worried about them. It took me a long time, for they have changed their names. But finally, my man Sims found them in Vale, a small town in the High Desert. Mr. Augustus Catledge, who now goes by the name of Augustus Smith, owns a small feed shop there.

"By the time we found them, unfortunately, Becky was gone. It was Becky whom Mrs. Hoskins was worried about. Becky has apparently been a rather unmanageable girl since arriving in Oregon. By all accounts, she has an uncontrollable temper, sees danger everywhere, and has been making what seemed to others to be wild accusations.

"But I suspect her suspicions are justified," Drake concluded. "If you have read Ellen Meredith's journals, you know of what I speak." He waited for Virginia to respond.

"You've read the journals?" Virginia asked.

He nodded. "It was I who arranged for Madame Morrissey to hold them, and for Rosie to keep a watch."

"I have not yet read them all," Virginia said. "But I think I have an inkling of what they contain. Please go on, Mr. Drake."

"It appears that when Sims found him, Mr. Catledge was ready to leave his business in the care of his wife and go in search of his daughter. When I informed Mrs. Hoskins of this, she requested that I join Catledge in his efforts.

"I have sent a message to Catledge to wait for me. I was almost ready to depart when I received word that you had visited Madame Morrissey's establishment. Mrs. Hoskins has requested that I ask if you'd like to accompany me. I have concurred, for I have heard of you, Miss Reed. I have heard stories that were hard to believe until I met you. You seem to know your way around the wilderness. So, on behalf of Mrs. Hoskins, would you like to join me in my quest?"

"Quest?" Angus said. "What quest? For the girl?"

"Yes, Mr. Porter, for the girl…and more," Drake said. For the first time since Virginia had met him, Drake looked excited. It occurred to her that if they found the Lost Blue Bucket Mine, his fortune would be made, and he would finally have a chance to be Mary's social equal.

Virginia turned to Angus, who looked confused. "How fast can you read, Angus?" she asked.

"I have no way of comparing, Miss Reed," he said. "But I believe that I read at a sufficient speed for what needs knowing."

"Good," Virginia said. "You and I will both read Ellen Meredith's journals as quickly as possible. By the time we reach Vale, I think we shall both have our answers. But I have already read enough to know that if we find the route of that lost wagon train, we will find gold as well."

"Gold?" he said.

"Yes, Angus," Virginia said. "Gold. If the stories are true, enough gold for you to return to England and buy a peerage. But that is not the real reason I am embarking on this journey. If we are successful, we will find the truth about the fate of the lost children, and God willing, give their spirits peace."

Chapter Fourteen

The Oregon Trail, August 1, 1845

Since we began this journey, the children of all three families in our little group have played together under the watch of the stowaway girl, Mary Perkins—all except for Jed, who made it clear that he thinks he is too old and mature for that, and who spends most of his time in the company of his stepfather.

Indeed, it might be said that it was the children's friendship that brought our small band together. We all saw the benefit of shared responsibility for them.

But though I did not see it at first, there is a divide among the children. Edwin and Becky are often together, while the rest of the children follow young Cager, who is the most adventurous of them. Mary has had her hands full trying to keep up with them, much less control them. None of us are overly worried, however. We know they won't stray far, and that all of them need to learn to handle themselves in the wild.

Although Mary is a mere wisp of a girl, and not much older than the others, she takes her babysitting duties very seriously. I think perhaps she never had a childhood of her own, and that she has been taking care of herself for most of her life. But as diligent as she is, she is slowed by the youngest of her charges. Nan and Mattie are too slow for the older children, especially Cager, who ranges far and wide, with his sister Allie always by his side and the younger children keeping up as much as their short little legs will allow.

As the months have passed, Becky has begun to spend more time with the women, helping with the cooking and mending. She is fourteen years old, and it is high time for her to act like an adult.

Edwin, meanwhile, has also grown tired of the children's games. He sits in the back of our wagon, reading one of his books, for hours at a time.

Perhaps I should have seen the trouble that would develop between my two sons, but I was blind to it for far too long. Edwin has always worshiped Jed, doing whatever his older brother does. I never expected that to change. But when Jed distanced himself, Edwin gravitated to Becky's equally strong personality.

This morning, Jonathan rode ahead to confer with some of the leaders of the wagon train. We are but a few days from the Blue Mountains, and once over this last pass, we will be in sight of the mighty Columbia River. I was driving the wagon, which I have learned to do over the last few months.

The day was warm, and I was nearly dozing. In truth, the horses would have followed the beaten path with or without my direction.

Shouting roused me, and I slowed the horses. Mary ran up, her eyes wide. One look at her expression and I knew there was trouble.

"What's wrong?" I asked.

"I can't find Mattie or Nan," Mary said. "Or Cager and Allie."

"What do you mean, you can't find them?"

"I don't know where they went!" Mary wailed. "I tripped and scraped my knee, and I was tending to it. When I looked up, the children were gone."

I sprang down off the wagon and ran to the back. It didn't make any sense to me. The landscape was flat and wide in every direction. Where could they have gone?

There…just on the horizon, there was a small mound of rocks. It was the only place they could be.

I threw open the wagon's canvas flap. Edwin look down at me, blinking, his book still open in his lap. "What's wrong, Mama? Why did we stop?"

"Go find Jed!" I shouted. "Mattie and Nan are missing!"

Edwin leaped out of the wagon and went running toward the Catledge wagon, which was a few hundred feet ahead of us.

I felt dread and a sudden surge of guilt, for I have been paying little attention to my youngest children. Dear Mattie and Nan, who never cause me worry, who are always just there; old enough not to be babied, but young enough to follow orders, except when Cager and Allie lead them in astray. But even then, it is mostly just innocent shenanigans. Until that moment, I'd been more worried about Edwin and Jed.

Edwin reached the Catledge wagon, shouting. Gus stopped and jumped to the ground. "What's wrong?" he demanded.

As Edwin began to explain, the back flap of the Catledge wagon opened and Jed and Becky emerged. They were both red-faced, and they wouldn't look at Edwin or at each other. Edwin stood there blankly. He couldn't seem to summon any words.

"Out with it, Edwin!" Jed shouted.

"Nan and Mattie have gone missing," Edwin finally sputtered.

The Catledge horse, Old Bitty, was tied to the back of the wagon. Jed jumped up on her, bareback. He reached down to Becky, and she leaped up behind him. They rode quickly back to our wagon.

"I think they are over there!" I shouted, motioning to the rock outcropping on the horizon. Just as I pointed to it, I saw a small figure climb on top of the rocks, waving its arms. Though it was only a blur, it looked like Mattie. It seemed to me that I could hear her screaming, though at that distance, it was probably only my imagination.

Jed and Becky went galloping away toward the rocks, with Edwin running after them on foot. I watched anxiously as they all reached the small figure and then disappeared from view. But only moments later, Jed reappeared, carrying someone in his arms. Edwin followed. Between them, they managed to get the limp body onto the back of the horse. Jed climbed the shelf of rocks and mounted the horse, and they galloped back.

I held my breath, certain that it was Nan. But when Jed lowered the body into Gus's waiting arms, I saw that it was Cager. The boy looked dead, his face drained of blood.

"What happened?" Gus said.

"Rattlesnake," Jed answered.

"Give me the horse," I said.

Jed looked at me blankly, as if not understanding my words.

"Jedediah, you hand those reins to me right now." I snatched them out of his hands. I led the horse over to the back of the wagon, climbed onto it, and then mounted the horse with a leg on either side of her, as a man would do. I'd always ridden that way back at the farm when I was by myself, but I doubt Jed had ever seen me do it. I didn't care. I spurred the horse toward the rock outcropping.

Edwin had seen me approaching and was waiting for me. Without a word, he led me over the rocks. On the other side, in a rock-lined depression, was a pool of water. Allie, Mattie, and Nan were huddled together beside the water, as if unable to move. Becky looked as if she was trying to coax them out. I started to climb down to them.

Becky grabbed my arm. "The rocks are infested with snakes," she said.

I looked around. There was a dead juniper tree that had tried to survive between the cracks of the lava rocks. I wrenched it from the thin soil. I broke off the branches until it made a thick walking stick. Edwin stood staring at me with his mouth open. He had little idea of the strength that flowed through me at that moment. I would have torn this rock pile apart if I had to.

"Follow me," I said.

I probed each step as we descended, making as much noise as possible. I didn't believe the snakes wanted anything to do with us.

When we reached the three children, they all tried to spring into my arms. I put my arms around them, as wide as I could manage. "Shush, children. You're safe now," I said. "We must leave this place. Becky, will you help me?"

Becky took hold of Mattie's hand and started climbing. Edwin put his arm around Allie's shoulder and followed. Nan didn't want to move, but I finally pulled her away. We managed to make our way slowly up the slope.

Halfway up, Becky froze. Without turning around, she put her hand behind her. "Give me the stick," she whispered.

I had never heard a rattlesnake, but the sound was unmistakable. Becky lifted the walking stick slowly, then slammed it down, so fast and hard that we all flinched.

"You can keep going now," Becky said.

As I reached the spot where she had stopped, I saw a huge snake, half coiled, its head split in two. Its fangs were splayed against the rock, still leaking their poison.

We reached the flatlands. Gus and Bart met us halfway and took Nan and Mattie, while the rest of us followed more slowly. At last, we reached the wagons.

The three families gathered, trying to decide what to do. Cager's leg was swollen and turning a threatening black and red. He was passing in and out of consciousness, moaning pitifully in either state.

"We can't fall behind," Jonathan said. "We're already trailing the rest of the train by a day or more."

"But Cager can't be moved!" Karrie objected. "The motion of the wagon will hurt him."

"We must stay here a day or two," Bart said, adding to his wife's argument. "We've had to delay for you often enough, Meredith. Surely you can wait."

"I'm not going anywhere," Gus said. "Abigail and I will stay with you no matter what."

"How did this happen?" Jonathan said, throwing up his arms. He looked over at Mary, who stood with her arms clasped around herself, a little apart from the rest of us. "Why weren't you watching them?"

"I…I'm sorry," Mary stuttered.

"It isn't her fault," Edwin said, standing up and facing his father.

Jonathan struck him across the face before anyone could react. The slight boy fell backward, and Becky was on her feet in a flash, running toward my husband.

I don't know what would have happened next. I truly don't.

But Jed stepped out of nowhere, snagged Becky, and held her tight. Then he turned slowly toward his stepfather.

"Don't you ever strike my brother again, Jonathan," he said. It was the first time I'd heard my son use his stepfather's Christian name rather than calling him Father.

Everyone watched my husband as conflicting emotions ran across his face: anger, surprise, but also a tinge of fear. I looked at the two of them and realized that Jed has grown into a man on this journey. He may not be as big as his stepfather, but he is fast and he is young, and it isn't clear to me which man will prevail if it comes to blows.

Jonathan backed down, as he had to. He was on the verge of being banished by the others, and I think he knew it.

I am sleeping alone again tonight, as my husband has gone off into the desert by himself, whiskey jug in hand.

Chapter Fifteen

<u>Testament of Virgil Conner</u>

<u>July 21, 1851</u>

It watched me eat, then lumbered away, back into the darkness at the rear of the cavern. It has apparently learned that its captives cannot live on raw meat alone. I have tried to learn from Tucker's mistakes, and have kept my little corner of the cave clean of the carnage that these creatures create. The insects are unavoidable, but at least they do not scuttle across my face as I sleep.

I often saw Tad Marshall writing in his journal, and I wondered on it. I found a blank notebook among the belongings he left behind and have decided to follow his example.

I write this with the awareness that I may never return home. If my body is found, if you find this testament, please contact my wife, whom I left in Saginaw, Michigan. Her name is Agnes Conner. Tell her I did not mean to abandon her. Tell her I planned to come home as soon as I made my fortune.

I *have* made the fortune I hoped for, but I will never get to spend it.

If you find this document, it is because Jonathan Meredith has murdered my friend Jake and me, and—though I have no proof of this— likely young Tad Marshall as well.

We should have known we were in trouble when Tad disappeared soon after we arrived here. At first we believed Meredith when he said that Tad had run away, even though all his belongings were left behind. After all, both Jake and I have thought of doing the same thing.

But Meredith is vigilant, watching us from the mouth of the cave, not letting us go outside with any of our gear. Even if I were to make a run for it, I would face miles of desert without food or shelter. It gets cold at night in the desert, even this far into summer. Nor do I know where we are—Meredith made sure of that by blindfolding us.

So we work each day trying to find the pure nuggets of gold that Meredith demands. We bring him sacks of the stuff, and he picks through the heavy rocks and discards most of them.

I thought it only right that I also take some of the pure nuggets, and I squirreled some away, but one night, a few days after Tad disappeared, Meredith asked to see what we had in our gear and in our pockets. He didn't point the shotgun at us when he made the demand, but the message was clear.

Both Jake and I had secreted away several nuggets. Meredith laughed and put out his hands. When we turned them over, he added them to his own collection.

"You can take all the gold you can carry," he said. "Just as I promised. But you must first dig up what I require. The harder you work, the more you dig, the sooner we can return home. We'll be rich men, all of us."

Neither Jake nor I answered him. And it didn't stop me from saving the best nuggets. But instead of hiding them among my own possessions, I found a hollow spot in a cave wall and have been putting some there at the end of every shift, covering the hole with a stone. One night, as I came around a corner, I discovered Jake stomping down some loose dirt. We exchanged glances, but I merely nodded, and he nodded back. There is enough gold for the both of us.

We just aren't sure there is enough gold for all three of us.

"This mine has been worked before," Jake said one day, surprising me a bit. My fellow miner says very little, so little that I sometimes think of him as mute. "I don't believe that fat old Meredith did all this digging."

"Yeah?" I asked, wondering if he was about to say what I'd been thinking. And he did.

"So where are the other miners? Why haven't we heard from them? A strike like this should be famous by now, but the only rich man I know is Jonathan Meredith."

"What do we do about it?" I asked. We've seen Meredith kill men—Indians, true, but still men.

"We wait until he lowers his guard and take one of his guns," Jake said. "That shotgun scares me. I'd rather he wasn't pointing it at me…at *us* all the time."

"And then what?" I asked, wondering how far Jake was willing to go. I may not be a good man, but I have never killed anyone. Jake has scars all over his body, and he'd been a sailor—he'd jumped ship in Portland—so I am not so sure about him.

"We'll make him lead us back to Vale," Jake said. "After that, he can scream and yell all he wants, 'twon't no one listen. I doubt he'll say much, though. He wants to keep this strike a secret. I don't care, as long as I get mine."

"Agreed," I said. "But if Marshall got away, it might be too late. He's probably already told everyone by now."

Jake looked at me funny. "Yeah...*if* he got away, he's probably done that."

We stared at each other, each trying to guess the other's intentions. I don't know why we didn't just say it out loud, because I'm pretty sure both of us have come to the same conclusion: as soon as we are in sight of Vale, we are going to bury Jonathan Meredith in the desert where he belongs.

It's as if Meredith can sense what we're thinking. He always has that shotgun in his hands and a pistol in his belt, even when he sleeps. Since it is impossible to move silently because of all the loose gravel on the cave floor, Meredith seems to awaken if we so much as turn over in our blankets.

At first, I figured he'd get tired, never sleeping at night, but I forgot that he has all day to rest. No doubt he takes long naps when we are out of sight.

It is Jake and me who are getting exhausted. We are filthy, and we stink; there is barely enough dirty water from the creek bed to drink, much less to bathe in. My muscles are so tight and sore from the strain of wielding the pickaxe that they quiver at night. And yet the moment I put my head on my pack, I am asleep. I awaken every few hours, my body in pain, but I always fall back to sleep.

I'm not sure how long we've been here. It is the same every day. I figure it was five days before we saw Meredith do anything out of the ordinary. We came back to the cavern and he was gone.

Jake went to the entrance and looked out. The last light of day was shining in. He turned to me and shook his head. "He's not outside, at least not that I can see."

"Now's our chance," I said. "We can grab our gear and run."

"I have to go back and get my stash," he said. "I know you got one too, Virgil, don't tell me you don't."

We didn't even have a chance to start back before we heard Meredith returning. He was coming from the left-hand tunnel, the one he'd always told us to stay away from.

"Quittin' early?" he asked.

"No more than usual," I said, turning away so he couldn't see my disappointment.

"You boys been right curious about this tunnel, now haven't you?" he said. "I've seen you looking. Come along, I'll show you."

I glanced at Jake and saw the same alarm in his eyes that I was feeling.

"Come on, boys, you might as well see what's there," Meredith urged. I looked over at the packs near the entrance that were half filled with gold. I didn't think he would leave until he'd gotten all he could carry. I also doubted he wanted to do the work himself.

So I followed him into the tunnel and heard Jake coming along behind me. The tunnel was narrower than the one we were working, but you could see the marks of tools on the walls. About a hundred feet in, there was a steep drop-off, a jumble of boulders leading down into a darkness that seemed to pull the light into it.

"There was a cave-in," Meredith said. "I lost my first crew here. Didn't want to tell you boys at first. I was afraid I'd scare you off."

I wasn't sure whether to be alarmed or reassured by the explanation. He'd said nothing about the tunnels being insecure. But it would explain why we had never heard of any other miners. I could tell that Jake was thinking the same thing.

"The gold was rich here, but I gave it up because of the cave-in," Meredith explained. "The tunnel you boys are working in now is much more solid. Haven't had any accidents yet, right?" He turned and waved his shotgun at us. I froze, and I saw Jake backing up.

Meredith snickered. "Let's head on back. You go first."

I started back up the tunnel, expecting to be hit by a shotgun blast at any moment. I've never before been so conscious of the small of my back. But we made it to the entrance, and Meredith sat down with a sigh, the shotgun on his lap but his finger off the trigger.

As I fell asleep that night, I wondered whether I should tell Jake what I'd seen.

There, in the rubble at the top of the rock fall, I'd seen the corner of what looked like a red bandana, the same kind of bandana that Tad Marshall was wearing the last time I saw him.

Chapter Sixteen

Diary of Ellen Meredith

The Oregon Trail, August 28, 1845

Our party has stopped at the base of the Blue Mountains. The Columbia Gorge is just beyond this last barrier.

The men were summoned to a meeting, and a vote was taken. It has been decided that we will go directly west instead of traveling north to the pass. There have been reports of Indian attacks in the mountains. Our guide, Stephen Meek, says he knows of a shortcut. If we strike across the High Desert, we will soon reach the Deschutes River, and from there we can travel north to the Columbia Gorge, saving us much time and strenuous effort in the mountains, as well as from the possibility of hostile Indians.

Apparently the vote was overwhelming, but I wonder if the same result would have happened if we women had had a say in the matter. By now, we have learned that our men tend to overestimate the danger of Indians. It is their duty as the men of the families to protect us, of course, and no one would argue with that. But our own dealings with Indians have been only peaceful, occasions to trade for much-needed fresh meat and hides.

And although I have only met Stephen Meek once, I don't think I trust him. He is a blustery fellow, and some of his pronouncements—as relayed to me by Jonathan, who never misses these meetings—have already proven to be in error.

But if it is true that he knows a better route, it will save us hundreds of miles and perhaps weeks of travel.

Almost immediately upon setting out, it became clear to me that it was a mistake. Until now, we have traveled roads well-trodden. Now we are forging a new trail, with all the troubles that entails. All able-bodied men have been requested at the head of the train, leaving the driving of the wagons to the women and boys. Now that we have again drawn close to the other wagons, their dust is blowing in our faces, and I already wish we had gone it alone over the Blue Mountains.

There are no landmarks, except perhaps those known only to Mr. Meek. The rest of us follow blindly on faith. There are no helpful signs telling us where to find water or fodder or firewood. There are only miles upon miles of sagebrush, with the occasional juniper tree dotting the landscape. These solitary, gnarled trees have become our landmarks, what we use to measure progress; without them, it would feel as if we hadn't moved at all or were merely going in circles.

It does not help that there is little socializing among our small group. Even the women have stopped talking to each other, out of loyalty to our men. Only the younger children seem immune to worry. As Cager slowly recovers, they have regained their spirits.

Among the older children, there is a different type of tension. Edwin will not speak to his brother or to Becky. The two people he most looked up to in the world have broken his heart. Becky and Jed seem to be avoiding each other as well, out of guilt, I suppose. I fear that this won't last, that there will be a breaking point. I am disconsolate that my two sons are at loggerheads. I fear that if the conflict escalates into fisticuffs, they may never speak to each other again.

Jed has volunteered to drive the Catledges' wagon, for Gus is with the other men and Abigail is not strong enough to handle the horses by herself.

Karrie drives the Parsonses' wagon, with Cager by her side on most days. He has mostly recovered, though the other day I saw his bare leg, and it is as if half of his calf is missing. The wound is still an angry red. He has a slight limp, though most of the time he is able to hide it. Still, I have seen him drag that leg when he is tired and he thinks no one is watching.

Edwin helps me harness the horses in the morning, and in every other way he can. I see him looking ahead at the Catledge wagon, no doubt wondering if Jed and Becky are together. I don't think he need worry, as least not for now. Becky is most often in the company of Mary Perkins and the younger children, as if she has decided that they need further looking after. Allie, especially, is causing problems. She has always been high-spirited, but much of her energy was expended with Cager, whom I had always thought was the ringleader of their troublemaking. I can see now that I was wrong. She seems angry that her brother has been taken away as a playmate, and she tends to be a little too rough in her playmaking with Mattie and Nan.

Once decided, the wagon train turned due west. We have been waiting to join the line, almost last, as usual. I foresee trouble already, for it is taking longer for the forward movement to reach us.

<u>August 30, 1845</u>

Once we were underway, it was easy to see why those ahead of us were so slow. Even sagebrush must be cleared if it is high enough, and the otherwise flat terrain can contain hidden surprises: gullies that can't be seen until we are right on top of them, or rocks that seem passable at a distance but that break wheels upon arrival. Those ahead of us are making a new trail, and it is easy to see where the lead wagons were forced to retreat, where they had to give up on a route, and where they had to circle around or backtrack. We have been spared that, at least, but the jostling and swaying is more than we are accustomed to. I wonder why the other wagons haven't already given up and sent the message for us to turn around. I'm quite certain I would have.

These men are stubborn and proud, like my husband, and once they decide on a course of action, there is little that can dissuade them. Otherwise the promise of difficulties and hardship would have been enough to keep them home.

The dust is ankle deep, and we have had to cross the Malheur River more than once as it winds through high bluffs and narrow passageways. The road is rough and rocky, and there is little timber except near water.

<u>September 1, 1845</u>

The road is bad. We have endured five days of this jarring motion. We are traveling less than ten miles per day sometimes, and if we weren't so close to our goal, I'd be worried about the winter snows. The trail continues to be strewn with broken rocks, and we travel up and down hilly ravines. The grass is dry. The oxen are giving out, their hooves bleeding. When we find a stream, there is not enough water for everyone. Some must go on, looking for other sources.

Jonathan returned to the wagon last night. He was covered in dust, his hands and arms were a tangled maze of scratches, and he was dog-tired. This morning, Gus and Bart also returned, so exhausted that they retired to the back of their wagons and fell instantly asleep. I'm amazed they can sleep through the bumping and jostling.

"This was a mistake," Jonathan told me over our lunch. "Meek is a humbug and a braggart. I don't believe he knows where he is going."

"Yet we travel west," I said.

"Yes, a shortcut, supposedly. But I can't help but I remember what my father told me: 'Never take shortcuts.' I thought at the time he was speaking in metaphor, but now I wonder if he wasn't being literal."

"We will reach our destination sooner or later," I said, trying to sound encouraging.

Jonathan did not seem encouraged. "I also wonder why, if it is so easy, no one else has taken this route before. This is a desert, though it is cold at night. There is very little water. Meek assures us that we will reach the Deschutes River soon, but the maps show differently."

"Then why do we follow him?" I asked.

"We can't go it alone," Jonathan said. "I tried my best to convince Gus and Bart, but the fools are too eager to reach their destination."

There is no help for it but to forge ahead. I am glad that my husband is back to drive the wagon, for I'd much rather walk beside it. It is beautiful territory, when my vision is not being jostled.

<u>September 2, 1845</u>

Water is starting to become a concern. We had enough to last us until the next waterhole—by way of the old route. Mr. Meek told us that we would reach water on this path even sooner, but there is no sign of it.

There is blood on the trail from the hooves of the oxen; at times, the poor beasts will simply lie down, and no amount of punishment will make them rise. There is more swearing than I have ever heard. Everyone is tired, and it is at this inopportune time that disease has struck our wagon train. We have been lucky until now. It is as if the fates were waiting until we were at our most vulnerable.

Those who are sick are put in the backs of wagons, and their moans are so loud that we can hear them far down the line. The group ahead of us, which consists of five families from Springfield, Missouri, have already lost one little girl. I wish Jonathan would let them get farther ahead of us, for I'd rather face Indians than cholera. I have forbidden the children from ranging ahead of us as is their wont. I have forbidden them to play with children other than those in our three wagons.

I had thought our trip strenuous and dangerous, but except for Sarah, I now believe we have not suffered as much as others—until now. Until we became certain that we knew better than those who came before us and struck out into new lands.

At the end of the day, we found some warm springs, a little above body temperature, but we still would not have had enough water were it not for an evening thunderstorm.

I only hope that God takes mercy on us.

Chapter Seventeen

<u>Columbia River, Oregon Territory, September 1851</u>

Dearest Frank,

I miss you terribly, and I hope that by traveling to Vale and talking to Mr. Catledge, I will clear this matter up.

Unexpectedly, Angus and I have been joined on our journey by three of Mary's employees. I've accepted their help, though I fear for their safety. They, of course, think they are keeping me safe. It is the youngest of them, a serious young man named Terrance Drake, who is in charge of the trio. It was he who found Augustus Catledge, and so I can't very well refuse to let him come.

You will notice that I mention Angus Porter. Yes, dear husband, I am aware that you have conspired with my father to send me a guardian. We will have a talk about that when I get home. I thought it foolish that the poor man traipse along behind me, so I have taken him under my wing. He seems a very interesting and capable fellow, and I enjoy his company.

I will mail this if I have a chance; otherwise, other letters may join it in the future as I continue to write.

Love,

Virginia

The gold in Virginia's rucksack was too heavy to carry across the mountains and into the High Desert. She exchanged the raw metal with a man on a side street, who gave her a usurious rate but who was unlikely to tell the authorities about her riches.

Angus stood watch nearby. When she emerged and they were walking away, he whispered out of the side of his mouth, "We've got company."

Virginia had already felt a tingling between her shoulder blades, and she simply nodded. She wasn't sure what to do about it.

"Keep walking, miss," Angus said, and dropped away into the shadows. Virginia continued on into the crowd. When he caught up with her again, he had a tear in one of his coat sleeves, but otherwise showed no sign of what he'd been up to. Virginia noticed him rubbing his chin and asked, "Are you all right?"

"One of the bastards caught me with a lucky jab, but no harm," Angus replied cheerfully. "They weren't used to their victims fighting back."

Virginia had enough money to buy them all passage to Vale by way of the road along the Columbia River Gorge, but Drake objected. "Mrs.

Hoskins told me to pay for everything," he said. "After all, you are doing this for her."

"You may pay for the horses and pack mules and provisions when we get to Vale," Virginia said. *If it becomes necessary*, she thought. She still hoped that by the time they got there, Becky would have returned home safely and Gus Catledge would have the answers Virginia sought.

They began the journey in relative luxury. A new freight line had opened in the last few months, though there were few goods or people heading east. All the better: they got a good rate, and the wagon was nearly empty, so they had space to spread out, even Sims, who for once wasn't forced to ride on top when the weather was bad.

And it was bad weather almost from the start, cold and wet, the kind of climate that Virginia was learning was the other side of the paradise that was fertile Oregon. The clouds glowered all day, whether it rained or not. She began to be glad that she had ended up in California, though the journey there had been a tragedy.

There was a single teamster driving the wagon. He seemed happy to have them along. As the lone woman in the party, Virginia was given the inside of the wagon to sleep in that first night.

To the south were the majestically severe slopes of Mt. Hood, already covered in snow. To the north was a gentler, rounder-looking mountain.

"St. Helens," Drake informed her.

The Columbia River cut right through it all. The slope of the road was gentle, though the road itself was winding and they had to take wide detours where the bluffs ran all the way down to the water. At other times, the water flowed just a few hundred feet away, looking gentle and calm. It was the widest river Virginia had seen since leaving the Mississippi River behind.

The sight of snow on the mountains gave Virginia the chills, as it always did. She awoke that first night screaming, certain that a wolf was creeping through the snow toward her. There was a gentle knock on the side of the wagon, and Angus's concerned voice asked, "Are you all right, Miss Reed?"

"I'm sorry to wake you, Angus," she said shakily. "It was nothing…just a dream. Go back to sleep."

They made good time on the well-traveled road. In some places, there had even been attempts to lay down timber and gravel to smooth the way.

"Is this part of the Oregon Trail?" Virginia asked. "My own path to the West went a little south of here."

Drake looked at her, and she could tell from the look in his eyes that he knew about her experience with the Donner Party. "It is part of the route, as I understand it," he said. "I came by boat." He turned to his man, Sims, who looked uncomfortable at being put on the spot.

"They've civilized it, miss," Sims said. "Just a few years ago, settlers on this route were still being attacked by Indians." He looked grim, and Virginia could guess how they had managed to civilize it.

"Civilized or not, Mary…Mrs. Hoskins would have been better served to have traveled this route," Drake said.

They stopped for several nights along the way, but the journey was still much quicker than it would have been only a few short years before. The teamster was able to change horses at stations along the way, and the travelers were fed hot meals. The biggest delay was getting out of the way of the constant stream of wagons going the other way, even this late in the season. Even though more wagon trains were heading to California now, there were greater numbers of settlers than ever heading for Oregon.

One morning, they awoke to frost on the ground. Not long after, the traffic coming from the east began to dwindle until there were long stretches where they were alone. The season for overlanders was over.

They came to a high plateau with the river far below. Two men on horseback were waiting for them behind a rockfall. There was something odd about them, and at first Virginia couldn't make it out. It wasn't until they spurred their horses forward that she saw that they were wearing bandanas over their faces.

Beside her, both Drake and Angus reached for their pistols.

"Hold off," she said, using her Canowiki commanding voice. It didn't always work on humans, but sometimes it did. Drake let his hand fall, but Angus kept his inside his coat. If they started firing, it was almost certain that someone would get hurt, and there was a good chance it wouldn't only be the bandits. *Let these bandits take what poor excuse for riches we have*, Virginia thought. As long as they reached Vale safely, they could replenish their supplies.

One of the robbers was holding a shotgun, which he pointed at the teamster in the driver's box. The other man dismounted and threw open the back of the wagon, then stepped back with a rifle pointed at them.

"Step out, gents," he said. He did a double take, and then added, "And you too, ma'am, if you please. I promise this won't take long."

Virginia got out first and stepped to one side. Angus moved next to her, while Sims and Franklin stood on the other of the door.

"We aren't worth the effort," Virginia said. "This is but an empty freight coach sent east to bring back goods." She glanced up at the teamster, looking for confirmation. He looked scared.

Oh, no, she thought as he reached for the shotgun propped next to the reins.

The bandit on the horse fired first. The blast caught the teamster in the lower face, blowing away his jaw. He slumped, letting go of the reins, but by some miracle, the horses didn't bolt.

Angus drew his pistol so fast that it was a blur and shot the horseman backward off his horse. Instinctively, Virginia pulled her bowie knife and threw it toward the robber on the ground, who was aiming his rifle at Angus.

Time seemed to stop. The rifle fired, and she felt the impact of the bullet slamming into the wood of the coach near her head. Virginia watched the individual revolutions of the knife as it tumbled through the air, and it seemed to her that the blade was going to strike the robber in the left eye. But the man flinched and reared back, and the hilt struck him square in the forehead.

He staggered back, dropping the rifle and drawing his pistol.

Sims charged him, pushing him backward, and they both fell to the ground, the bigger man on top. There was a single shot, and Sims slumped.

"Get him off me," came a muffled voice. "I can't breathe."

Angus hurried over to Sims and put his fingers to his neck. He looked up and shook his head.

The bandit was continuing to complain, but sounded weaker with every second. Finally, Angus and Drake pulled Sims away. Then they took turns punching the robber until he stopped moving.

"Why did Sims do that?" Virginia fumed. "The man was beaten; he was going to run."

Drake was white-faced. Virginia suspected he had never seen anyone killed before. "Sims never backed down," he said.

"What I want to know," Angus growled, "is why that idiot teamster reached for his gun. These men weren't killers unless forced to be. They look like farmers down on their luck. They would have taken our money and gone on their way." He climbed up to the driver's box and tipped the dead man over onto the ground unceremoniously. "Ah ha!" he said. He pulled out an iron box and tried to lift it, then grunted and let it slam back down. "Unless I'm mistaken, this is full of gold."

Franklin whistled, and they all looked at him. He had a huge grin on his face. "We're rich, boys…er, and lady. If Porter can't even lift that box, it must have enough gold to make us all rich."

No one said anything. They simply stared at him until his grin fell away. "I mean…we could…" His voice trailed off.

"Here's what I want you to do, Franklin," Angus said, finally. "Find something you can write on, and make a sign that says, 'This be the End for all Thieves and Murderers.'"

Franklin's mouth fell open, but no words emerged.

"Get to it, Franklin," Drake ordered. He walked to the middle of the road, bent over, and picked something up. Then he walked back to Virginia and handed her bowie knife. She blushed and looked down, embarrassed. Her Canowiki fighting abilities didn't seem to work as well with humans. The blade had missed, though getting hit with the hilt had distracted the bandit.

She looked up to thank Drake and saw the admiration in his eyes, and she blushed again.

The surviving robber was starting to stir, and they got him to his feet. They tied his hands behind his back and put him on his horse.

"Please," he said. "I've got a family. I wasn't going to hurt no one. I just needed enough money to make it through the winter and to buy seed for planting time."

Virginia forced herself to look at him. He was telling the truth. He was skinny and malnourished, his skin blotchy from fear and hunger. He kept swallowing, his prominent Adam's apple bobbing up and down.

Franklin emerged from inside the coach with a roughly made sign. It was barely readable, but he hadn't had much to work with, only some charcoal and a page out of the teamster's journal. He pinned the sign to the robber's shirt with some sharp twigs.

There was no discussion, no ceremony. The men threw a rope over a low branch and put a noose around the bandit's neck. He was silent now, his eyes closed, his face and hands drained of blood.

"God damn you," he said softly.

Angus slapped the rear of the man's horse, and the murderer slid off the back. There was the merciful sound of his neck snapping, and then he was swinging in the late afternoon wind as snow began to fall.

Chapter Eighteen

<u>Diary of Ellen Meredith</u>

<u>The Oregon Trail, September 3, 1845</u>

In the distance, we see Fremont Peak, a large, round rock at the peak, like a castle. In the morning, the fog is so thick that we find it hard to gather up the cattle. The climb around Fremont Peak was steep, but there was good fodder at the top. We can see pine trees on high.

<u>September 5, 1845</u>

We are lost. None of the men will say these words aloud, but I can see it in their eyes. We have traveled too far from Vale to go back, though there has been talk of it. On one thing, all agree: Stephen Meek is a fraud and a humbug. He says one thing to us in the morning, only to deny that he said it in the evening.

"We will reach the Deschutes River by nightfall," he says, then later implies that he meant something entirely different. The next day, the whole charade begins again. We travel west, that is all we know for certain.

The wagon train is starting to splinter into factions. Our own party has moved up to the center of the pack as others falter. As bad as we believed our situation to be, it turns out we are in better shape than most: an unforeseen advantage, I suppose, of taking up the rear and not having to blaze the trail as others have done. All those hundreds of miles of eating their dust have brought their reward.

The leaders of the entire wagon train have asked that those of us who are better supplied begin to share with those less fortunate. Last night, I came across Jonathan in the back of our wagon, hiding food and water. He didn't acknowledge my presence, and I did not say anything. I am torn, for I see the suffering of others, but I have four children of my own to look after.

Bart and Gus have been more generous, as might be expected. When Jonathan offered his paltry portion, I saw both men look at each other as if to say "I told you so," and I was ashamed.

The going has become rougher, either because of our position farther up the line or because it is a new trail for everyone. Today we had to travel up a gulch as rough as any we have encountered. Jonathan says that the men removed ten thousand stones before we could go on.

Our wagon has begun to break down in small ways, and rarely does a mile pass before we come across a disabled wagon, the men working furiously to fix the wheels or the axle. We have also come across dead livestock alongside the trail, as there is not enough water for both man and beast. As important as our beasts of burden are to us, when one is thirsty, it is hard not to drink all the water oneself rather than give it to mere animals.

When we do find the rare source of water, it is quickly despoiled. Oxen and cattle can't be held back, and men and women struggle to fill their water pails before it becomes mud. If we come across a small stream, it is soon almost buried under the trampled banks, and we must scramble upstream to reach fresh water.

We want to stop but know that we cannot, for we also need food, and this land is quickly being stripped of all resources. I wonder if we will not eventually drain the rivers themselves.

The terrain is the same, mile after mile, and yet the land is never level, nor the path ever clear. We strain our eyes to see the Cascade Mountains that are supposed to be directly ahead of us.

"We will see a lava butte we can travel toward," Meek tells us. "Beyond that is a bend in the river where we can cross."

But there is no butte; there is no river. There is nothing but sagebrush and rock, mile after mile. The sandy soil coats everything in gray-brown, and our throats are dry, our eyes gritty. We came across freshly dug graves this morning, and it made me cold in the midst of a hot day. We are all on the edge of oblivion, with no relief in sight.

Mr. Meek has ridden ahead, I think as much to avoid the wrath of those he has led to this place as to actually find a way through. I hope that no other company that follows is as gulled as we have been.

"He's a fool," Jonathan raged last night at our fire. "We have already gone far beyond where he told us the Deschutes River lies. I wonder if he has ever traveled this way."

"Yet the river must be there, eventually," Gus said.

Jonathan snorted. "Aye, and so must China be…eventually."

"If we strike north, we will reach the Columbia Gorge," Bart said. "We can find the well-traveled path. Better that we be late than that we never arrive."

"Gerald Simmons has already decided to do so," Jonathan said. "He is leading a group north tomorrow. I say we should join them."

There was silence at that. Jonathan is no longer in a position of influence, as he once was. Gus is the man whom Bart listens to, and so whatever Gus decides, we do. It drives Jonathan mad with indignation, but he never shows it to others, only to me, late at night. I have learned to listen to his resentment and not express an opinion either way, and hope that it dissipates.

Gus finally spoke. All were listening, the women and children as well as the men. "We will stay with the main body for now. There is safety in numbers, and we can always turn north if need be."

And so we continue into the dust and sun, day after day. Jonathan grows frustrated, sure that by the time we reach Oregon all the land will be gone, or at least all the good land. That isn't possible, I think. It is a big country, and I will be surprised if we are not among the first of multitudes yet to come.

But first we have to reach the Willamette Valley safely, with our possessions and our lives. I fear for both.

September 6, 1845

The road is all short turns, sidling places, hard pulls, and rolling stones. We traveled up a ravine so narrow that there was no way to avoid the large, sharp rocks. We made it through without incident, or so we thought.

On a flat plateau, our wagon finally broke. We were not even on a rough road, and perhaps Jonathan relaxed; he struck a rock that splintered the right front wheel, and the entire wagon tipped over, throwing those of us riding in it against the side and almost crushing Edwin, who was walking beside it.

Once again we have been saved our friends. Gus and Bart immediately pulled aside, letting the others pass, and the rest of the day was spent putting our spare wheel onto the wagon. We tried to reach one of the campsites before dark, but ended up simply pulling off the trail and going to bed without the warmth of a fire or food in our bellies.

September 7, 1845

This morning, we hurried to get underway so that we didn't fall in with the last group of wagons, for if that happens, by the time we arrive at any watering hole, we will find the water gone or spoiled.

During all this, Cager has stayed in the back of his wagon, reading. As we started off, the wagon became hung up on a ledge of stone, and we could only get it off by rocking it back and forth. Jonathan was behind the wagon, and he saw Cager inside and it enraged him. He started yelling, "Get out here and help us, young man!"

Allie came to her brother's defense. "Leave him alone!" she screamed. "He's hurt!"

Jonathan wasn't mollified. "He can walk, I've seen him."

I was too embarrassed to speak. Here these kind people had spent an entire day helping us, and Jonathan was repaying them by yelling at one of their children.

Allie flew at Jonathan then, and I believe if she had had a knife in her hand, there might have been blood. Jonathan easily held her off, but he had an astonished expression on his face.

Bart heard the commotion and came running, and the two men nearly came to blows. Gus managed to separate them, but I fear that our long association may be over. I don't know what we'll do by ourselves. I believe that without the other men around, nothing will keep Jonathan from expressing his unhappiness in dangerous ways.

<u>September 8, 1845</u>

We went on without speaking of yesterday's incident. Cager has come out of the wagon and is doing what he can to help, but it is clear that he is not healthy enough to do much. I am so embarrassed that I have stopped visiting with the other women.

It is very hot and dry, and there is nothing to cheer us. The road remains broken and rocky, with no way to get along quickly. The majority of the overlanders have decided to travel on through the night in hopes of finding water. Men travel ahead, lighting beacon fires of sagebrush. We tried to reach the fires in hopes that they had found water, but, exhausted, we have stopped to make camp without finding grass for the animals or water for any of us.

Some of the men want to stone Stephen Meek or hang him. We have now been traveling more than a week past where he said we would encounter the Jay River.

Fremont Peak has disappeared behind us; ahead is only rocky, inhospitable, broken ground.

I heard another overlander say, "If Meek doesn't lead us out of this land, his head won't be worth a chew of tobacco." Yet other men insist that—even though we are lost—he still has more knowledge of the terrain than any of the rest of us.

We descended into a deep valley, wheels locked, dragging the biggest logs we can find to slow our plunge.

Will this trip never end?

Yet as intolerable as it has been for our small company, we have heard that in other companies, people are dying. This morning, we were told the entire King family, including a month-old babe, has perished, as well as Delaney Norman. Mr. Fuller lost his wife and daughter. I have little doubt that when we join up with other companies, we will find that many others have died. I believe that because of the strain these last few weeks have put on us, we are all prey to any sickness we encounter.

<u>September 9, 1845</u>

We have stopped again. The two groups following us have decided to turn north, and we have decided to join them. If we can only reach the Columbia River, we believe we can stop long enough for repairs and to rest. It was not really discussed; it was clear we all wanted to try something different.

When Harrison Semple, the leader of this offshoot of the wagon train, turned his wagon north, we followed. But it was not long before we realized that we are lost again. We have no real idea where we are, and it is not a simple matter of continuing north. The terrain appears to be almost impassible. From a distance, it seemed to be the same flat terrain we have been traveling over for the last few days, but we quickly realized that there are deep gorges in our path, with no easy way across them. We have been traveling eastward because it appeared that the steep sides of the main gorge flattened out in that direction, but instead, as we turned into the morning sun, we found that the gorge only deepened.

Most frustrating of all is that we have traveled miles in the wrong direction. We have made camp on the edge of the gorge. All night, the winds have been blowing upon us, as if there is an angry god at the bottom of the deep, black ravine.

<u>September 10, 1845</u>

We have reached a low, stagnant lake, surrounded by tall rushes and full of ducks, geese and cranes. Elfie Packwood died today, and many others are sick and feverish.

Once again, we are trying to decide whether to continue or turn back. There seems to be no choice, for the gorge appears to be impassable. We have begun following our own tracks back west, and then once more to the south. We hope that when we reach the spot where the trail turns west again, we will not be too far behind the others to catch up.

Though the terrain is flat in this direction, the sagebrush grows so high and thick that we must take turns breaking through it. We spend much of our time compelling the unwilling oxen forward. The nights are turning colder, as autumn is upon us.

A young child died today. Because of what we have done, I will not say her name. We buried her without a marker, and then drove over the grave to hide it. We have heard that the Indians are digging up the graves to take the clothing of the dead.

I believe that God will forgive their desecration more readily than ours.

Chapter Nineteen

<u>Testament of Virgil Conner</u>

<u>August 2, 1851</u>

On Meredith's orders, we have begun to load the mules with the nearly full packs of gold. The animals stagger under the weight, and I fear they will not make it back to Vale. Then I laugh at the thought, for I am convinced that Jake and I will not make it back either. Meredith watches us work with gun in hand and an impassive expression. Occasionally, he'll say something that he no doubt means to be encouraging: "You're going to be rich, boys. Any day now."

Jake and I have decided we can no longer wait to make our escape. We aren't even hiding our stashes of gold from each other anymore, since both of us already have more than we can carry. I intend to carry as much as I can for as long as I can, but will shed the weight if my survival depends on it.

We are just waiting for Meredith to turn his back. I don't want to hurt him, but if I have to…

<u>August 3, 1851</u>

We all realize we are near the end. Meredith never comes near us and always has his weapon in hand. He acts casual, even friendly, but there is something threatening in that. I'd rather he seemed resentful that we were taking his gold. That, at least, would mean he means for us to keep it. I keep writing this testament because if things go wrong, it may be the only thing I leave behind.

Jake fears that Meredith will rob us, but I fear something far worse. I don't believe Meredith means to leave any witnesses. We might have been blindfolded, but I do believe I have a sense of how far we came and in which general direction. I have told Meredith otherwise, of course. From the moment we arrived, when poor Tad exclaimed about how turned around and lost he was, I chimed in my agreement.

But I can't help but think about the journey to this place, reconstructing it, adding it to what I know of the local terrain, and I think I may have a fix on where we are.

I must leave. There is something wrong with the air, the earth, the sounds and smells. It all brings back memories of the past. Yesterday, I saw my daughter. She was floating in the air before me, wearing the look of disappointment that I always remember when I think of her. I cried out, and the figment disappeared. I leaned against a rock and closed my eyes, my heart pounding. She had seemed so real.

For the rest of the day, as I was digging, the terrible thought came to me that if I had not neglected my poor daughter, Tina, she would still be alive. If I hadn't been carousing around town every night, my wife Agnes would still love me. The feeling of remorse won't go away. I remember that last argument with my wife, how mean-spirited I was, and regret washes over me. It is as if there is something pulling my innards down into the dirt. My heart feels raw, as if rubbed by sandpaper. I am hollow but for my roiling fear.

Yesterday, I turned to Jake, ready to confess that I could not take the darkness any longer, and I realized that he was weeping. Jake Tanner, weeping. A man who could outdrink, outfight, and outcurse any man I have known. Crying silently, the dirty streaks of his tears running down his furrowed cheeks like a flash flood in the desert.

I am not a thoughtful man. I know this about myself. How can I think about the past when I am trying to survive the present? When the occasional bad dream surfaces, I ignore it. I have lived as I must.

It was never my fault that these things happened.

So I believed until now. Now all I can think about is how I should have done things differently. How a few kind words to Agnes might have kept her my willing bride, and how, had I said a few words of encouragement to Timothy, perhaps he wouldn't have run away.

Last night, as I returned to the front of the cave, I found Meredith frowning down at the ground, as if he was thinking sad thoughts. It was a strange sight, for Meredith rarely shows any emotion at all.

The gold does not warm me. At first, I was dazzled by it, but now it is merely more rocks. Gold doesn't light the darkness, and it doesn't have the warmth of human companionship. I'm tired, and I want to see the sun, to swim in a river, and most of all, to talk to someone who isn't as dirty and tired as I am—man, woman, or child, even a stranger. I long to join civilization again. Tomorrow I leave, whether Meredith wishes it or not. He will have to shoot me to stop me.

This morning, I woke to a rumbling noise. I tried to rise, but the ground was shaking so violently that I was thrown to my knees. Jake also tried to rise and cried out as he was thrown against the rock wall.

When the shaking ended, we were in darkness. I couldn't see the dust, but it filled my throat, and I coughed until my sides hurt and I nearly vomited. I swiped at my eyes, which made things worse, grinding the grit into them until the tears were flowing down my cheeks.

I couldn't even remember which direction the entrance was. I reached out blindly and touched one of the walls and began to feel my way forward. I stumbled on the rocks of the cave-in before I reached the now closed-off entrance.

A flicker of light sent my fragmented shadow shooting up the crumbled walls of the entrance. Jake had lit a single match. I wiped my eyes as the light filled the cave. Then the light blinked out with a cry from Jake as the flame reached his fingers.

"Hold off," I said, and my voice had a muffled quality, as if I was enclosed in a small space. The entrance of the mine was small, but until then, I hadn't understood how I'd come to depend on that sliver of natural light for hope, for reassurance, and as a reminder that there was a bigger world outside. "We need to start a fire," I said.

"Where are you?" Jake said. "Come toward my voice."

I reached out and stumbled toward him. My fingers brushed against him, and he reached up and grasped my hand. "Here…I think I've found the remains of the campfire," Jake said.

He lit another match and set it to the leftover tinder from the previous night's fire. The welcome light filled the room, and we both sighed in relief. Jake's face was black with dust, and his eyes were white and frightened. No doubt I looked just as bad.

"He left us here," Jake said. "He took all the gold."

"He took the food and water, too," I said. "We can't live on rocks."

Jake didn't respond. It was clear that he hadn't thought of that. He moved off into the shadows and came back with his empty rucksack. "He even took my gold."

Despite knowing it was a foolish reaction, I hurried to my own hiding place and found my pack empty as well. "We had the purest nuggets," I said. "He must have known that." For several days, Meredith had rejected almost all the diggings we had brought him, despite having one more bag he said he wanted filled. The pile of tailings—rejects that in any other mine would have been considered rich—filled one side of the cave.

Only then did the anger surge up in us. And if I was angry, Jake was furious. He started cursing, stomping about the chamber, kicking at loose rocks. "We should have rushed him while we had the chance," he growled. "Even if we'd failed, it would have been over quickly." He struck the wall so forcefully I was afraid he'd injure his hand.

"Careful," I said. "We're going to need to dig our way out of here."

Jake laughed. "We have no tools. We have no water. There is no way we can dig our way out in time."

"We have to try," I said.

Jake lowered himself down beside the fire and stared disconsolately into the flames. I slid down across from him and joined him in his silence.

<u>August ?, 1851</u>

I don't know if the day has turned. Surely it must have, but time has slowed down so much that it seems like every breath is an eternity. I've heard that a fire will suffocate a man if there is no outside air, so I insisted we put out the fire, over Jake's objections.

It was only when the darkness became so oppressive that Jake began whimpering that I told him to light a match and rekindle the fire. It occurs to me that we have wasted precious time and air by not beginning to dig our way out. But simply examining the rockfall is so dispiriting that neither of us has moved so much as a single stone. If anyone knows how much stone can be moved in a few days, it is Jake and I, and both of us have judged it to be impossible.

I have spent my time on this testament instead. It seems like time better spent.

It is hopeless, but I know that we will eventually try to get out, probably after it is too late and we are so desperate that we will ignore the truth of our doom. The fire has begun to flicker, and we have run out of things to burn. Soon we will be thrown into the final darkness.

***

I felt the breeze in my sleep. I awoke, suddenly certain that there had been a breeze all along and that the flickering flames were bending with it, but that it was so slight that I hadn't noticed until now. The smoke had become thick in the cave, but not as thick as it should have been. I now believed there was a current of air coming into this chamber.

I woke Jake, who grumbled and said something about just letting him die.

"There's another opening," I said. "Can't you feel it?"

"Feel what?"

"A breeze…ever so slight. It comes from below, I'm sure of it."

"I'm not going back down there," Jake said. "If I must die, I want to die with the sun and the sky only a few feet away, not buried deep in the earth."

"What does it matter?" I asked, exasperated. "We become bones either way."

"I'm thirsty," he said.

"Remember when we first got here? Meredith said there was a stream in the lower parts of the mine. Maybe that wasn't a lie."

"Don't say his name," Jake said. "Everything he said was a lie."

"The gold wasn't," I said. "And why would he say such a thing if it wasn't true?"

I continued to feel the draft, though I was beginning to wonder if it wasn't just my imagination. But I think Jake felt it too. And both of us had felt it before, though we might not have recognized it at the time. We'd be sweating in our labors and a coolness would come over us. We probably thought it was coming from the entrance, but in hindsight, I seemed to remember that the breeze hadn't felt dry and warm like the air outside the cave, but had had a tinge of coolness, even moistness.

"We have to try," I said, finally. I could barely speak the words, my throat was so dry. Jake didn't answer, but I sensed he was assenting. I reached out until I felt his arm and ran my hand down it until my hand grasped his. "Let's see where it leads."

We began tentatively, stumbling across loose stones. We hadn't gone very far before Jake stopped, wrenching his hand out of mine. "I'm not leaving without some gold," he said.

I wanted to tell him he was crazy, that it was foolish, that we'd be lucky to escape with our skins intact. But in truth, I had the same urge. If I was going to die, I wanted to die a rich man. I laughed, and it hurt, which only made me laugh harder. Yes, sir. I was going to die rich.

We felt our way to the pile of tailings. Both of us had grabbed our nearly empty rucksacks, but once we were upon the pile of rejected ore, we couldn't see.

"I've still got matches," Jake said. "But we need to burn something. What about that book you keep writing in?"

"I wanted to…to leave something behind," I muttered. "A testament."

I could sense him mulling this over in the darkness. "You only need one more page," he ventured.

I pulled the small notebook from my pocket—the same book whoever is reading this has discovered. I ripped out the pages from the second half of the book. It didn't seem to matter. Either we would escape, in which case I wouldn't need the book, or I wouldn't be alive long enough to write more than a few more entries.

We quickly grabbed the more glittering of the rocks, and it didn't take long to fill our rucksacks. In the light of day, we may find that we have nothing but tailings, but I believe even this residue will prove rich.

The fire went out before the sacks were full, but it doesn't matter. In our weakened state, the rucksacks are heavy. I will be surprised if much of the ore won't be dumped before we reach safety.

As we turned to where we knew the tunnels to be, I saw white lights in the distance. At first, I was sure they were a mirage, a leftover image from the light of the fire. The two lights floated in and out of sight, and suddenly, I felt despair such as I'd not yet felt. I wanted to drop the rucksack, fall upon it, and curl up and die. It was pointless. We were going to perish.

"What the hell are those?" Jake asked, confirming that I'd indeed seen something.

"They are our guiding spirits," I said. I felt that the opposite was true and that the lights were going to lead us to our doom, but I thought Jake was already so disconsolate that he would give up then and there if I voiced my feelings.

"Guiding spirits, my ass," Jake said. "I've seen them before. Those are ghosts."

Chapter Twenty

Diary of Ellen Meredith

The Oregon Trail, September 11, 1845

The ground is encrusted with salt, and its fine grains blow into our faces, making us ever more thirsty. Gus rode off to find water and lost his horse. Luckily, Edwin found him and gave up his own horse so that Gus could make it back; he was barely alive. Edwin made it back to camp a few hours later. Some hundred cattle drifted off, and we spent much of the day rounding them up.

I began shivering in the midafternoon heat. When it came time for Edwin to spell me at driving the wagon, he took one look at me and exclaimed, "Mother, are you unwell?" His cry brought Jed and Jonathan. Until that moment, I'd hope it was a passing hot flash, for I have begun to experience these waves more often as the trip wears on, which I am secretly grateful for, for I hope that it means I can no longer conceive a child.

Jonathan still comes to my bed at night, but there is no tenderness in his touch; it is as if I am merely a receptacle for his lust.

Both my husband and my eldest child blanched upon looking at me, and they insisted that I get into the back of the wagon. Jonathan carried me the last part of the way, for I became dizzy on my feet.

As sick and worried as I was, I cannot but confess that I felt gratitude at the alarm in my husband's face. Perhaps I read too much into it; after all, I have no doubt that he needs me, if only to take care of the children. But I cannot but hope that the concern he showed for me was more than that.

I fell into a fitful sleep on the baseboard of the wagon, too tired to even cushion myself. I awoke with a crook in my neck. I was sopping wet, for my fever had broken. The wagon wasn't moving, and there was darkness outside, broken by the flicker of a campfire.

Relief washed over me, and tears came to my eyes, for no fever that breaks so quickly can be serious. It was a mere cold, not cholera nor dysentery nor any of the other illnesses that so afflict travelers. I rose up, dampened a cloth, and wiped myself, and then changed into my Sunday dress. I will wash both dresses on the morrow, if I am still feeling well.

I climbed out of the wagon and went to join the others, who were deep in discussion around the campfire. But first I kept to the darkness and observed them. Jonathan stood by himself, and even Jed was standing with the others. They were having a heated argument, with my husband on one side and everyone else on the other.

"We should try the northern route again," Jonathan insisted. "If we keep following the others, we will meet the same doom as they. We know that there is a well-traveled trail along the Columbia."

"That may be true, but there is no trail from here to there," Bart said. "At first, I too believed that we should go north, but after our experience over the last few days, I think that is foolhardy. The land is unknown by all. At least if we stick with the others, we know that a trail will be found, and if not found, it will be forged. We must do our part."

Everyone turned to Gus, who as usual would have the deciding vote. He stared into the fire as if unaware that everyone was waiting. Finally, Abigail spoke up. "What do you think we should do, Augustus?"

He roused himself and looked around. He looked tired. "I can't decide tonight," he said. "Let us sleep upon it and make our decision tomorrow."

I decided it was time to reveal myself, and I was met by greetings of relief and support. Jonathan joined me by the fireside and even grasped my hand. It hurt, but I was so grateful that I didn't say anything.

I cannot sleep. I've rested through the day, and now it is as if it is full daylight. My mind churns over the dangers of the present and the hopes for the future, but mostly, I question whether I made the right decision in marrying Jonathan.

The truth is, even if I had known what he was really like, I would have had little choice but to join myself with him. A single woman on the prairie, already deep in debt, with small children to take care of—I don't know what would have become of me.

<u>September 16, 1845</u>

I have unable to write in this diary for the better part of a week. Things have become so desperate that I have begun to believe we will not survive.

On the evening of September 12, we found a small spring. We were loath to leave it, for we did not know if we would ever find water again. We interrogated Stephen Meek, who seemed at a loss and unwilling to give directions, which was just as well, as none of us would have believed him.

Over the next few days, more and more groups arrived at our small spring. The camp became dirty and the food and water scarce, and all the fodder was consumed. Over one hundred men went out searching for water, but none was found.

There was more talk of hanging Mr. Meek. Some of the oxen collapsed, having gone as far as they could. The horses were ridden in search of water until they could go no further.

We found Indians in possession of missing horses, and some of our men charged them. The Indians fled, miserable creatures possessing only bows and arrows.

On the morning of September 13, we started off, but returned to the spring when informed that little water has been found. A few small creeks have been discovered, but they are not sufficient even for three or four wagons, much less our large party. So we remained in camp.

This morning, the decision was made to forge northward. We have filled all available containers with water from the dirty, muddy spring we camped beside for so many days. We are sick at heart and of body. We have been forced to kill some of our livestock, but there is little doubt they would have died anyway.

It was decided that if any water was found, three shoots were to be fired. We have traveled all day in hopes of hearing that gunfire, but it never came. We have used up all our water.

There is a full moon, and the night is clear and silent. I sit in the back of the wagon, writing in the dark, for I do not know when or if I will be able to write again.

<u>September 17, 1845</u>

We have been saved. Water has been found!

When word came, we all rushed forward. The cattle ran ahead of us and drank from the pool until we had to drive them away. I didn't care how dirty the water was; I plunged my face into it and drank until I could have burst.

Gus shouted for joy, while his wife wept silent tears of happiness. Edwin clapped his hands. Young Becky came to me and gave me a hug. I believe that even Jonathon was overcome with joy. Most of us simply sat on the ground after drinking our fill and stared at the water as if it was a mirage.

God has given us another chance.

Abigail has a fever this morning. We have decided to rest for one more day, work on repairs, and give Abigail a chance to recover. I'm hoping it is the same illness that I recently recovered from and not something more serious.

The children are driving us crazy with their energy. They are not affected by the adults' worries. To them, it is all still a big adventure, and they seem confident that we will reach our destination.

Allie asked Mary Perkins if she and some of the younger children could go exploring. "Please, Miss Mary, we don't have anything to do!" she pleaded.

"I must take care of Mrs. Catledge," Mary answered.

Karrie Parsons looked up from her cooking. "I think it will be all right as long as they stay in sight of the wagons."

Mary didn't look so certain. I nearly laughed, for I knew that Mary had more experience with the children by now than any of the other adults. Still, what harm could there be? They couldn't go far, and they were driving us to distraction.

"All right," Mary said. "But be careful, and don't wander far."

Karrie handed Allie a blue bucket. "Collect some tinder while you're out there," she said. "Look for water."

In the end, Becky and Edwin joined Allie and Cager, and my own girls, Mattie and Nan. They took two more blue buckets with them. Ordinarily, the girls might have been left behind, but they could now walk as fast as Cager, who was still weak and hobbled by his injury, so the older children reluctantly agreed to let them come.

The rest of the afternoon was taken up by chores. Clothing needed to be washed and mended, the wagons needed to be repaired, and a thousand other little tasks needed to be completed. In truth, I didn't even notice that the children were gone, except perhaps to be grateful for the silence. But when it started to get dark, I noticed Karrie looking up from her mending more and more often, and finally, as the sun sank below the horizon, she stood up and examined the terrain anxiously.

"Sooooeeee!" she bellowed, which always makes me jump no matter how many times I've heard it before. She learned the pig call in the hollows of West Virginia, and it is a piercing cry.

I added my meager voice. "Mattie! Nan!"

Mary Perkins came out of the back of the Catledge wagon, where she was taking care of Abigail. "What's wrong?"

"They haven't returned," Karrie said.

Mary didn't look as concerned as I might have thought she would be. "They know to start back when the sun goes down," she said. "Do you want me to go look for them? Abigail is feeling better. Her fever has broken."

"Would you, please?" Karrie asked.

Mary went to the wagon and retrieved her shawl. A slight breeze was picking up. It can become brisk when the sun goes down, especially if there is a wind.

"Which way did they go?" Mary asked. "Did anyone see?"

"I think they went south," I said. I had a vague recollection that I'd heard them playing near a stand of junipers on the horizon, and I motioned in that direction. Soon after, the children had wandered out of sight, but I hadn't been concerned at the time. By now, they have traveled thousands of miles and are well accustomed to unexplored terrain. Most of us have gained a sense of how far they might wander and in what direction.

Mary strode off, not looking worried, but certainly moving more quickly than normal. She reached the copse of trees and disappeared.

I couldn't concentrate on my mending after that. I sat at the fire, staring into the flames, wondering what kind of mother would let her children wander away into a land of bears and rattlesnakes and savages. Certainly, nothing like this would have happened closer Independence, but we had become accustomed to the hardships of travel, and things that have once been unthinkable are now things we take for granted.

I heard the children laughing, first. The laughter of children travels far, perhaps even farther than Karrie Parsons' pig call. The sound of my own children's laughter travels with gladness and joy, and my ear seeks it out. I immediately relaxed, for such a sound melts away worry and fear. It is the sound that makes all of the travails worth it.

I couldn't even be angry with them, for they had already been heading back when Mary found them. Karrie also softened at their approach, and simply took Cager under her arm and helped him to the wagon, for he was limping. But he had a bright smile on his face, along with the strain and the pain.

Becky was carrying her blue bucket with both hands, as if it was heavy. Edwin had one of the other buckets, and though he was carrying it with one hand, I could see that he too was straining. The third bucket was balanced on top of Allie's head, and she was taking great delight in it.

"What have you got there?" I asked.

Edwin plunked the bucket down. The bottom third was full of rocks.

"What on Earth is that?" I asked. "Why did you bring these back?"

Edwin looked a little embarrassed. "They were so pretty, Mother. They were just lying in a dry creek bed, but the nicest ones were in the hillside above."

All I saw were white rocks, catching the last of the sunlight. There was a glitter that flashed for a moment, then was gone. I tried to lift the bucket and nearly toppled over, it was so heavy. We certainly didn't need to add this to our animals' burden.

"Can't we keep them, Mother? Please? You can put them in your garden," Edwin wheedled.

He knew how to reach me. I had a vision of my dream garden, lined by white, shining rocks. "I suppose…" I started to say.

Mary came around the side of the wagon before I could finish, with Becky Catledge following her. Mary lifted one of the blue buckets and began to dump it out.

"Please, Miss Mary, can't we keep them?" Becky pleaded.

Mary snatched one of the empty flour bags out of the back of our wagon. I nodded permission, and she poured the rocks into it.

Jonathan's deep voice came from behind me, and I froze. "Won't you be needing the cloth, dear?" he asked.

I didn't turn around, afraid to look him in the face while I dared to contradict him. "We are almost to Oregon City," I said. "If we need to, we can dump the rocks out then."

"To what purpose?" he asked. He reached over and took the pail from Mary. He lifted one of the rocks and examined it. He frowned, and then his face became impassive. I felt a chill, for I knew that when he became impassive like that, he was at his most dangerous. I wasn't sure what had caught his attention and breathed a sigh of relief when he shrugged.

"Please, Jona…Mr. Meredith," Mary said. "The children have so little."

"I don't suppose it will hurt anything," Jonathan said. "I suppose old Clyde and Peter can pull a little extra weight a few more miles."

<u>September 21, 1845</u>

We have resumed our journey, following the lost wagons ahead of us, hoping that by the time we catch up, they will no longer be lost. I did not sleep last night. The vision kept coming to me of my husband reaching out for the blue bucket and his hand lingering a little too long on Mary's,

and the way she went still, as if afraid. I remembered that she had begun
to call him Jonathan before remembering her place. And I tried to
remember whether I had seen either my husband or Mary all afternoon.

Jonathan came to bed but did not want me, and for that, I was glad.
He could not see the tears that flowed from my eyes like a stream flowing
over stones.

Chapter Twenty-One

<u>Testament of Virgil Conner</u>

<u>August ?, 1851</u>

The lights flickered deep within the tunnel to the left, the passageway that was caved in. I sensed the draft came from there as well. It was as if the spirits or apparitions were expecting us. I couldn't see Jake's expression, only the outline of his body, but I could tell he was ready to go. It was either dare the ghosts or become ghosts ourselves.

Whether malevolent or benign, the spirits lit our way. I could dimly see the walls and loose rocks upon our path. Our weird guides stayed well in front of us, and we followed them. My vision couldn't quite grasp them in full. If I stared at the lights too long, they disappeared. I closed my eyes and wondered if they were an illusion. It was when I didn't look directly at them that I could see their glow.

Once, as we rounded a corner, one of the apparitions appeared to be waiting for us.

"Tad, is that you?" I whispered. Beside me, Jake started in surprise, but then turned to the light as if he too was curious.

The light shot down the tunnel and disappeared. We were left in darkness.

"Maybe you shouldn't talk to them," Jake muttered.

We waited, as if we both sensed the apparition would come back. "Maybe they are leading us deeper into our graves," Jake said.

"What choice do we have?" I asked.

"They give me the creeps," Jake said. "They make me think upon my past, every damn thing I ever did wrong. Things that can't be helped. Things I had to do. But now I look back and think maybe I could have been a better man, a kinder, more generous man." He paused. "Ah, to hell with that," he said bitterly.

Gnawing guilt was mounting inside me as well, along with the kind of doubt that comes late at night, when the mind can't let go of the idea of what should have been. Perhaps it was the nearness of death, but I couldn't help but notice how the remorse built the longer and the more closely we followed our guiding spirits. I pushed the doubts down, as I always do, but they kept rising up like a nightmare.

"Mary and Joseph and Baby Jesus," Jake said.

The smell struck both of us at the same time. We had reached the cave-in, the place that Meredith had led us to before. The ghosts—I had begun to think of them as such, for there was no doubt they were unnatural—had dipped over the drop-off and disappeared into the darkness.

"It's Tad," I said, not knowing I was speaking aloud. "It must be."

"Jesus!" Jake repeated, and I sensed he was making the sign of the cross, as I'd seen him do before in times of danger and trouble. "You really think it's him?"

"Meredith wouldn't have let him escape, any more than he let us," I said. The familiar guilt surged inside me, and I could barely breathe. "We should have looked for him."

"Meredith would only have killed us earlier," Jake said. "Hell, the bastard didn't really need us all that much after we opened up the mine. He could have dug up the gold himself without much trouble if he weren't such a lazy bastard."

I saw a light appear far below. It seemed to be beckoning to us. I started to ease my way down over the rocks.

"I ain't going down there," Jake said. "Damn ghosts want us to join them. They want company."

"We aren't dead…yet," I said. My voice cracked as I said it, as if there wasn't enough moisture in my throat to form words effectively. "Come on, Jake. Why would the spirits bother with us if they didn't have somewhere they were leading us?"

"Leading us to hell," Jake said. "Leading us to the bottomless pit."

I laughed, and once I started laughing, I couldn't stop. Jake didn't join me, but I could sense him reluctantly grimacing. "We're just getting a head start," I said. "This way, they won't have so far to drag us down."

The vast regret I'd been feeling over the last few days confirmed what I've always known—it is too late for me. Too late to make amends, too late to become a better man, too late to return to my darling Agnes and become the husband she always hoped I'd be.

I started down the scree again and heard Jake following. Halfway down, the stench forced me to breathe through my mouth, but even so, the odor of death seemed to coat my lungs. I coughed and retched, and heard Jake doing the same thing. It was dry heaves; neither of us had enough water or food in our guts to do much more than that.

A single light shone at the bottom. It was hovering over Tad's body. It seemed to me that it had the shape of a girl, with a wide, round face and staring eyes. It wasn't my Tina, but a strange girl about the same age, eleven or twelve. The ghost floated over a jumble of what looked like clothing. I went closer and saw something squirming, and realized that bugs were swarming about the body, already picking the bones clean of flesh. Maggots and beetles were fighting for the remaining raw meat.

The ghost of the little girl backed away slightly, as if in respect. I could see by her light.

There was some paper clutched in Tad's skeletal hands, and I removed the sheets gently, careful not to tear them. It was too dark to read them, but I realized that poor Tad had had the same idea as me: to record his doom. I shuddered, for I wondered if I would meet the same end and whether sometime soon, someone would find this book.

Tad had apparently survived the fall for a time. His belt was wrapped around one leg, and I could see splintered bone through the shredded cloth.

"There're other bones down here," Jake said.

I tore myself away from the sight of Tad's yawning skull. "What's that?"

"There's another body down here," Jake said. "And it ain't buried under no rocks, neither." He leaned down and examined the skull. "There's a bullet hole in this one."

"We were lucky Meredith didn't plug us when he had the chance," I said.

"Maybe," Jake said. "Or maybe he did them a favor."

We stared down at the collection of bones, and it was strange to realize that someday others would look down on our bones the same way. I shuddered. I realized that I was resigned to dying, but I didn't want to become a ghost.

Our guiding spirit was hovering in the air, moving away and then back again, as if urging us to hurry. I started after it, and within moments, we came across two more skeletons. These bones were smaller, older. I sensed that they belonged to our child ghosts.

A wave of sadness came over me. Strange that I should feel it so strongly, but I've always been affected by the misfortunes of the young. A child beggar always gets my coin, if I have one.

Worry about yourself, I thought.

We were no longer in a tunnel fashioned by tools but in a natural cavern, like a crack in the earth. It was smooth in places and nearly impassible in others. I felt the moisture in the air, and when I reached out and wiped my hand along the stone, it came away wet. I put my dampened fingers into my mouth, and it helped.

I heard the trickling water from a long way off, and it gave me added strength. Jake, who had been grunting and complaining the whole way, suddenly fell silent, and he almost pushed me aside in his eagerness.

The ghosts stopped, and as we came upon them, we saw that they were hovering over a dark pool of water. Jake and I dropped to our bellies and plunged our heads into the pool, drinking deeply. It was freezing, but clear.

I gasped, raising my head, feeling awake and alert for the first time since we'd begun our journey.

The ghosts whirled about us, and again memories bombarded me with regrets, but instead of it dispiriting me this time, I felt hope, for I wanted to return to Agnes, to start over. I'd never look for gold, never leave my job, again.

We filled our waterskins. Our bellies were full of water, and I could actually hear the sloshing as we walked. I smiled and then marveled that I could still find humor in our ordeal. The water had the strange effect of satiating my hunger a little bit but at the same time reminding me of just how hungry I was.

The breeze that had been so slight that it could have been a zephyr of imagination now felt strong on my wet face. I hurried forward, my eyes on the floating ghosts who were leading us out of the subterranean burial chamber. We reached a wide spot in the cave, and then they swooped into a hole near the base of a wall. The ghosts disappeared into the hole, and I followed.

The floor disappeared beneath me, and I tumbled into a pit, smashing into loose objects that clattered about me. Jake followed with a grunt.

The ghosts appeared to brighten. Amid miles of dark soil and rock, the clattering objects at our feet were a bright white. All the dread and regret of a misspent life came down upon me at that moment. It was a necropolis, a catacomb of bones, thousands upon thousands, with the round shapes of broken skulls dotted among them. And all the souls were still here, still raging at the living.

These were not the ghosts of children, or of people who were like us in any way. These were the ghosts of an ancient and long-lost tribe.

"Oh, God!" Jake cried. He dropped to his knees, crossing himself again and again. The ghosts swirled around him as if excited, and he cried out, "I'm sorry, Betsy! I didn't mean to hurt you!" He toppled over and curled up in a ball. "Forgive me, Betsy. Please, dear God, forgive me. I didn't mean it to happen!"

I stared down at him in shock. I too was roiled by memories, but his undoing was so complete that for once I was able to shove aside my own guilty thoughts and worry about him. Perhaps this saved me; I don't know.

Betsy had been his first wife. He had told me that she had abandoned him, but with a chill, I heard his words and understood their meaning.

"Come on, Jake," I said. "We've got to get away from here."

The ghosts still swirled around us, and now they were passing through us as well. Each time one of the lights went into Jake, he jerked as if being stabbed. He'd stopped babbling, stopped moving at all.

"Jake!" I cried, and then the ghosts concentrated on me. They swirled around me, and each time, I had visions: of Agnes as she was on our wedding night; of Timothy as a young boy, when he'd still looked up to me; and most of all, of Tina, my beautiful little girl whom God had called home.

I wanted to go back to my family, to my gentle memories, not these horrid thoughts of abandonment and shame.

"Stop it!" I cried. "Stop!"

The lights swirled about me again and then moved away, as if warded off. In their place were the brighter lights of those who had led us to this place, the ghosts of the children. For the first time, they fully coalesced. Their feet reached the ground, and I could see their features clearly: a young girl, a boy with a misshapen leg, and a taller, handsome older boy— a young man, really. They didn't say anything, but I could sense them judging me.

I turned and ran deeper into the blackness. I found a small hole on the other side of the chamber, and I scrambled into it. It led to a tunnel leading upward. I left the chamber of bones and the avenging spirits behind. God help me, I left Jake behind.

The breeze grew stronger until it felt like a wind, and I saw a light far in the distance, far above. I scrambled up the slope, slipping, falling more than once. I knew that if I survived this day, I would be nothing but bruises, but I would be alive. I would return to Saginaw, and I would seek out Timothy and help him if I could, and I would put flowers on Tina's grave every day, and I would never leave my home again.

I could feel the warm air halfway up the slope. My fingers scrambled on the hard rock, bleeding, fingernails shredded, and I crawled those last few feet, to a hole that was just big enough for me to fit through.

I felt the hot desert sand and rolled over on my back, blinded by the midday sun. I closed my eyes and breathed in the air, and extended my arms and grabbed handfuls of sand and let them run through my fingers. The sun was low in the sky, but it was still hot out.

I knew that I was not yet safe, that perhaps the most dangerous part of my return home lay ahead of me. But I had no doubt that I would survive. When the sun dropped below the horizon, I forced myself to stand and walk.

I was walking blindly through the dark when I came among them.

There in the blackness, I sensed other men, who could see me even if I could not clearly see them. Savages.

I waited for the deathblow. I wasn't afraid. *If I must die*, I thought, *then let it be here in the open, while I am free.* I could not even blame the Indians for wanting me dead.

And then they were gone. Maybe they'd never been there. Maybe I had imagined it. When morning came at last, I saw moccasin prints in the sand, and I understood that by some miracle, they had decided to let me live.

Meredith had done his best to confuse us by blindfolding us, and if you'd asked me a few days earlier, I would have thought us lost. But I seemed to have an unerring sense of which direction to go. The territory really isn't as large as he'd tried to make us believe. He must have led us in circles, crossing the same creek more than once.

I reached the creek bed where we had been blindfolded. It was dark again by then, and I saw a campfire where the guards Meredith had hired to patrol the perimeter were eating dinner. A few days earlier, I might have been frightened, but now I detoured around them without a qualm.

The guilt I'd been feeling began to fade like a bad dream, but the resolve the guilt had engendered in me remained. I hefted my pack, which I'd managed to hang onto through my escape. It was heavy with nuggets.

I don't know how much gold is in there, but I know I'll never return for more. It will have to be enough.

I am going home. The rest of the gold can stay buried for all I care.

Chapter Twenty-Two

<u>Vale, Oregon Territory, September 1851</u>

Dearest Frank,

We reached Vale without trouble. I have given these letters to a wagon master who is heading for Oregon City and who promises to see them forwarded from there. First thing in the morning, we intend to find the Smith Feed Store and, hopefully, Gus and Abigail Catledge. I hope they have enough information that I might combine it with what Mary has told me and what is in Ellen Meredith's journals and get a full accounting.

However, I also wish to fulfill Mary's request and find Becky Catledge and make certain she is safe. From what I have learned from the journals, this will probably mean confronting Jonathan Meredith, for he seems to be at the center of all these mysteries.

It will be a dangerous confrontation, I suspect. But I have good men around me. Terrance Drake is an admirable young man, and of course Angus knows how to take care of himself. Franklin also seems a capable fellow. If it must be done, I cannot think of better support than these three men. Don't worry, dear husband. I will endeavor to stay safe.

Love,
Virginia

Virginia sealed the envelope, wondering if she'd said too much. She'd started the letter intending to downplay everything—thus telling Frank that the journey to Vale had been uneventful, which was far from true. But she couldn't lie to him. Whenever she did that, it only caused problems later on. She hated to worry him, but either she would come out safe, in which case his worries would be resolved, or she wouldn't, in which case her warning might help prepare him.

She handed the letter to the wagon master, along with enough money to pay for him to find way to get the letter to California. It was only money, which Virginia could get more of at any time. Keeping in touch with Frank was far more important.

I will ask him to come with me next time, she thought. *I mustn't lose him.*

They had arrived in Vale after dark and found the one hotel in town already closed. Virginia pounded on the door until a grumpy woman answered and let them in. She was going to refuse them lodging until Virginia opened her pack and brought out a stack of money.

"Two rooms?" The woman looked from Virginia to the three men accompanying her with raised eyebrows. It wasn't the first time Virginia had found herself being judged by others for being a woman traveling with three men, none of whom were her husband.

"My employees can sleep in one room," she said. "I would like a private room for myself."

The hotel owner seemed reassured by that. Virginia had already learned that having retainers was less frowned upon than having three men as colleagues.

As soon as they were unpacked, they went to the nearest saloon. Again, Virginia got looks, but she stared the men down defiantly. She asked the saloonkeeper if anyone was heading to the Willamette Valley, and he pointed out the wagon master. After giving him her letters, she left the men to their drinking and went back to her hotel room.

The travelers met up in the morning in the hotel dining room. Angus, Drake, and Franklin were nursing hangovers, but they had managed to find out where the Smith Feed Store was—not that it would have proven difficult, for it was right there on the main street, not far from the saloon.

When they got to the store, they found that it was busy and, by all appearances, prosperous. A grizzled old man met them as they entered the lot.

"What can I do for you gentlemen?" he asked. He nodded to Virginia, but it was merely a courtesy. It was the men who would conduct the business, obviously. Virginia turned to Angus, who took her cue.

"Would you be Augustus Smith?" he asked the man.

"Lord, no. My name's Cole Johnson. I'm just the foreman. Gus isn't here right now, but I am authorized to do anything that he can do."

"What about Abigail Smith?" Drake spoke up. "Is she here?"

"Why would you want to be talking to her?" the foreman asked. It was clear that he'd been warned not to let anyone near Mrs. Smith.

"Don't see how that would be your business, my good man," Angus said. "But as it happens, Miss Reed here is friends with her."

"I see," Johnson said, sounding uncertain. He glanced over his shoulder, as if looking for someone from whom to ask permission. Virginia saw that there was a small cottage behind the barnlike structure of the feed store. "I suppose it would be all right for her to go on, if you gentlemen will wait here for her."

Angus looked as if he wanted to object. Virginia cut him off. "That would be fine, sir. My men are looking for livestock and supplies for our trip. I'm hoping you can help." She turned to Angus. "Mr. Porter?"

"Yes, miss?" he answered, so obsequiously that Virginia nearly broke out laughing.

"You have my full authority to purchase whatever we need for our journey. I shall return shortly."

"Yes, Miss Reed," Angus said. "You certain you don't want some company?"

"I'm sure I'll be fine," Virginia said. Now that it had come to it, she realized it was probably a good thing for her to proceed alone. Gus and Abigail Catledge would be nervous about any visitors, and she wanted them to trust her. Angus, Drake, and Franklin were good men, but they had a rough feel about them.

She strode up the path to the little house, which looked like the houses she remembered back in Illinois: painted white with green shutters, a small flower garden in front.

She knocked on the door, wondering what to say. No one answered, but she heard a pounding noise from out back, and she left the porch and went around the side of the house.

An old woman was splitting firewood in the backyard. She was putting some muscle into it, for she was a large, portly woman who obviously knew how to wield an axe. She was a pioneer woman, and in a pinch, she could do almost anything a man could do.

"Mrs. Smith?" Virginia pitched her voice so it was just loud enough to cut through the noise, but not so loud as to alarm the woman.

Abigail turned, her axe raised high, then lowered it slowly when she saw it was a slender blonde woman addressing her. *A good thing I came alone,* Virginia thought. *And that I don't look as strong as I am.*

"Lord, you nearly frightened me to death!" Abigail exhaled. "Who might you be?"

"My name is Virginia Reed," Virginia said. "I'm looking for…"

"Virginia Reed?" Abigail interrupted. "Of the Donner Party?"

Virginia fell silent, wondering if her being recognized was good or bad. Abigail looked around as if she expected wolves to be lurking in the shadows.

"You'd best come in the house, girl," Abigail said. She slammed the axe into the chopping block and wiped her hands. Then she led the way through a small vegetable garden to the open back door of the house.

She went into the kitchen, took out a teapot, and began boiling water. It was clear she was buying herself time to think, and at the same time, trying to avoid the inevitable.

"I am looking for Abigail and Augustus Catledge," Virginia said, finally.

The old woman didn't stop bustling around the kitchen. Not until the water was boiled and the tea brewed did she turn around. "Sit down, Miss Reed. I didn't think you were here to find Abby and Gus Smith."

Virginia sat at the table, and Abigail poured her a cup of tea. She took a polite sip. It seemed to burst on her tongue with the taste of roses and cinnamon. "Yum," she said.

"I grow the flowers in my garden," Abigail said, taking a sip of her own tea. She leaned back. "I've heard of you, of course. Mary Perkins talked of you often, and when we heard the stories of the Donner Party, we recognized your name. But how did you find us?"

"I didn't," Virginia said. "That was Mary 's doing."

"Mary? Mary Perkins?" Abigail looked surprised, as if it was the last thing she had expected. Then a troubled expression came over her face, and she looked away as if ashamed. "Is she…well?"

"Yes, very much so. She is Mrs. Oliver Hoskins now, married to a very wealthy man." Virginia decided not to mention her doubts about Mr. Hoskins.

"I am so very glad to hear it," Abigail said, and her relief was genuine. "I wanted to help her, but…well, we were having our own problems."

"That's why I'm here," Virginia said. "I understand your daughter is missing. Mary asked me to look into it."

"You?" Abigail looked at Virginia's slender frame and delicate features doubtfully. "I don't understand."

"I am more capable than I look, Abigail."

The old woman stared at her a while longer, then nodded. "I believe that you are. I've heard stories. Very well. What do you know about what happened?"

"I have been given Ellen Meredith's journals," Virginia said. "And of course, Mary has told me what she knows."

"Then you know of our problems with Jonathan Meredith," Abigail said. "But you don't know what happened after Ellen died." She took a long drink of her tea. "Poor woman. I am glad that she never knew what happened to her sons, at least."

"Jed and Edwin?" Virginia asked. "I assumed they were still with their stepfather."

"Oh, there is much more to the story than that," Abigail said. She got up and closed the back door, as if she was afraid of being overheard. "But much of it is too strange to be believed."

"I have traveled all the way from California to hear your story, Abigail. I am prepared to believe anything you tell me. I don't know what stories you have heard about the Donner Party, but the experience taught me that there is more danger in this life than what you see on the surface."

"Yes," Abigail said. "Of that, I am sure."

"Where is Mr. Catledge?" Virginia asked. It had seemed to her that Abigail hadn't wanted her to ask that question and wouldn't have answered it until she was sure that Virginia didn't pose a threat.

"Before I tell you that, I think I need to tell you about everything that happened after poor Ellen died," Abigail said.

Chapter Twenty-Three

<u>Diary of Ellen Meredith</u>

<u>The Oregon Trail, September 24, 1845</u>

Disaster has struck our little party. We've traveled across the continent and lost but one person, which, no matter how precious she was to us, was a smaller price than most have paid. But today has come a reckoning. Cager and Allie are missing. Kerrie and Bart awoke early, and normally they have to roust their children out of bed to help with the chores. But this morning, they found only neatly folded blankets, as if the children had never been to bed at all.

Karrie thought Bart had put the children to bed, and he thought that she had, so it is possible that the children have been missing longer than just the night. Nobody can remember when they saw them last. They were at the midday meal yesterday, that is agreed, but after that…

A search party was quickly organized. All the men mustered, including Jed and, for the first time on one of these ventures, Edwin, leaving the women and children behind. Jed rode ahead and was able to gather more men from the wagon train to help. They have split the surrounding territory into quadrants, each with three men.

No one knows what to expect. We have not seen any sign of Indians, and even the wildlife is sparse in these lands. Over the last few days, we have seen a huge owl, a few jackrabbits, and plenty of coyote tracks, but little else. Most likely, one of the children met with an accident and the other child is staying at his or her side, waiting for rescue.

Jonathan chose to cover the quadrant that includes the area we have already traveled through, taking Jed and Edwin with him. The men are grim, for the nights have become cold, nearly freezing. If the children are exposed to the wind, they are in great danger.

After the men left, the camp felt empty, abandoned. The families have retreated to their wagons, and there is little conversation or movement. I can hear Karrie sobbing, for she is bereft, already certain that her children have met their end. I feel the same, though there is no real reason to think so.

Abigail has taken Karrie under her motherly wing, and it good that she has done so. I feel for the woman, but I cannot express it. I've become stoic, more stoic than I was before we left. I no longer see this journey as a fresh start, but as an ending. I sense that Jonathan is tired of me, tired of the children, and that nothing will keep him from leaving us once we reach our destination. I fear for the future, for I have nothing to offer any man. I'm old and fat, and I have no skills other than mothering, if such skills I have, for I have begun to doubt even that.

The children are uncharacteristically quiet. It occurs to me that they were silent yesterday as well, even before Cager and Allie disappeared. Something happened that they refuse to talk about. I wonder if the disappearance of two of their number is connected to it. I cannot imagine what has caused such disquiet.

Mattie and Nan cling to me, and I pat their heads, but the comforting words do not come. I have no comfort to give.

The search parties returned by nightfall, empty-handed.

"We searched all the places they might hide," said Carl Lundgren, one of the men from the larger wagon train.

"Hide," Gus echoed. "Why on Earth would they hide?"

Lundgren didn't back down. "If they are lost, why would they not make themselves visible? If they are injured, why have they not answered our cries?"

No one said anything, for we all knew the answer. If they had not sought high ground, if they were not answering summons, it was because they couldn't.

"We will search farther tomorrow," Lundgren said. "We will go directly to where we left off searching and expand our range. But if we do not find them tomorrow, it is difficult for me to believe that they could have gone farther than that."

"Let's not borrow trouble from the future," Gus said. "Surely we will find a sign of them, if we keep searching."

Bart stood up abruptly. He walked to the edge of the light and stood there, his back to us. Everyone fell silent, and for the rest of the evening, we were all aware of his intensity, of him staring into the abyss of the desert night. We were all getting ready for bed when we heard him cry out, "Cager! Allie! Come home!"

<u>October 6, 1845</u>

The search parties spent two days scouring the High Desert within the boundaries of territory the children could possibly have traveled. Of course, searching every nook and cranny was impossible. There are more gullies and ravines than can be counted, some of them mere depressions in the earth where a body could not be seen from more than a few yards away. There are rock outcroppings with passages between them where a battalion of soldiers could hide.

The men decided to fire their rifles every mile, and throughout the day, the gunfire echoed back to the camp. Each time, Mattie and Nan trembled at the sound, though they knew the reverberations were coming. Even the farthest-away shot could be heard in the camp, which meant that the children would have had to be twice the distance away not to have also heard it. If they were not answering the shouts or the gunfire, it was because they couldn't or wouldn't.

The next morning, there was frost on the ground. It was the first frost we had encountered since leaving the Rockies behind. The campfire was difficult to start that morning, and the men lingered longer around it than in previous days, trying to get warm.

At the end of a badly cooked breakfast, Carl Lundgren stood and spoke for the other rescuers. "We can't stay any longer," he said. "Our water supplies are running low, and we don't know when we'll reach a more hospitable place. We would like to help you search further, but…"

"Then help us," Gus urged. "The children have only been gone a few days. They could be someplace where they can't hear us. They could still be waiting for us to find them."

Lundgren shook his head. He didn't have to say what he was thinking.

"Let him go," Bart said to Gus. "They have their own families to look after."

"We'll stay," Gus said, looking toward Jonathan, who, somewhat to my surprise, nodded.

"Let me go with you this time," Becky said. "I can help."

Jonathan looked as if he was going to object, but Jed spoke up first. "She's a better shot than any of us. And she can probably walk farther and faster."

"Very well," Jonathan said to Becky. "But you must do as I say."

Bart, Jed, and Gus struck out to the north and the west, while Jonathan, Edwin, and Becky went to the south and the east. They had searched all the obvious places; now they were going to check out the smaller ravines, the rock outcroppings, anyplace that could hold two small bodies, though no one said so out loud.

When they returned that night, I noticed that Jonathan and Edwin weren't talking to each other, and that Becky seemed distressed. I tried to question my son, but he shook his head and didn't answer. I figured he and his father had probably gotten into another argument.

Two more days were spent searching. Our water ran out at the end of the second day, which made the situation desperate.

The following morning, Bart harnessed his team and led us away. It was his decision. I'm not sure who among us would have given up the search if not for Bart's surrender. We followed the tracks of the rest of the wagon train, the last of the wayfarers. A half-day's journey later, we came across a crude sign pointing north of the trail that said, "Water."

We refilled our water barrels and continued on. Two more days' journey, and we saw that the bulk of the wagons had turned north again. Once again, we had a meeting to decide which path to follow. There was little disagreement. We followed the wider trail north.

Within a few days, we saw the Columbia River flowing below the plateau, and there were campfires spread out along the dark water. Whether it was our own companions or another wagon train, the sight lifted our hearts. For a moment, I almost forgot about Cager and Allie.

Bart cried out to his mule team, and they began winding down to the river to join the others.

We were welcomed with hot food, fresh firewood, and fodder for our livestock. Most of the rest of the wagon train appeared to have heard about the missing children, and they were very solicitous toward all of us, but especially toward Bart and Karrie. I have never seen anyone as undone by grief as they are.

One we were safe, I felt the energy drain from me, and for a full day, I did not leave my bedding. Mattie took up the task of feeding the family, and her cooking was surprisingly good. Tears squeezed from my eyes. No one really needed me. I was useless as a mother and a wife, and even a child could take my place.

"What do you think happened to Allie and Cager?" I asked my husband that night. Nestled among the hundreds of other settlers, I was finally able to express my fears.

"There is no way of telling," Jonathan said after a long moment. "Those last few days, I even looked for the circling of buzzards."

"Jonathan!"

"Even if they were only injured, the carrion birds always know," he said pragmatically. "They're always waiting. But there was nothing. Wherever they are, they are out of reach."

I wanted to put my head on his shoulder. I wanted him to wrap his arms around me. But I turned away. "Where were you?" I asked quietly.

"What?"

"On the day they went missing, I saw you leave and go toward the east. Where did you go?"

I felt him propping himself up on his elbow and sensed that he was glaring down at me. "What are you saying?"

I heard the anger in his voice, and perhaps it should have reassured me. But I have learned that Jonathan can summon his anger at any moment, and that anger serves to hide his lies.

"I will forget you asked that," Jonathan said, turning his back to me.

<u>October 25, 1845</u>

We have reached Oregon City! I am feeling such relief as I thought I would never feel again. We are safe. My family has arrived at our destination without harm, except for poor, dear Sarah. Most of our possessions are still intact.

The last two and a half weeks of the journey were slow, almost leisurely. The trail was well worn, and there were few dangers: no rivers to ford that didn't have ferries or bridges; no steep cliffs that hadn't already been surmounted. There were even general stores along the route, though their prices are usurious. I spent my last pennies on candy for Mattie and Nan.

Even Jonathan has become more lighthearted. One morning, I heard him tell a terrible joke to Gus, who responded with a belly laugh that made me glad. Then they both glanced at me, as if the joke was unseemly. I pretended I hadn't heard a word.

No one laughed or told jokes when Bartholomew or Karrie were near, however. They withdrew from us, keeping close to each other, and I could hear Karrie crying at night. I feel strangely guilty that this tragedy befell them and not us, and then I remember my dear children and I shake the guilt off. It could have happened to any of us, but it happened to them. God keeps his mysteries.

We spent one last evening together by the campfire, and this morning, we hugged and shook hands, and the children cried at leaving their friends.

Now we have gone our separate ways. Jonathan is determined to move on to Portland and start a business there.

We have not slept together since I questioned him, but to my surprise, he shows no sign that he intends to abandon his family. Despite myself, I have begun to hope for a future for us, though my doubts remain.

Jonathan has not turned out to be the man I thought he was, but I am his wife and he is my husband, and there is little I can do about that.

Chapter Twenty-Four

<u>Diary of Ellen Meredith</u>

<u>Portland, Oregon Territory, November 3, 1848</u>

I have not written in this diary for over three years. I had thought my journey over. I had thought that nothing unexpected, nothing exciting would ever happen again; that life would return to normal, a wonderful ordinariness.

And for a time, it did.

Jonathan's lumber business was successful from the start. We quickly progressed from our clapboard house by the river to a mansion in the hills. To be honest, I would have been happy in the more modest domicile, but my husband insisted that we must display our success. After a few social occasions at which I was too petrified to speak, he didn't demand that I attend any more. Once a year, I summon my courage and invite his friends over for a soiree, and because it is held within the familiar, comfortable surroundings of my own home, I am able, for that one night, to pretend to be a gracious hostess.

The more successful my husband becomes, the more distant he is to me. He no longer comes to my bed, and I am fearful that he will find a younger woman and try with her to have the sons he has always wanted. I know that he visits other women at inappropriate times, and some of my neighbors take pains to hint that he is being unfaithful, but I pretend that I don't understand. If he visits women of the night, it is nothing to me.

He keeps me in luxury, but I am merely a prop for his respectability. I manage the household, I provide him meals, I take care of the garden and the children, I command the servants, but we might go days without speaking a word to each other.

Perhaps he has not discarded me because he has finally accepted Jed and Edwin as his sons. Jed especially has been given great responsibility in the business, and Edwin has been working with his brother after school and in the summers. I don't see much love between my sons and my husband, but they no longer yell at each other.

Jed has become nearly as distant to me as his stepfather. Edwin is always busy. If not for my girls, I would have no one. From the outside, I live an enviable life. The clerks and the livery drivers all treat me with respect. My mother told me not to expect happiness, and I never have. I should be content with my family's prosperity.

This is a life that I would have accepted, that I would have been grateful for, if not for my nightmares. During my waking hours, I find myself daydreaming about dear Cullum, whom I never appreciated enough, who always tried honorably to do the right thing. I never told him how much I loved him. At night, I dream of his death. I see him riding along the trail above our farm, something leaping from the shelter of the trees, him tumbling out of his saddle and landing on his neck.

I see the creature standing over him, biting into him, tearing at his flesh.

When I awake, the feeling of horror won't go away. I can't help but remember how Goldie found his way back to Jonathan's stables without a mark up on him. I try to see the creature's face, but I cannot. But when Jonathan enters the dining room for breakfast, I feel a sudden terror. I hide it as best I can, but I have seen him staring at me with cold eyes, as if he knows what I am thinking.

I began this diary again because I sense that the consequences of our journey across the continent are not yet over.

<u>December 13, 1848</u>

I try to have my yearly celebration between the other wives' bigger ones, midway between Thanksgiving and Christmas. Even then, not all my RSVPs are answered. Still, enough guests show up that we are not embarrassed, though most are my husband's business associates.

To my great surprise, I recognized an old friend this year. I sent an invitation to one of Jonathan's new partners, Mr. Oliver Hoskins, and his wife. When Mary Perkins walked in the door, draped on the arm of a distinguished gentleman, well, I was so surprised I almost couldn't speak.

She saw my discomfiture and came to me and embraced me. "I'm so happy to see you again, Ellen," she said.

I looked upon her in amazement. She was a beautiful young woman, her green gown matching her bright green eyes, her red hair piled ornately atop her head, held in place by a diamond tiara.

It was also the first time, I believe, that she ever called me Ellen and not Mrs. Meredith.

"Does Jonathan know?" I blurted.

"I think my husband has told him that we are acquainted," she said. "But whether Jonathan remembers little old me, I couldn't tell you."

"Of course I remember you," Jonathan boomed, entering our little circle. "Without you, our children would have run wild on the trail."

I watched Mary carefully and saw a faint blush upon her cheeks.

Jonathan and Oliver Hoskins shook hands, and I wanted to disappear. Here were three handsome, vibrant people, in the prime of their lives, and dumpy little me, wearing last year's dress and hoping no one would notice. I couldn't speak after that, simply nodded dumbly to what anyone said to me.

Mary took me in tow, doing all the talking, and it was clear that she'd had practice at this sort of thing, that she understood what it was like to be the wife of a tycoon. When the men retired to the library for cognac and cigars, Mary took me aside.

"Are you all right?" she asked. "Is Jonathan…Mr. Meredith treating you kindly?"

"He…is treating me…well," I said haltingly. The memories of our journey together were overwhelming me. I'd thought to leave it all behind, but Mary's presence was bringing it all back vividly. "Have you seen the others? Gus and Abigail? Young Becky?" I paused and took a deep breath. "Whatever happened to poor Karrie and Bartholomew?"

"The Catledges left me a letter," Mary confided. "They have left the territory and changed their name. They asked me not to try to find them."

"Left?" I echoed. "Whatever for?" But even as I asked, I sensed the truth.

Mary didn't answer. Instead, she said, "Karrie disappeared not long after we arrived. I haven't been able to find her. Bart…you can find him down at the docks. He sweeps out the taverns and does whatever odd jobs he can find. He is usually drunk. I have offered to help him, but he refuses."

"Oh, dear," I said. I sounded like my mother, old and staid. I hated what I had become and envied this beautiful young woman, which is something I never would have thought possible.

Mary dug into the tiny, jeweled purse she was holding and handed me a piece of paper. She leaned over and whispered, "If you must reach me, send a message to this address. Don't try to get to me at home."

She looked around to see if anyone had overheard or noticed, and then gave me a bright smile. "Let us speak of happier things. How are Edwin and Jed?"

"They work with their stepfather," I said. I was surprised that I had used the term "stepfather," because with most people, I pretended they were his true sons. "They are well."

"And Mattie and Nan?" Mary asked, smiling.

I returned the smile, and for the first time all evening, I felt like myself. "They are turning into young women before my eyes. Both have been going to school. Mattie has announced that she will become a doctor!"

Mary laughed. "I wouldn't be surprised."

The men started venturing back into the dining room, and Mary quickly said, "We must get together soon. I have more to tell you."

Since that night, she has sent me several messages, but I haven't answered them. I am certain that what she wishes to tell me is something I'd best not hear.

I'm a coward, but I have fought my battles. Now all I want is peace.

Last night, I dreamed of the creature who attacked Cullum. The creature had Jonathan's face.

<u>January 12, 1849</u>

I asked Carter, our butler, to arrange a carriage ride down to the waterfront. He objected, but I insisted. I could see him wondering if he should tell Mr. Meredith, but in the end he acceded to my request, on the condition that he accompanies me.

We drove up and down the streets, and I examined the rough-looking men lounging outside of the taverns and flophouses.

"Who are you looking for?" Carter asked.

"A friend," was all I answered. It was none of his business.

I was about to give up for the day when I saw Bart Parsons. It was his shock of blond hair that alerted me; otherwise I never would have recognized him. He was sitting with his back to the boardwalk, his head down, but I was sure it was him.

Carter helped me get Bart into the carriage, and we went to a nearby restaurant, a respectable if not lavish establishment. They almost didn't let us in. Bart stunk to high heaven. I pleaded for them to let us have one of the back rooms, and when Carter produced a fair sum of money, they let us in.

Bart didn't recognize me. I had to tell him my name more than once. Finally, he looked at me blurrily. "Ellen? Ellen Meredith?" Then he looked panicked. "Is he with you? Is he looking for me?"

"My husband doesn't know I'm here," I said. Carter gave me a sharp look and opened his mouth to say something, but I stared back at him steadily and he subsided. I'd never done that before, but I was more determined than I'd been in a long time.

"Where's Karrie?" I asked.

"I need a drink," Bart said. "Give me a drink and I'll tell you."

I sent Carter off to get a drink. The moment he left the room, Bart leaned forward. His eyes cleared for a brief moment. "She went looking for our children," he said. "She never came back."

"Where did she go?" I asked, mystified.

"Ask your damn husband."

"Jonathan? Why would he know?"

Just then, Carter returned with a shot glass of amber liquid. Bart downed it with one gulp.

I turned to Carter. "Give him the rest of the money."

"But, ma'am…"

"I don't want your charity," Bart said, standing up unsteadily. "I don't want his money."

He lurched out the door, and I rose to follow him. I felt Carter's firm hand on my arm. "Pardon me, ma'am. You must respect his wishes. Give him that much dignity."

The next thing I knew, I was in the back of the carriage going back to our mansion in the hills, as if I'd blanked out the time since leaving the restaurant. Carter was across from me, looking at me speculatively. When he noticed I was back among the living, he gave me a smile—the same smile he gave me every morning, and just as false.

"You will not mention this to Mr. Meredith," I said. "I have asked very little of you, Carter. And you've had little to fear from me. But do not cross me on this."

Carter looked surprised, then a twisted smile came over his face— twisted, but at least genuine. "As you wish, ma'am."

<u>February 10, 1849</u>

My daughters are ill. It was a light fever at first, and I made both girls go to school. Nan was sent home, shivering and flushed. I sent Carter to fetch Mattie from her school and sent for the doctor.

It is typhus, the doctor told me. "They are young and healthy," he said. "They can recover."

Jonathan is on one of his business trips. I have asked Carter to go get him, but I don't believe he will return in time to make a difference.

I felt the fever come upon me. I went to my bed, telling no one. In the morning, when I rose, the walls and floor rippled as if made of cloth, and the light pierced my eyes and entered my head, filling them with pain. I stumbled to my children's room, where the doctor sat, drowsing.

"He poisoned us," I said loudly.

The doctor looked confused. "Poisoned? It is typhus, Mrs. Meredith. I assure you." He rose from the chair and led me to it, helping me sit. He put his hand to my forehead, then stepped back. "You must go to your room, ma'am. You must rest."

"I will sleep here," I said. "You can take care of all of us here."

The doctor didn't object. I'm sure it made his job easier. A bed was brought in, and I asked for this diary, in which I have written as long as I can. I can't see the letters anymore, only the white of the paper. I can't hold the pen firmly; it slips out of my hand. But I will struggle on and hope that whoever reads this can make sense of my ramblings.

I summoned my maid, Bridget, and I have instructed her to deliver this to Mary Perkins…no, Mary Hoskins, I now remember.

If I lose Mattie and Nan, I have no more reason to live. Today their condition took a turn for the worse, and even now I hear Nan struggling to breathe. Mattie has not been conscious since this morning. My own mind grows confused. I fear for us all.

Mary, if you are reading this, the worst has happened.

I must tell you now what I have always known but never admitted it to myself. My husband is an evil man and a murderer. This is not the fever speaking, this is the truth finally coming out. When Cager and Allie Parsons went missing, I caught my husband that same day washing his hands clean of blood. He told me it was from dressing a rabbit, but there was so much of it, and it was thick upon his hands.

When gold was discovered in California, I remembered the blue buckets and the shiny rocks, and I asked Jonathan about them, but he professed not to remember the incident. But I know when Jonathan is lying, as he has been lying about almost everything for a long time now.

Be careful, Mary. If you see the Catledges, tell them to remain hidden, especially young Becky.

I can write no more. I can't see the paper now, nor feel the pen.

May God forgive me.

Chapter Twenty-Five

Dearest Frank,

It was fortunate that I finished Ellen Meredith's diary before reaching Vale. Otherwise I might not have understood the story that Abigail Catledge told me upon arriving. I might have thought she was exaggerating, even delusional. But the evidence is beginning to add up, and it is clear that the culprit is gold, as it always seems to be these days. It is clear that the children found gold while lost in Eastern Oregon, and that Jonathan Meredith learned of it.

Beyond that, all is supposition, with no real evidence to support it. I believe that I am going to have to find the Lost Blue Bucket Mine if I am to confirm my suspicions. This won't be easy. It is, after all, truly lost, except perhaps to Jonathan Meredith, and he won't so easily give up the location. He is a rich man and able to buy the rough men he needs to protect his secrets.

If I am interpreting Ellen's diaries correctly, there is only one of the children still alive or not missing who knows where the mine can be found—and that is Becky Catledge. I'm disappointed to find that she is not here in Vale, but Abigail has provided information that should allow me to find her.

Love,
Virginia

Abigail Catledge got up from the table and poured both of them another cup of tea. She bustled around the kitchen, putting away things, rearranging things, and Virginia understood that taking comfort in her domestic chores was the woman's way of giving herself time to think. Finally, she sat down across from Virginia with a sigh.

"Jonathan Meredith became extraordinarily successful in a very brief time," she said. "It was as if he already had money from some source or other. At first, my husband and I didn't think too much about it. We'd learned that Jonathan was an aggressive and ambitious man.

"But one day, Gus saw him coming out of the gold exchange office, and on a whim, he went in and questioned the clerk.

"'Mr. Meredith is our best customer,'" the man said. 'He doesn't complain about our exchange rate, which is admittedly not as good as he could get in San Francisco or Seattle. He understands the difficulties of being in a less populated and prosperous area.'

"'He's come in before?' Gus asked.

"'Many times,' the clerk said. He broke off and suddenly seemed doubtful, as if he realized that perhaps it wasn't a good idea to be telling a stranger tales about his best customer. 'Sir, unless you have business to transact, I must get back to my work,' he said.

"That is as far as my husband took it. It probably seems strange to you now, but you must understand that at that time, we were not yet aware of the gold strikes in California. It wasn't until a few months later that we understood the full significance of it. We simply assumed that Jonathan had brought his riches west with him, which gave him a head start in his business ventures.

"The Merediths were soon too wealthy to acknowledge the likes of us poor farmers. I think Ellen would have liked to visit, but Jonathan kept her in that mansion, surrounded by servants, and I think she was too embarrassed to make the effort.

"Gus and I purchased land outside of Oregon City, and it was every bit as fertile as we'd been told back East. We did well the first two years. The weather was good, the crops grew well, and we had enough money left over to purchase seed and supplies for the next year's crop.

"Kerrie and Bartholomew Parsons purchased land nearby, but they did not do as well. Bart began drinking, and Kerrie rarely left the house. We tried to help them, but Bart was too proud to accept money, and his farm was in such arrears that Gus couldn't take enough time from our own crops to make a difference.

"I'm not sure Kerrie noticed or cared that their farm was failing. Bart and Kerrie seemed to live two separate lives, even while inhabiting the same ramshackle cabin. For the first two years, they came to our house for Christmas Eve dinner. On the second Eve, Bart drank throughout the evening, and for once Kerrie also drank, which I had never seen her do before.

"Before the meal was over, she was ranting, telling us that her children had been murdered. Bart tried to shush her, which only sent her into a greater rage.

"Kerrie was practically screaming, 'Jonathan Meredith knows what happened to my babies, I'm sure of it! I'm going to make him tell me!'

"Not long after, Kerrie disappeared. No one knows what happened to her, but I couldn't help but remember how she'd threatened to confront Meredith. Bart quit trying to work the farm at all and soon lost it to the bank. He too disappeared, but Gus saw him a few months later on a trip to Portland. Bart was falling down drunk on Burnside, Portland's skid row.

"It was all very sad, but we'd seen many families fall apart on our trip west, and more since we arrived. We could not force Bart to accept our help. Our own farm was doing well. Becky was growing into a beautiful young woman, and she had no shortage of admirers. But I think her heart was still set on Jed Meredith, who was by then working full time for his stepfather and by all accounts doing well.

"It was Edwin who visited us, however. He was always infatuated with Becky, and on the trip west, when he was a mere thirteen years old, it was cute. But now he was nearing fifteen, and he was as interested as ever. Personally, I thought him the better match, despite his being two years younger than Becky. When you reach my age, two years doesn't seem like so much, not if your husband makes you happy, but at their age, the gulf seems vast.

"Edwin was strangely subdued on his visits, not the ebullient child I remembered. He was going to school, and also working with his brother and his stepfather. I had the feeling that he wanted to leave Portland. He talked of going back East, of attending college, or of heading south to San Francisco.

"Becky was kind to Edwin, but she did not encourage his attentions and made it clear that she was interested in Jed. However, Jed never visited, though he did write one or two rather formal letters. Becky clung to those letters as proof that he was still interested in her.

"I'm ashamed to say I hoped she was right. Jonathan Meredith was becoming an important man in this territory, and Jed was his heir."

Abigail paused in her story and took Virginia's hand. "Much of this you may already know from Ellen's journals. I tried to keep in touch with her. Even though she never answered, I assumed she read my letters."

Virginia shook her head. "She spoke mostly of her own family, though she does mention running into Bart Parsons."

"Then you know nothing about what happened to Edwin and Jed?"

"No," Virginia answered. "I assumed they were still working with their stepfather."

Abigail shook her head sadly. "Now we come to the part of the story where the Catledges ceased to exist and the Smith family took their place. To sum it up, Miss Reed, we ran away."

"Tell me what happened," Virginia said.

Abigail took a sip of now-cold tea and stared out the window at her garden. She didn't speak for a long time. Virginia waited patiently.

"It was Becky who figured it out," Abigail said, finally. "Gus and I heard that gold had been found in California, but we didn't think much about it. Gus threatened to join the rush to the south—Oregon City seemed to empty of men overnight—but I forbade him. Our farm was doing well enough for our modest ambitions.

"One day, Becky came into the house with one of the old blue buckets that we'd used for water and that we'd carried for thousands of miles across the Great Desert. It was dirty and filled with cobwebs, and at the bottom were dirt-encrusted quartz stones. The moment Becky pulled one of the rocks out, we saw the vein of gold running through it.

"It may seem strange that we didn't think of it before, but when we came to Oregon, it never occurred to us that we would stumble across precious minerals of any kind. The richness we sought was the dark, fertile soil of the Willamette Valley.

"Obviously, we were excited, and Gus wanted to take the gold to Portland at once to see how much it was worth, but Becky told us to wait. When we asked why, she asked us to just trust her.

"She was quiet for a few days. Then Edwin showed up and the two of them cloistered themselves away together, not allowing Gus or me to overhear them. When they emerged, they told us a strange story."

Abigail rose from the table and went into the next room. She came back with a blue bucket in her hand. It was clean and empty, but it was obviously the blue bucket from her story. She put it on the table, as proof, Virginia supposed.

She resumed her story. "Does Ellen Meredith speak in her diaries of the disappearance of Cager and Allie Parsons?"

Virginia nodded.

"We searched for several days, but in the end, it was only our small group that was still actively searching. Becky pleaded to join the search, and against my better judgment, Gus allowed her to go. You must understand that our daughter is a very level-headed and capable young woman, and as we were shorthanded, it was not completely strange that Becky should join in the search.

"Jonathan included Becky in his own group, along with Edwin. They soon returned, not having found a trace of the missing children. Becky was very quiet, but I didn't think anything of it at the time.

"Now, she informed us that Jonathan Meredith had acted very strangely during the search. They had been crisscrossing the desert, but there was a prominent hill on the horizon, and Becky thought that if she was lost, that's where she would go.

"But Jonathan refused to go there. He told her that he had already searched the hillside and there was nothing there. Becky said that as they returned to the camp that night, she thought she saw something glitter on the hillside and once again asked to detour to the site. Jonathan became angry with her, accusing her of harboring false hope.

"She told us, 'Edwin and I are both certain that the hill that Jonathan refused to search was the very same hill where we had filled the blue buckets with the shiny rocks.'"

Abigail fell silent, letting the full portent of that revelation sink in.

"Why has no one confronted Jonathan Meredith?" Virginia asked. "Everything leads back to him."

"I don't think you understand, Miss Reed," Abigail said. "Unless I'm mistaken, Jonathan Meredith has been confronted more than once, and each of the people who have challenged him have disappeared. Including Edwin."

"Edwin?" Virginia said.

Abigail nodded sadly. "We agreed to investigate further, and Edwin promised not to say anything to his father. Yet soon after came word that Edwin had left home. He supposedly left a note saying he was heading for the gold fields of California, but of course, we never believed that."

"What did Becky do?" Virginia asked.

"Gus and I insisted that she come away with us," Abigail said. "The truth is, we ran away, Miss Reed. I'm not proud of it. But we had no proof of anything, and Meredith is a very rich and powerful man. We sold our land, turned in the gold from the blue bucket, and left the Willamette Valley. We didn't have the heart to leave the Oregon Territory altogether, but we thought that Vale was far enough away to be safe.

"Becky wasn't happy about leaving, but she was the last of the children who had filled the blue buckets with gold, and she realized that she was in danger. We began our lives over, Miss Reed."

"But something happened, didn't it?"

"We haven't prospered here," Abigail admitted. "We have fallen deeply into debt, and there seems no way that we can ever pay it back. Becky was never happy here, and I'm certain that she started writing Jed not long after we arrived. I'm also certain that she fixed it in her mind that she would find the gold mine and bring back enough wealth to pay our debts.

"Not long ago, Jed showed up to visit. The next day, they were both gone. They left a note telling us that they were going in search of the lost mine. Gus and I were frightened for them, of course, but we didn't know what to do. A week later, we got a letter from Becky telling us where she was. Gus set out at once to find her.

"And it is in this state of affairs that you find us. I haven't heard from Gus, and I am worried. If you would go after them, I would be forever in your debt, Miss Reed."

"I promised Mary that I would help, Mrs. Catledge," Virginia said. "I will promise you the same thing."

Abigail lowered her head, and a teardrop splashed into the teacup in front of her. When she looked up, the expression of gratitude on her face made Virginia rise and go to her side and put an arm around her shoulders.

"We'll find them, I promise," she said.

Abigail rested her cheek against Virginia's hand. "Thank you," she whispered.

"Do you still have Becky's letter?" Virginia asked.

Abigail rose from the table, looking flustered for the first time. "I don't know if Gus took it with him. Let me look." She went into one of the rooms next to the kitchen. There was the sound of rustling papers, and then she emerged, triumphantly holding up the letter.

Virginia smoothed the sheets out on the table and began to read.

Chapter Twenty-Six

<u>Vale, Oregon Territory, September 1851</u>

Dear Mother and Father,

Forgive me for leaving so abruptly.

I will try to give you a full explanation for why I left. As I told you, when the Parsons children went missing, I suspected that Mr. Meredith tried to keep me from searching the hillside where we had gathered the gold, what is now being called the Lost Blue Bucket Mine. If I had known that there was gold involved, I would have insisted on exploring that hillside, but though I was troubled at the time, I could not conceive of any reason why Mr. Meredith would lie about already having searched the area.

What I didn't tell you is that even though the wagon train was lost at the time, I clearly remembered the landmarks nearby and kept track of them as we continued our journey. I intended to return and search for Cager and Allie as soon as possible, even if only for their mortal remains.

When we reached Oregon City, I realized that you needed my help, and as time went on, the urgency left me. Cager and Allie were gone, and there was nothing I could do about it. Nevertheless, I am certain that I can find the same location again. I want to prove, once and for all, that Jonathan Meredith is a murderer, that he made Cager and Allie lead him to the gold, and that he then killed them. If so, their remains must still be nearby. There might not be enough evidence of his crime to have Mr. Meredith arrested. Perhaps the only justice I can provide is to reveal the location of his riches so that he can't have any more of them.

At the end of this letter, I give detailed directions to where I think the Lost Blue Bucket Mine is. If I do not return, be certain to publish these directions wherever you can, so that every gold miner in the territory will converge on the area. Perhaps Mr. Meredith has not claimed ownership because he is afraid of claim jumpers. If so, I intend to fulfill his worst fears.

But first I need to examine the area, so that he doesn't have time to cover up his crime. When you insisted on moving away from our prosperous farm in Oregon City, I was doubtful of the wisdom of it, but I now know that you were right. It may be only a matter of time before Mr. Meredith finds us. When he does, I fear not only for my own safety but also for yours, my dear parents. He will want to make certain that I did not tell you where the mine lies.

He has the gold to buy all the men and resources he needs. But when I am done with him, I hope that I will have deprived him of his riches, and even more importantly, that he will no longer have any reason to threaten us once the location of the gold is revealed—though even then, he might take revenge.

I don't feel as though I have any choice in the matter. Either way, we are not safe. If we must live in fear, I'd rather try to find justice for poor Cager and Allie.

I have been planning this for a long time. I have arranged all the necessary supplies. I promise you, we aren't venturing into the wilds without adequate preparation. You needn't worry about that. But even though I have been ready to leave for some time, I have hesitated. I love you both, and I worry that once I set these plans in motion, anything could happen. I convinced myself that if I did nothing to reveal our location, we would be safer if I tried to go find Cager and Allie.

Jed showed up at our door while both of you were at the store. He was frantic, for Edwin is missing. Though his brother left a note detailing his plans to go to California to look for gold, Jed is certain that the letter was coerced or manipulated out of him, and that Mr. Meredith has done something to him. I didn't feel that I could wait any longer, as Jed would have left without me, inadequately provisioned. So I have taken the packs from the shed that I had hidden there, and I have taken old Gussy, whom Father never uses anymore at work. She may be old and fat, but she hasn't forgotten how to be a pack mule.

I have written most of this letter on the first night of our journey. There are travelers camping near us who are heading to Vale, and I intend to leave this missive with them. I'm sorry to have left in such a hurry and without warning. I'm not sure when I will be able to contact you again.

Just know that I will be very careful, that I have Jed, who has become a capable young man, at my side, and that we will endeavor to avoid any confrontation. I look only for evidence of Cager and Allie. I don't care about the gold, except to deny Mr. Meredith the use of it, but I feel that if I find any, it would only be fair to take some to help secure the future of your business. Beyond that, let the claim jumpers come!

Please do not come after me. I give you the directions to the mine because I want it to be general knowledge, not because I want you to follow me. Please trust that I am safe and that I will fulfill my goal.

All my love,
Becky

Virginia looked up from the letter. "How long after you received this did Mr. Catledge go after her?"

"The next day," Abigail said. "Just as soon as he could pack. I copied the directions, and he took our best horse and a couple of mules he borrowed from our neighbors. I haven't heard from either of them since."

"A week ago, then?" Virginia said, looking down at the date.

"I guess so…yes."

"I'm sorry I didn't get here sooner," Virginia said. "I might have been able to go in Mr. Catledge's stead."

Abigail was standing near the stove, and she looked at Virginia with a strange look in her eyes. "But you're just a girl yourself, Miss Reed. Nor is it your responsibility. I'm not entirely sure why you are here."

Virginia suddenly saw herself as Abigail Catledge must see her: a strange woman who had shown up on her doorstep, acting as though she was more important and more capable than Abigail's husband, a grown man. How could she explain? If she told Abigail about her duties as a Canowiki, the woman would probably see her to the door. Nor was this a situation that necessarily called for the talents of a Canowiki. There was nothing supernatural here, at least as far as she could see, only ordinarily human greed and evil.

And yet, something was compelling Virginia to see it through. There was something otherworldly here—she just couldn't put her finger on it. But it was something that made her believe that before it was over, her talents would be needed.

"I have had…experience in such matters," Virginia said.

Abigail examined her as if Virginia was a horse she was thinking about buying. "I can believe that. You remind me of my daughter, actually. People often tend to underestimate her."

"I have admired her from afar," Virginia said.

They sat in silence for a time, sipping their tea. It was clear that Abigail was debating with herself about whether to trust the young woman who had come to her door. Finally, she sighed. "I will let you copy the directions to the mine, Miss Reed. I am worried about my husband. The Umatilla tribe is killing trespassers in their territory, and the gold mine is right at the center of it."

"I have men in my employ who are quite capable of doing whatever needs to be done," Virginia said. She stood up. "The manager of your store wouldn't let my men follow me here. Would you be so kind as to allow them into your house?" She smiled. "I can't vouch for how housetrained they are, Mrs. Catledge, but I don't think they'll do too much harm."

With a nod from Abigail, she left the house and found Angus, Drake, and Franklin sitting with the shop manager, Cole Johnson, in the back office, halfway to getting drunk. Virginia frowned at Angus, but he waggled his eyebrows at her and said, "We're not nearly drunk enough, Miss Reed. This is just an afternoon's respite."

"Well, I need you to come with me back to the house," Virginia said. "We've got a journey to plan."

Once they were in the kitchen, Virginia set Drake to copying the directions to the Lost Blue Bucket gold mine. He took one look at the letter and glanced up sharply. "Is this what I think it is?"

Virginia nodded.

"You are trusting me with the location to a gold mine?" He sounded completely amazed.

"Mrs. Catledge is trusting me," Virginia said, "and I am trusting you. Should I not trust you, Mr. Drake?"

He flushed and looked down at the letter again. "I am a man of honor," he muttered.

"I never thought differently," Virginia said. She turned to Angus, who was watching with a knowing smile. She pulled him aside so that Abigail couldn't overhear. "I want you to buy supplies for a two-week trip into the High Desert. Buy the very best; spare no expense. In fact, buy more than we really need. I can afford it, and it seems that the Smiths need a little help."

"Leave it to me," Angus said, winking. "Nothing but the best for Miss Reed and company." He turned to leave.

"And Angus?"

"Yes, ma'am?"

"Make sure you buy plenty of ammunition."

Chapter Twenty-Seven

<u>Oregon Territory, October 1851</u>

Dearest Frank,

We have in our possession a crude map with the directions to a gold mine! Many people have searched for the Lost Blue Bucket Mine in the last few years, driven by the legend. No one is certain how this story became so well known when there was only the vaguest information about it. The lost Meek Cutoff wagon train, the blue buckets, the gold—that's all anyone seems to know about, but such scant information has given rise to more than one forlorn expedition into the High Desert. There are usually no names attached to the myth.

Certainly Jonathan Meredith wouldn't have spread the tale. Nor, according to Abigail, have the Catledges told anyone. Perhaps Bart Parsons is drunkenly rambling about it on the Portland wharfs. In any case, there is many a man who would kill for these directions to a dry creek bed where the placer gold is so rich one needs only to lean over and pick it up. Or so it is said.

I suspect it won't be as simple as that. If the mine were that easy to find, someone would have found the location by now. The directions are specific only for the last few miles, but without those last instructions, there would be no way to find it. We could wander by only yards away and not know it.

The expedition is complicated by the fact that the tribes of the Columbia Plateau are on the warpath. The California miners have arrived in southern Oregon, and some of them have made their way north. And there have been gold deposits found in northeastern Oregon, not far from where we are now. Miners have begun encroaching on tribal lands.

My companions have been steadfast. Lesser men might be seduced by the possibility of finding gold, take the map, and steal away in the night. My companions don't seem to care about riches. Drake is infatuated with Mary, and Angus tells me he's too old to care about money anymore. Franklin is a dutiful follower.

I will make sure that all three are rewarded for their loyalty by paying them with my own Skoocoom gold—which, fortunately for us, no one has told any stories about.

Love,
Virginia

The directions to the Lost Blue Bucket Mine, at least for the first part of the journey, were simple enough. Virginia and her companions merely needed to find the location where the lost wagon train had intersected with the Columbia Gorge after traveling northward from its wanderings in the middle of the territory. This spot, according to the map, was about three days' travel west along the riverbank. It was a place Virginia had noticed on the eastward trip to Vale, where the high bluffs gave way to a sharp ravine with a dry creek at the bottom.

The way south from there was also relatively easy to follow, until the ravine ended and a high plateau began.

As the travelers reached that spot, they saw the smoke of a campfire on the horizon, a welcome sight with dusk falling and a cold breeze blowing briskly across the high plains. The firelight seemed to be flickering out of the ground itself, and as they neared, they saw that it came from the bottom of a depression, as if the earth had given way to a sinkhole that had, over the years, partially filled back up with earth and sand. There was a mule at the bottom, a fire against one wall, and a man huddled over the fire, warming his hands, unaware of their approach until they were right on top of him.

"Ahoy there," Angus called out.

The man shouted in surprise and turned, a shotgun in hand, pointing it up at them fearfully.

"Whoa, there, friend," Angus said, holding out his hands. "We're not the enemy."

The man lowered the gun. "You startled me," he said. "Come on down, I'm cooking some stew."

There wasn't enough room in the hole for the travelers and their mounts, so they tied their horses to the branches of a lone, scraggly juniper and climbed down.

The man had set aside his gun and was trying to stand. He had a bandaged leg and was having a difficult time staying upright. He had a thick black beard with gray streaks in it and watery blue eyes, and his features were those of a grizzled farmer. His hands shook a little, but evidently from age rather than fear.

The remains of a gutted rabbit had been thrown against the base of the incline on the other side of the fire. A blackened pot nestled in the coals, stew cooking within. Virginia's stomach growled at the savory smell.

"Are you Gus Smith?" she asked.

The man hesitated, then nodded. "And who might you be?"

"Abigail sent us," Virginia said. "She gave us directions."

"Oh?" He looked suspicious. "And why would she do that?"

"We know about your situation, Mr. Smith…or should I say, Mr. Catledge."

His hand drifted toward the shotgun, but Virginia thought it was an unconscious reaction, for he stopped halfway. Beside her, she felt Angus tense, his own hand reaching inside his coat.

Virginia said quickly, "My name is Virginia. I am a friend of Mary Perkins. She asked me to help look into the missing Parsons children."

"Why would she do that?" Gus growled. "What business is it of yours?"

Virginia could see that he wasn't going to be as easy to convince as his wife had been.

Angus spoke up for her, his voice aggrieved for her sake. "I assure you, sir, Miss Reed only wishes to help. She is quite well off. She doesn't need a gold mine. She only wants to find the truth."

"Virginia Reed?" Gus asked. "Of the Donner Party?

Drake was standing on Virginia's other side, and he gave a short laugh. "Amazing that everyone knows about you, Miss Reed. Evidently you make quite an impression."

"Aye," Franklin said. "I've heard things too."

Gus appeared to relax slightly. He shrugged. "Is it such a surprise? It is what we all feared would happen to us: starving and freezing, without anyone to help. All the way across the continent, we feared it. So when it finally happened to someone else, we all paid attention. We also noticed that the events didn't all add up. That's where the rumors about Miss Reed come from."

"Rumors?" Drake asked. He didn't appear to have heard them.

Virginia broke in. "We're happy to have caught up to you, Mr. Catledge. We thought you'd be far ahead of us by now."

The stew had started to boil, and Gus reached over with his bare fingers and lifted the pot, almost dropping it into his lap and then blowing on his fingers. He picked up a spoon and began eating it absently, not offering any to anyone else.

"I hurt my leg," he said. "I thought I'd give it a day or two's rest and hope it got well enough to walk on."

"May I see it?" Angus asked. "I have some experience with injuries."

"No!" Gus said, almost shouting, and Angus stopped after moving a few steps toward him. "I'll be fine. I'm going to leave some of my supplies here and ride one of the pack mules."

"Have you seen any sign of Becky or Jed?" Virginia asked.

Gus seemed surprised by the question. "Uh…not yet. I expect we'll find them soon enough."

"We'd like to accompany you, if you don't mind," Virginia said.

It looked to her as if Gus wasn't happy with the thought but couldn't think of any reason to object. "Sure," he said. "Listen, I'm sorry I'm so grumpy. I haven't had to rough it for a few years, and this injury is dispiriting." He looked down at the half-empty pot of stew and suddenly seemed to realize he'd been eating it in front of them. "Would you care for some of this stew? I was so hungry I forgot to be a good host."

"I wouldn't mind," Angus said, stepping forward. After pulling his coat sleeves up over his hands, he lifted the pot with the spoon in it and started eating. He looked over at Virginia and Drake, who both shook their heads. Drake pulled some jerky out of his backpack and sat down near the fire, chewing and staring into the flames. Franklin waited until Angus was done, and when offered the pot, hungrily finished the stew.

Virginia had some hardtack in her pack, and that sufficed for her dinner. As she ate, she considered Gus and the fact that she wasn't sure how she'd respond if strangers came along and got involved in her business. Gus was being protective, and she was going to need to win him over.

As she spread out her blankets, she saw Angus standing nearby, watchful, with the posture of a picket guard. She smiled to herself and fell asleep.

***

When Virginia awoke, most of the others were already up and ready to go. Gus Catledge was leaning against his mule as if contemplating trying to get on it.

"We're all packed, Miss Reed," Angus said. "Thought we'd let you get a little extra rest."

She'd slept hard, and there was a crook in her neck. She reached up and rubbed the spot until it loosened up. She'd slept in her clothes, and as soon as she was on her feet, she realized that she didn't need to do anything but mount up.

"I'm ready," she said. "I don't suppose anyone brewed up any coffee?"

Angus magically produced a cup of the black liquid. "I've seen that you aren't clear-headed in the mornings till you have a cup," he said. "I saved you one. A bit cold, I'm sorry to say."

It tasted awful, but Virginia felt her mind clearing before she reached the dregs. She chewed on the grounds, sucking the last bit of energy from them. "Angus, you are proving to be a boon companion in more ways than one," she said.

Gus pulled himself onto the mule, refusing Drake's help.

"Why don't you head back home, Mr. Catledge?" Virginia said. "We'll find Becky and bring her back, I promise."

"No," Gus said. "She's my daughter. I'm not leaving her out here."

He turned south, and they followed him. He seemed to know where he was going. Whenever they reached a spot where they had to decide which path to follow, he chose a route without referring to the map.

That night, when they set up camp, Virginia saw Gus testing his leg, and it seemed he could put some weight on it. He was much more cheerful at that night's campfire, telling stories about the wagon train's trip across this land.

"I notice you haven't had to refer to your map," Virginia said.

"I remember this place, as it happens," Gus said. "Which is a bit of a surprise. If you'd asked me, I would have said I wasn't paying much attention by the time we reached here. We were so close to our goal of the Willamette Valley, I was focused on that. I didn't realize anything had happened. I mean, we were all devastated by the loss of Cager and Allie, of course. But I thought it was likely an unfortunate accident, like so many others. We were near our new home, and that's what I remember most. I don't even remember seeing the blue buckets or their hidden cargo."

"You were never tempted to go look once you found out?" Angus asked.

"You've met Abigail," Gus said. "She is all the wealth I need."

"Hmmm," Angus said.

"Oh, don't get me wrong," Gus said. "If we find gold, I won't turn it down. I wouldn't mind indulging Abigail for the rest of her life. Knitting, gardening…whatever she wants to do…without worrying about money. No, I wouldn't mind that at all."

"How much farther?" Drake asked.

Gus didn't answer for a time, and his eyes glazed over as if he was referring to a map inside his head. "I think we're close," he said at last. "Maybe one more day."

"We should keep an eye out," Virginia said. "If we're close, we risk running into Jonathan Meredith. I don't think he'll be happy to see us."

"We need to watch out for Indians too," Drake reminded them. "I'll take first watch."

It took longer than usual for Virginia to fall to sleep that night. She sensed that she would learn the truth on the morrow, whatever the truth might be. She rose up at one point to stir the fire and caught the glint of Gus Catledge's blue eyes peering at her. She shuddered. No doubt he was imagining the worst. There was no sign of Becky or Jed having come this way, which Virginia thought was strange. Surely Becky must have suspected that her father would come after her and would leave clues for him.

Drake was still on watch, and Virginia went over and relieved him, over his objections. He gave in at last, rolled himself up in his blankets, and was instantly asleep. When Virginia turned and looked back at the fire, Gus had rolled over, turning his back to her. She turned away from the light and let her eyes adjust to the darkness. She stood watch the rest of the night, letting Angus and Franklin sleep in.

The stars above were brighter than she ever seen, and she had to admit to herself that she loved life on the trail. She thought of Frank, back at the ranch, and felt uneasy. She wanted to be a dutiful wife, but…

She turned her eyes away from the stars and stared into the darkness.

Chapter Twenty-Eight

In the morning, Virginia took the map out and looked it over. To her left was a cone-shaped butte, and to her right was a deep gully. According to the map, there should be a small creek directly to the south of them. According to the X on the map, the Lost Blue Bucket Mine was only a few miles beyond it, halfway to another creek.

Once again, Gus didn't refer to his own map but led the way confidently, as if he already knew where he was going. Within an hour, they came to the top of a small bluff, and there at the base was the creek, which was almost dry. It was lined by aspen trees, whose leaves were shaking in the slight breeze. It was an idyllic spot, a place Virginia could have imagined staying for a long time.

"You go on down," Gus said. "My mule is laboring under me. I'd like to give him a rest before I continue." He slid off the mule and leaned up against it. Then he hobbled a few steps and grinned at the others. "I'll mosey on after you. You folks go ahead, water your horses, have a repose. We're almost there."

So Virginia and her companions went on, and as they approached a copse of trees sheltered in a sharp bend in the creek, Virginia smelled a campfire. She stopped, holding up her hand. Angus must have smelled it too, because he already had his pistol out. Over the heavy breathing of their horses, they heard the faint sound of men talking. They were speaking English.

Virginia relaxed a little. They'd been lucky not to run into any Indians. These were probably miners, trying their luck in a new creek bed.

"I'll go on ahead," she said. "You wait here."

"I'll be damned if I'll let that happen," Angus said. "I'm not letting a woman stroll into a miner's camp alone."

"I'll be safe because I'm a woman," Virginia answered. "They'll be less likely to be alarmed."

Angus glanced over his shoulder to where Gus was making his way slowly down the hill toward them.

"If I shout, you come running," Virginia said. "I'll be fine."

Angus looked at Drake, who seemed bemused and merely shrugged. "She'll be safe enough," he said. "They might shoot you or me as claim jumpers." He nodded to Virginia. "We'll wait for Mr. Catledge and come on over when you call."

Franklin watched the exchange, looking troubled, but he didn't say anything.

"You packing?" Angus asked Virginia.

She pulled back her coat, revealing the small gun nestled in her belt.

Angus gave a resigned sigh. "You be careful, miss. Let them know you're approaching. They must be rather jumpy, what with the Indian attacks."

Virginia rode into the camp from the side, where she would be the most visible. Her horse neighed when it smelled the other horses picketed nearby.

"Who's there?" a man shouted. She had unknowingly passed the latrine. He appeared from behind her, buttoning up. He wasn't armed. He was barely clothed, just wearing his long johns.

"A fellow traveler," Virginia said. "I'm looking for someone."

He walked over to her, squinting up into her face. "Well, you'd best come into the camp."

There were five men in the camp, two of them lying on their blankets as if they were just waking up, though it was nearly midday. The three others stood tending the campfire. They were rough looking, as if they'd been out here for weeks. Virginia looked around; there was no sign of mining or any other activity that would explain their presence here.

The oldest of the men looked to be in his mid-forties, with a long mustache dropping down below his jowls. His hair was a tangle, matted down around the forehead where his hat would sit. He looked annoyed to see her.

"Whose turn was it on guard duty?" he asked. None of the others answered, but they all looked toward the young man who'd led Virginia into the camp. He was the youngest looking, clean-shaven because he probably couldn't grow a beard if he wanted to. He'd sheared his hair close to his head.

The older man spit off to one side. "Well, damn, Samuel, you are worthless."

"Well, shit, Clement," the clean-shaven youth said. "We ain't seen no one we weren't expecting to see in weeks. What does it matter?"

"Lucky it's just a girl," Clement said, "and not a band of savages." He turned back to Virginia and took hold of her horse's bridle, jerking it down. The horse tried to rear up, but he kept an iron grip on the bridle.

"Come down from there, young lady. You're putting a crook in my neck from having to look up at you."

"Why are you camped here?" Virginia asked instead of dismounting. Now that she was among them, she sensed there was something wrong here.

"Well, now, that's our business," Clement said. "We aren't paid to answer questions. Now I really insist that you come down from there."

"Don't you want to know why I'm here?" she asked.

"We aren't paid to ask questions either, ma'am. Are you coming down from there, or do I need to drag you down?"

She dismounted on the other side of the horse from where Clement and the others were standing. When she came around the horse, she had her pistol in her hand.

"If you gentlemen would please back away from the campfire," she said. None of them had been armed when she'd ridden in, and her appearance hadn't alarmed them enough to fetch their weapons, which were among the backpacks near the bedrolls spread about the clearing near the fire.

"Now, ma'am, that isn't necessary," Clement said. He took a step toward her.

Virginia raised the barrel, pointed it between his eyes, and held it there steadily. "I assure you, sir, I will have no trouble killing you if you come any closer." She used her Canowiki voice, and he froze in place. While the five men stood staring at her, she moved toward the packs and found a loaded pistol lying on top of one of them. She took it up in her other hand.

She sighed in relief. One pistol might not have been enough if they'd decided to rush her. They might have figured their odds were good. But two pistols meant she could take two of them down, and that changed the odds.

"Come on ahead!" she shouted at the top of her voice. She couldn't be sure if her words would reach her companions, but they had the added benefit of letting her opponents know she wasn't alone. She lowered her voice and said, "I'll repeat…why are you here?"

"We were just about to cook our dinner," Clement said. "We'll be glad to share. Really, ma'am, there is no need for guns."

"When my friends get here, we'll talk about that." Virginia was quite willing to rely on Angus, Franklin, and Drake, all of whom were practiced gunmen, against these five men, of whom only Clement looked like a real threat. The other four had obviously been picked up off the streets; just men who would follow orders, who could point and shoot but probably didn't aim too well.

She heard horses approaching from behind her and took a quick look over her shoulder. Drake, Franklin, and Angus were leading their horses forward on foot, followed by Gus, who was limping behind them.

During that brief glance, Clement had begun to make a move, and Virginia raised her pistol warningly. She kept the gun pointed at his head while her friends approached. When they reached her, she turned to Angus and started to hand one of the guns to him. "Keep your eye on…" She stopped as she saw the look in her bodyguard's eyes.

"Raise your arms up, boys," Gus Catledge said. "Let her know how things stand."

Virginia's companions raised their hands above their heads.

"You aren't Gus, are you?" Virginia said.

"I would never have claimed to be," Jonathan Meredith said, "if you hadn't so assumed. It was hard to take on his old-shoe manner, I'll tell you. Not my way at all." He was standing only a few feet away, his shotgun pointed at the backs of all three of her companions. "I won't hesitate to shoot, Miss Reed. This close, the spray will take out at least two of your men. Give your pistols to Clement before I get tired of waiting."

She let her hands drop. She let Clement take the guns from her.

"Take a look at Miss Virginia Reed, boys," Meredith said. "The Angel of the Donner Party."

They all stared at her, impressed, especially the young man, Samuel. "Well, I'll be damned," he said. "No wonder she got the drop on me."

Clement laughed. "You had your pants down, Samuel. A five-year-old girl could've got the drop on you."

"Enough!" Meredith said. "Tie these folks up."

"Even Miss Reed?" Samuel asked.

"Especially Miss Reed," Clement said. "She's a witch or something. Not natural, a woman being this way, ready to shoot a man between the eyes."

"Just do it," Meredith growled.

Virginia was led over to one of the trees, and her arms were pulled back around the trunk and tied. Angus, Drake, and Franklin were tied to their own trees a short distance away. Meredith kept his gun on them the whole time. Only when they were secure did he waver. He almost dropped the shotgun and stood swaying until Clement rushed over and held him up. They staggered to the campfire, where Meredith was set down.

"I've got a bullet wound to my leg that needs dressing," he grunted. He turned to one of the three other men. "Caruthers? You can remove a bullet, no? Get some water boiling."

"So you ran into Gus Catledge?" Virginia asked.

Meredith looked over at her, frowning; then he shrugged. "The old man had the drop on me. But he didn't have the guts to finish it. I did."

Virginia felt her heart sink. She'd come to like Gus Catledge and his family through Ellen Meredith's diaries. Meeting Abigail Catledge had only reinforced the impression. There was no doubt, from Meredith's tone of voice, that Gus was lying dead somewhere in the desert.

Caruthers came over with a pot of boiling water and clean rags and proceeded to pull the soiled bandage from Meredith's leg. He cursed but didn't move. There, in his calf, was a single round bullet hole, which Caruthers began to clean.

"Becky and Jed?" Virginia asked softly.

Meredith winced. "Careful!" he snapped at Caruthers before turning back to Virginia. "I wouldn't have even known they were out there if not for you. I've got to thank you for that, at least. I've always hated Becky…snotty little girl. But I'd rather not have to kill my stepson. He's always had potential, once he got out from behind his mother's skirts."

"What about Cager and Allie?" Virginia asked. "And Edwin?"

Meredith stared at her. He wasn't going to answer, she realized, but it been worth a shot, since he was being so voluble.

"What about them?" he asked.

"Did you kill them too?"

"Why would I do that?" he grunted.

"They showed you the gold mine, didn't they? You had to keep it a secret." Virginia could see that Meredith was getting uncomfortable—not because he was feeling guilty for killing the children, but because he wanted to keep his secret above all. "You haven't even told your bully boys, have you?"

"Told us what?" Clement asked Virginia. "That he's got a gold mine somewhere out there? Hell, lady, we knew that. He didn't have to tell us. But he pays us damn well to pretend we don't know. Personally, I'd rather earn my money sitting here with my gun in hand than over there digging up…" His voice trailed off as he realized his boss was staring at him, red faced.

"Probably shouldn't have let Mr. Meredith know that you know," Virginia said. "People who find out tend to disappear."

"Like I said," Clement muttered. "We don't care about no gold."

Despite what Clement said, it was clear that at least a couple of the other men hadn't known what they were guarding. They exchanged glances.

"Well, it was time to share the wealth anyway," Meredith said. "Time to let you boys take your pick of the gold. No need to dig, Clement. It's just lying there. You can have all you want, all you can carry. I've got all I need. There's more than enough for all of us."

Virginia wondered if the others could tell as easily as she could that he was lying. Is it my Canowiki powers? She wondered. No…they know.

They were keeping silent, not looking at each other.

All but Samuel.

"Woo-hoo!" he shouted, and after a few moments, the other men joined in, except Caruthers, who was finishing up tying Meredith's bandage.

"We'll start in the morning," Meredith said. "Best keep a two-man guard tonight. We don't know who's out there."

Chapter Twenty-Nine

<u>Oregon Territory, October 1851</u>

Jonathan Meredith couldn't believe everything had gone so wrong so quickly.

He'd planned one last trip to the mine, this time by himself. He hadn't been looking forward to the drudgery of digging out the entrance, but he didn't want any complications. He'd gotten away with murder so far, but he couldn't be certain his extraordinary luck would hold.

No, he'd figured to take one more load, probably from the scrap heap he'd told his workers to leave near the entrance. He'd pay off his men, who might know there was a gold mine somewhere within the territory they were guarding but wouldn't be able to narrow it down to a specific site, especially if he covered up the entrance.

Just one last trip and he'd be wealthy enough to live without working for the rest of his life. If he ran out of money, he could always come back, but he didn't believe he would need to. His businesses were profitable.

Jonathan didn't plan to stay long. The voices in his head got louder every time he visited the mine. At first, he'd wondered if he was going insane. Never before had he felt anything when he killed or robbed someone. Ever since his first murder, that of his neighbor, Cullum, he'd been able to live with his deeds without the slightest twinge of guilt. Perhaps it was finally catching up with him.

The voices got louder the deeper he went into the cave, he soon discovered, and before long, he could go no farther than the entrance without being so distracted that he was a danger to himself and others.

Memories of past misdeeds came to him, but they had no meaning. After Sarah died, he'd been hollowed out, and anger and pain had rushed in. He walked among the living determined to make others feel the same anger and pain. There was no other goal. Money was only a weapon, which he could use to inflict misery on others.

Only the thought of Sarah could disturb him, and he sensed that whatever was driving the guilt he saw in others would eventually reach him. So he'd hired bums off the streets of Portland and brought them, blindfolded, across the desert. He'd had every intention of fulfilling his promise of letting them carry gold away. But when a rockslide killed the first two workers he'd hired and he was able to walk away with the gold they had dug up for him, he realized that he didn't need to pay anyone. It wasn't greed—there was plenty of gold—but the idea that word would soon get out that the Lost Blue Bucket Mine had been discovered that worried him no end.

There'd be no peace after that. Besides, he hadn't claimed the site, nor would it have mattered if he had. The government's treaty with the Umatilla tribe was binding, at least for now, and they would have the rights to any gold found on their land.

So it was important that Jonathan keep the secret for as long as possible.

He hadn't actually had to kill anyone working the mines. He had simply closed off the entrance, which, after all, could have happened by accident at any time, even without his help.

He'd headed out from Vale alone, taking just one packhorse along, which he figured could carry enough gold, along with his own mount, to get the job done. He'd intended to pay off his men who were guarding the boundary. He was looking forward to the time by himself.

He had been amazed to come across Gus Catledge, camped on the high plateau two days' journey south of the Columbia Gorge. Meredith had spent a small fortune sending men out looking for the Catledges, and here was old Gus, sitting by a campfire, his rifle still in its holster near the saddle, his pistol removed from his belt.

There was only one other person left on Earth who also knew the location of the Lost Blue Bucket Mine, and that was Becky Catledge. For some reason that Jonathan couldn't fathom, she hadn't gone after the gold, but he was convinced it was only a matter of time.

"Hello, Gus," he'd said, stepping into circle of light from the fire. He was holding the reins of his horse in one hand, his gun in his other hand, hidden behind his coat.

Gus surprised him. The old man's pistol, which hadn't been evident when Jonathan observed him from the darkness, suddenly appeared in his hand, and something struck Jonathan's lower leg so hard he was knocked off his feet. He let go of his horse and heard it and the packhorse galloping off into the desert. The gunshot echoed as he dropped to the ground and rolled, planning to bring his own weapon to bear.

But Gus had managed to get to his rifle and already had the barrel pointed at Jonathan's head.

"What the hell, Gus!" Jonathan cried. "What are you doing?"

"Let me see your hands," Gus demanded.

Jonathan stayed crouched on the ground. He let go of his gun, hiding it under the folds of his coat, and raised his hands. "Why are you shooting at me?" he cried, the aggrieved, innocent party.

"You're a snake, Meredith," Gus said. "I should shoot you right now. But I want to know if you've seen Becky. If you've…done anything to her."

"Done anything?" Jonathan said. "What are you talking about?"

Gus stared at him, trying to gauge his truthfulness. Jonathan didn't even have to lie; he could just put his full innocence on display. He hadn't known that Becky was out here. He was wide-eyed and slack-jawed, and truly shocked by the turn of events, and that must have come through. But Gus didn't lower his gun.

"I wasn't sure Becky was right about you," Gus said. "I knew you were a hollow man, without a conscience, but I couldn't believe you were a killer. But seeing you out here…whatever reason could there be but the gold?"

"Of course I'm here for the gold!" Jonathan said, continuing to tell the truth. The best way to slip in a naked lie was to clothe it in truth.

"Which you decided to keep for yourself."

"Of course," Jonathan said. "You'd have done the same thing, Gus. Don't tell me different."

"No," Gus shook his head. "I would have told you and the Parsonses. Hell, I might have told everyone. I certainly wouldn't have killed to keep the secret."

"Killed?"

"I didn't want to believe it at first, but as the years went by, I couldn't think of a better explanation for Allie and Cager's disappearance. To my shame, I didn't do anything but run away and change my family name, may my father forgive me. I managed to keep a rein on my daughter, though I could tell she was unhappy with the silence. But when Edwin disappeared, I couldn't keep Becky from running off. She's out here somewhere, searching, and I'm going to find her, and I'm not going to let you do anything to her."

The old man raised his rifle and pointed it at Jonathan's head. "I believe you when you say you haven't seen Becky and Jed. I got no reason to keep you alive, Meredith. I'd be doing the world a favor by killing you right now and letting the buzzards and coyotes have you."

Gus's finger tightened on the trigger, and Jonathan began to reach for his own gun, on the ground under him. He would be too late, except perhaps to get off a return shot, but he was going to go down fighting.

Then, surprisingly, Gus lowered the rifle. "You ain't worth it, Meredith. Get back on your horse and go back to Portland. You're done here. As soon as I get back to Vale, I'm going to let everyone know the location of the mine."

Jonathan got to his feet, almost falling over as his wounded leg gave way, snatching up the pistol as he rose. He aimed the gun at Gus's stomach and fired.

The old man toppled backward with a groan that sounded like an acknowledgment of his own stupidity, as if, in those last moments, he realized what his mercy had brought down on him.

Gus was still breathing when Jonathan walked over and kicked the rifle away. "Be assured, old man, if I find Becky, she's as dead as you are. She was a pretty girl. I'll be she's a lovely woman."

"Please," Gus said weakly. "Leave her be. You can have the gold."

"I don't need your permission," Jonathan said. He kicked the old man in the gut, right where the wound was. Gus huffed once and passed out.

Jonathan looked around the campsite. Gus's mule hadn't bolted and was still tied to a small juniper near the campfire. He sat down and looked at the pot of stew Gus had been cooking, judged it edible, and started scooping it into his mouth. When he was done, the fire was almost out.

He picked Gus's pockets clean. There was nothing worth anything. The old man was still breathing, his eyes closed. Jonathan packed up all the rest of the gear and loaded the mule, then mounted the skittish beast. He slapped the animal hard on the neck, and it settled down. Then he rode off, leaving Gus behind for the buzzards and coyotes.

Jonathan rode as far as he could that day, feeling the blood dripping from his wound. For some reason, it was only a trickle, as if the fatty part of his leg had closed over the hole, but it became more painful with every mile.

He was nodding off when the mule stopped so abruptly he almost slid off. A depression in the ground had nearly swallowed him and the mule. He slipped off the animal and hopped down into the hole on his one good leg. He managed to coax the mule down, and he was pretty sure the creature wouldn't try to escape. He started a fire and bandaged his wound. Then he brought out Gus's stewpot and began cooking some of the meat and potatoes he'd found in the old man's pack.

He was taken completely by surprise when Virginia and her companions found him. But when they'd addressed him as Gus, he'd quickly fallen into character. He couldn't believe his luck.

He was amazed that the woman was Virginia Reed, about whom he'd heard so much. Why she was involved, he couldn't imagine. But he thought his boys would like the look of her.

Chapter Thirty

Virginia slept fitfully, slipping in and out of consciousness throughout the long night. Even if she could somehow get free, she couldn't leave her two companions behind. In the middle of the night, as she slept, someone—she thought it was probably Samuel, the youngest of her captors—threw a blanket over her. In the morning, there was thick frost on the ground. The white flakes slid off her blanket when she stirred, sprinkling onto the dark soil and sparkling in the morning sun.

She didn't know what Meredith was planning. He hadn't killed them immediately, which meant he had something else planned for them. She was shivering violently when Samuel came for her and led her to the campfire. She was allowed to soak up some of its warmth. She watched as her fellow captives ate breakfast, which consisted of a thick gruel. She didn't have an appetite and turned down a plate.

"You best eat something, miss," Angus said. He was struck hard in the face, nearly knocking him over. The others got the message and stayed quiet.

When they were done eating, they were tied up again.

It took most of the morning for Meredith's men to pack up. They had been camped here for a long time, it seemed. Their gear was spread out everywhere. They were leaving most of it, a scattered mess. Finally, just after noon, they released the prisoners from the trees.

Virginia felt the blood coming back into her hands and arms in a painful rush.

"On your feet," Caruthers said, pulling her up roughly. She staggered, her legs numb, and nearly fell over. Her hands were tied behind her back again. It was clear that she and her three companions weren't going to be allowed to ride their horses, which were led away by their captors.

They were steered toward the creek and pushed forward. Virginia carefully ventured into the freezing water. The creek was nearly empty, and at the deepest spot only reached her knees. But it was slick, and she nearly lost her footing several times. Beside her, Drake went face first into the water, where he struggled to lift his head above the surface. Finally, Samuel took pity on him, lifted him up, and helped him across the last few yards to the far side of the creek.

At the top of the bank, Virginia saw three patches of freshly turned soil. The digging had been done in a rush, and the areas didn't have the well-defined contours of graves, but she was certain that's what they were. Who the unfortunate victims were, she didn't know. Gus was lying somewhere exposed in the desert, according to Meredith, and unless he was telling a lie—and Virginia couldn't imagine why he would be—he hadn't yet encountered Jed or Becky.

Caruthers tied a rope around her neck and mounted his horse. She struggled to keep up on foot. These men didn't have a clue how much danger they were in. Virginia was certain that any trespasser on what Meredith considered his territory was in danger, and that probably included Meredith's own men. Virginia wracked her brains for a way to warn them—and to make them believe her. She thought it pretty unlikely that Meredith had ever intended to reveal the location of the mine to his men, but once the secret was out, he had no choice.

"He doesn't want you to know where the gold is," she said abruptly. "He won't let you get away."

Caruthers leaned down from his saddle and raised his fist as if to strike her, and she subsided.

There was no way Meredith was going to get the drop on all five of his followers, which meant he had to winnow them down, pit them against each other somehow—which suited Virginia's goals as well, if she and her friends could just survive long enough. She would watch and wait for her opportunity.

The knife strapped to the inside of her thigh chafed as she walked. Meredith had ordered her searched, but, out of modesty, Samuel hadn't discovered it. If she could get her hands free long enough…

Despite the frost of the night before, the day was warming up quickly. By midafternoon, Meredith's men were drinking from their canteens, and Virginia's mouth felt dry, her lips cracked.

"If you want to keep us alive," she said, "you'd best give us some water."

None of her guards reacted. Meredith was riding at the head of the group. He didn't seem to hear her at first, then she heard him say, "You'll live, bitch. We're almost there. You can drink once we arrive."

Virginia looked around. The desert looked the same as the day before and the day before that, an endless sea of sagebrush and lava rocks, small hillocks, and gullies, but now that she knew what to look for, she saw a small butte ahead of them, bare of vegetation, covered by rocky scree. As they approached, the land dipped downward steadily to the bottom of a dry creek bed. Bare rocks rimmed the bottom, rounded and worn smooth by water, so apparently the creek wasn't dry all year long. Dark sand filled the spaces between the rocks.

There was evidence of a recently occupied campsite on the banks, and against a small juniper tree leaned a shovel. Below the shovel was a spot in the creek bed where the soil was darker than the rest, with a glistening of moisture atop the dirt and rocks.

Meredith dismounted and strode over to Virginia.

"Clement, keep your gun on her," he said. He cut her bonds, then took two steps over to the tree and grabbed the shovel. Marching back, he shoved it into Virginia's hands. "You want water, girl? Then start digging."

She hefted the shovel. Meredith was within striking range; one quick blow and her enemy would be down forever. Without him, chances were good that the others would set to squabbling over the gold mine—if they could find it.

Clement was watching her. His eyes were glinting as if he could see her intentions and was daring her. No, she decided. She might take out Meredith, but she'd die in the effort, and his men would probably shoot the rest of the prisoners too.

Besides, she'd promised to find Becky Catledge, and she intended to fulfill that promise.

Virginia shoved the spade into the dark sand, turning it over and reaching water within moments. She dug down several feet, slopping the wet sand over the sides of the hole. She stood back and examined at the murky water, and almost put her face down to it, silt or no silt. But even as she watched, the water began to clear.

She felt arms wrap around her waist and lift her away from the hole. Clement grabbed the shovel and tossed it back against the tree. He leaned down and filled his waterskin. One by one, the other men joined him, until the water was down to a few inches of muck at the bottom of the hole.

"There's your water, miss," Clement said, walking away. In his disdain, he didn't retie her hands. She was a mere girl to him, someone he could lift bodily, and he obviously didn't believe she posed a danger, reputation or no reputation. Her hands drifted down to her thighs.

But what could she do with only a knife? She would only get them all killed. She decided to leave the blade where it was for now.

Meredith supervised the unloading of the packhorses and mules. "Leave that one," he said, pointing to one of the mules, which was loaded down with shovels and picks. "We'll be needing those tools to open the mine. You boys stay behind for now. Caruthers and Clement, get your personal gear and follow…"

"Hey, boss!" Caruthers called out.

Meredith turned, frowning, annoyed at being interrupted.

Caruthers was pointing up the rocky hillside. "There's someone up there!"

Meredith marched to his horse and pulled his rifle from its holster in one swift move. He motioned for Caruthers and Clement to follow him. At the last second, he paused and turned, speaking to his three other men. "Keep on eye on the prisoners. If they try anything, shoot them."

Virginia examined the hillside. She thought she could see movement about halfway up. She tried to get a better view, careful not to make any sudden motions. Samuel glanced nervously back at her, and then toward his boss, back and forth with gun in hand, as if he couldn't decide where the greatest danger lay.

Meredith and his men marched to the base of the hill and start climbing. It was only when they were almost to the mine that Virginia saw the small hole in the hillside and the pile of rocks around the entrance.

A head poked out of the hole, long blonde hair glinting in the sun.

Becky Catledge, Virginia thought.

"Stay back!" a woman's voice shouted. "I've got a gun trained on you!"

Meredith stopped abruptly. The barrel of his rifle rose slightly, as if he was considering defying the challenge, but then he lowered the weapon.

It was a stalemate, and Virginia couldn't see how could be easily resolved.

Shoot him! Virginia thought. But from everything she had read in Ellen Meredith's diaries, she doubted Becky was that cold-blooded. Yet if she let Meredith get away, it was only a matter of time before he and his men would storm the hill.

Or worse, they would simply wait. The only water was in the creek bed, and Meredith had time on his side.

"Is that you, Becky?" Meredith said. His voice was even, almost friendly sounding. "Is Jed with you?"

"I'm here, Jonathan," a man's voice called from inside the cave behind Becky.

"Well, I'm glad to see you," Meredith said. "Why don't you let me in, or better yet, come on out? I've got fresh supplies to share. We can talk this over. There's plenty of gold for all of us."

There was silence, and Virginia wondered if the pair inside the cave were actually considering Meredith's offer. She wanted to shout out a warning, but of course, Becky and Jed knew better than anyone how little Meredith could be trusted.

"We found them, Jonathan," the girl shouted. "We found their bodies."

"Found them?" Jonathan echoed. "Found who?"

"You know who, you bastard! Cager and Allie…and Edwin."

"I don't know what you're talking about."

In response, there was the loud crack of a gunshot. A rock just above where Meredith was standing spun and slid down downhill, generating a small rockslide that nearly tossed the man off his feet.

"Get away, and don't come back," Becky called.

Meredith caught his balance but remained where he was. Caruthers and Clement turned tail, however, and went sliding down the hill toward the camp.

"I'm not going anywhere," Meredith said loudly. "And neither are you."

He stood defiantly for a few more moments, as if daring her to shoot him. Only then did he turn and make his way down the hill, not looking at all rushed.

Virginia heard a furtive movement behind her, as if an animal was running for cover. She turned to look, and at the same moment, there was the sound of a gunshot.

Caruthers, who had almost reached the bottom of the hill, slapped his hand to the side of his neck. Blood welled out from under his hand, then squirted between his fingers. He fell to his knees, then toppled over.

Two more shots rang out. Franklin dropped to the ground, unmoving. Behind Virginia, the small tree the shovel was leaning against splintered. She couldn't make sense of it at first. Were Becky and Jed shooting at them? Why now?

A fourth shot rang out, and one of the horses squealed and staggered. The shots were coming from behind them, at the edge of the copse of trees. Furtive shadows darted forward, and Virginia saw their bare skin. Indians, she thought.

She tried counting them, and probably counted some of the attackers twice, but she was certain there were at least a couple of dozen men, quickly flanking and enveloping them.

Two of Meredith's men were caught in the open, and both went down in a flurry of gunshots.

"Run for the mine!" Virginia cried.

Perhaps her Canowiki voice helped, for they all obeyed—prisoners and guards alike—at once. Samuel ran over to the horses and tried to lead them away, but they were too panicked. Several broke away, and he quit trying to coax the others and turned and ran.

Virginia, Angus, and Drake were the last to reach the base of the hill. By then, Meredith had reached the mine's entrance. He stood at the entrance, his hands outstretched, his pistol dangling from his fingers. Everyone paused for a moment to see what would happen, even as bullets continued to strike around them, sending ricochets off the rocks.

Meredith ducked into the opening, quickly followed by Clement and Samuel. Virginia pulled out her hidden knife and cut the ropes binding Angus and Drake. Angus stumbled as they began the ascent. Virginia grabbed his arm and helped him gain his balance. Drake lurched forward on his own.

Bullets flew past them, tugging at the edges of their clothing and packs, but miraculously missed them.

Should we throw ourselves on their mercy? Virginia wondered. It was clear that Meredith and his men had done something to anger the Indians. Her thoughts went back to the three freshly dug graves. Could Meredith have been so stupid?

She continued to scramble up the rocky hillside. It felt as if she was sliding back a foot for every two feet she climbed, but eventually she reached the opening to the mine, which was bigger than she had expected. It wasn't big enough for one of the pack mules, but she could duck into it without having to crawl.

A last gunshot rang out. The rock above Virginia's head shattered, showering slivers into her face, barely missing her eyes.

Uncertain what she'd find on the other side, Virginia dove into the darkness.

Chapter Thirty-One

<u>Vale, Oregon Territory, September 1851</u>

When Jed showed up at the Smith Feed Store in Vale, it was barely dawn. Becky, an early riser, was sitting on the porch. Her heart leapt to her mouth, and she felt uncharacteristically shy as he approached. He was tall and handsome, and so mature that she felt like a little girl in his presence.

"Hello, Jed," she said softly.

He stood before her, looking as though he wanted to embrace her, but instead stiffening into a ramrod correctness. "Miss Catledge," he said.

A few years before, she would have squealed and run into his arms, but now she blushed and looked down at the ground like a proper young lady. She had spent most of the last couple of years in hiding, dreaming of the day when Jed would appear before her, and she had fashioned a thousand greetings, but now that the time had come, she was dumbstruck.

Jed seemed equally tongue-tied, but he managed to ask Becky when she would be free to go for a stroll. She looked around for the manager, Cole Johnson, and motioned him over.

"Will you take over the front?" she asked.

"Certainly, ma'am," Johnson said.

She turned back to Jed, who raised an eyebrow. "Ma'am?"

Becky curtsied. "I'm free right now, sir," she said. At the word "sir," both of them laughed, and it seemed to break the tension. But a "sir" was what he looked like. He'd filled out, and no longer looked like a scarecrow in castoff clothes. He had a short beard, neatly trimmed, and a mustache that he curled up at the ends.

Becky had filled out as well, and she caught him staring when he thought she wasn't looking.

As they walked down the dusty street, they relaxed, and, chatting, they soon fell into their old conversational rhythm.

"Where's Edwin?" Becky finally asked. The question ended their easy familiarity.

Jed stopped dead in the street and looked down at his shoes. "That's…that's why I've come."

Not to see me, Becky thought with a twinge of disappointment.

"Edwin's gone, Becky," Jed said. "He left a message that he was going to California to join the gold rush."

"He always was a romantic," Becky said. "Good for him."

"No," Jed said curtly. He caught himself and took a breath. "Sorry, but you didn't hear how he used to disparage the gold hunters. 'You'd make more money selling them shovels,' he'd say."

They started walking again. They had no specific destination, and there was little open that early in the morning. Eventually, Becky intended to lead Jed back to the house, but for now she wanted him to herself.

"So where did he go?" she asked.

"I think he went looking for Cager and Allie," Jed said. "At least, so I hope."

"But you think there is another possibility…" she prompted.

"My father…stepfather…was traveling around the same time. Edwin was always asking to go along…"

Becky felt her heart sink. It was a fearful possibility, for they both suspected that Jonathan Meredith was responsible for Cager and Allie's disappearance, though neither had ever dared to broach the possibility, for if either of them admitted it, they would have had to do something about it.

The tragedy had tainted the friendships of all the small company who had spent so much time together on the long westward trail. They'd all felt the same helpless guilt. When Becky's parents had insisted on moving away and changing their names, Becky had agreed, but only because she thought it was a temporary solution. She'd thought she'd be separated from her friends for only a few months; a year at the most. Surely Mr. Meredith would meet justice, if not for this crime, then for another.

"How did you find me?" she asked.

"Your letters," Jed said. "You always sent one of them near my birthday, and finally I followed the man who delivered the letter and questioned him. I have a great deal of money now, Becky. I bribed him into telling me who'd given him the letter."

Becky didn't say anything for a few moments. Then she turned aside, climbed the stairs in front of the general store, and sat on the empty bench outside the door. Inside, she could see Mildred and Paul Davies getting ready to open the store.

"How long ago?" she asked.

"What's that?"

"How long ago did you find out where I was?" she repeated.

Jed sat next to her and put his hand on hers. "I've known for a couple of years, Becky," he said gently. "But I wasn't sure you wanted to see me. You disappeared, after all."

"What about your stepfather?" she asked. "Does he know?"

"Of course not!" Jed said, sounding shocked. "He never knew I received any messages from you, and I certainly wouldn't tell him."

Becky believed him, but she was still troubled. If Jed had a "great deal of money," Jonathan Meredith had a great deal more of it.

"Becky, I'm going to look for Edwin," Jed said. "Will you come with me?"

Becky didn't have to ask where Jed planned to look for his brother, for they both knew there was only one place he was likely to go. "Let me write a note to my parents," she said. "We need to be gone before they wake up."

***

The Lost Blue Bucket Mine was easier to find than Becky had expected. It was as if she could remember each individual footstep she'd taken on that long-ago journey, but most of all, she remembered the places that Meredith had avoided in the search for Allie and Cager.

Jed followed her without question. Unlike most men, he treated her as an equal, for he'd seen how she'd handled herself on the long trek westward. She'd turned down more than one proposal for marriage, waiting for him. Sadly, it had taken Edwin's disappearance to finally bring Jed to her side.

Becky went unerringly to the exact spot where she had once bent down to pick up the shiny quartz from the creek and fill a small blue bucket with it.

She'd learned a thing or two about gold since then: how placer gold was washed down a creek from a source upstream, which could be anywhere amid so much territory that a miner could spend his life looking for the mother lode.

She examined the hillside above, immediately spotted the fresh rockfall, and sensed that the slide had been designed to hide what was beneath it.

They camped by the dry creek and found a spot where someone had dug into the sand for water. In the morning, they set to work pulling the rocks away from the entrance of the mine. It took them most of the morning, but it wasn't as bad as it looked, and by early afternoon, they managed to open a small hole.

It took them the rest of the day to widen it so that it was large enough for someone to slip through.

"We should shore it up," Jed said dubiously as small rocks continued to slide by them.

"We'll only be inside for a short time," Becky said.

Jed picked up some dry branches and examined them. "Someone's used these before," he said. "You go down and fix supper, and I'll see if I can stabilize this a little."

"You go make supper," she said. "You're the better cook." She grabbed the branches out of his hands, laughing.

He pretended to be shocked. "All right," he said. "We'll both starve. Come on, the quicker we get this done, the quicker we can go to bed."

His voice trailed off at those last words. Each night of the trip, they had slept in separate bedding near the campfire, but close together for warmth. Becky had wanted to turn to Jed and open her arms to him, but she well knew where that would lead, and while she might have welcomed it, she knew that Jed thought of himself as a gentleman and would think less of himself. She tried not to entice him, but each night, it had become harder not to give in to temptation.

It was nearly dark by the time they finished shoring up the entrance, and as much as Becky longed to light a torch and explore the mine, they descended the hill and returned to camp. They gnawed on some jerky and hardtack, washed it down with silty water, and went to bed. Fortunately, the hard labor of digging had made them so exhausted that they both immediately fell asleep.

In the morning, it seemed as if they were both reluctant to approach the mine entrance.

We don't know what we'll find, Becky thought.

When they finally stood in front of the mine, they stayed there for the longest time. Then, with snort of exasperation, Becky ducked down and crawled through the hole they'd made. She heard Jed following her.

The first thing she saw was the gold. There was enough light to see the shimmering in the walls, and Becky instantly knew that this was the mother lode, but instead of it making her glad, her heart sank, for it was final proof that Jonathan Meredith possessed a secret important enough to kill for.

There was a stack of torches near the entrance, constructed of juniper branches wrapped in grasses. She lit one of them and went to the back of the chamber. There were two tunnels there, but one was obviously unused, while the other showed footprints in the dust.

She turned and looked at Jed, who appeared pale and ghostly in the torchlight. He swallowed, then nodded her on.

They crept forward, frightened every step of the way at what they might find. They reached the end of the tunnel. There was nothing there except tool-marked rocks. Quietly, they went back to the front of the mine. Becky wasn't sure if she was relieved or disappointed. It was clear that they would have to explore the other tunnel, but she was so exhausted that she was ready to call it quits, even though the day was only half over.

Jed agreed that they should rest, and they went down and gathered their camping gear and brought it up to the mine.

"What about our horses?" Becky asked.

"I'll hobble them loosely," he said. "They won't go too far, but they'll be able to forage."

"Unless the coyotes get them," she said.

He shook his head, smiling. "They'll be safe enough. And I'm looking forward to not being so cold. Let's get a fire going."

The fire warmed up the cave quickly, especially when Jed got up and covered the entrance with one of the horse blankets. The stone floor was harder than the desert sands, but Becky felt safe and secure. Jed lay only a few feet away.

What would happen if I kissed him? she wondered. Would he kiss me back? Would he take my in his arms? Would he…?

She felt a surge of guilt at the thought, as if she was somehow betraying Edwin. Poor Edwin, who had always had a crush on her. She'd tried to gently discourage him, and he had never taken it very far, but she knew he had never fallen out of love with her.

The world shrank down into guilt and shame.

It was as if everything Becky had ever done wrong, every unkind word, every discourtesy, every angry argument, besieged her mind with regret. Beside her, Jed moaned, and she looked over to see if he was asleep. His eyes were glittering, staring upward in torment.

She fell in and out of sleep, until she couldn't tell where reality began and nightmare ended. Part of her realized that what she was seeing and feeling was in the past. She would wake up from the memories, and then, just as she began to wonder upon it, she'd be dragged back in.

She remembered hiding from Edwin, not wanted to have to deal with his puppy love, and it seemed like a terrible thing.

At last, she sat up with an anguished cry, and Jed sat bolt upright next to her. And then he did what she'd always hoped for; he reached out for her.

They embraced, and it was as if all Becky's hopes came together in that one moment, illuminating the truth that neither of them could avoid; that they were meant to be together forever.

"I'm sorry, Becky," Jed said. "I should have come to you sooner. But my father…disapproved of you. I thought if I could prove my worth to him that he'd come around. That he'd accept our union." His voice cracked, and it seemed to shock him. He pulled away from her. "I'm sorry, I don't know what's happening to me. I've never felt this way."

A shudder went through him, and Becky took him back into her arms. She didn't think any less of him for his emotions, but she knew that he was embarrassed.

"I never thought Jonathan would hurt Edwin," he said. "I wondered if…I wondered about Allie and Cager, but wouldn't let myself believe it. But Edwin…"

She tried to reassure him despite not believing her own words. "We don't know that anything has happened. Perhaps he did go to California, as the letter said."

"No," Jed said. "He wouldn't do that without telling me first."

Becky stared at Jed in the darkness, and it appeared to her that a faint light was glowing around him. The same light swirled around her. If she concentrated hard, she could push the lights away for a moment and again see what was real.

And then the guilt overwhelmed her again.

Allie and Cager. She'd known what had happened to them. They had all known. But none of them had done anything about it, because they couldn't prove it.

But that none of that should have mattered. She should have tracked down Jonathan Meredith and made him pay for his crimes. Instead, she had run away.

And because of that, Edwin was dead.

She realized she had known that he was dead the moment they'd crawled into the mine. She had sensed the ghosts of Allie, Cager, and Edwin immediately, though she couldn't admit it to herself. It was as if they had been waiting for her. She didn't say anything now, but saw the same distress on Jed's face, as if he too was feeling their presence.

They held and comforted each other for a time. Then, suddenly, he was kissing her, his hands reaching under her clothes, and she knew she should stop him, but she wanted him to continue. In the darkness, surrounded by ghosts, they made love.

And yet, the spirit of Edwin didn't seem to blame or haunt them. It was as if they had been forgiven, which almost made it worse. The guilt and shame didn't lessen, but intensified. Allie, Cager, and Edwin had been left abandoned in the dark, with no one to mourn for them. If it had been Becky, she would have been angry and vengeful.

She tried to speak to the spirits in her mind. Once, as she was drifting off the sleep, she heard Jed say, "Is that you, Edwin?" But the ghosts seemed only vaguely aware of their own existence. There were no thoughts there, only emotions, fear and regret and, most of all, bewilderment.

***

In the morning, neither of them wanted to leave the front of the cave. But as they lay in each other's arms, the guilt and shame returned. Jed broke away from her. He had a grim look on his face. "We need proof," he said. "We have to find them."

They decided to explore the second tunnel, which looked much like the tunnel they had explored the day before, but instead of ending in a dead end, this shaft ended in a cave-in. There was a huge gap above them and a steep slag-filled slope below them.

They hesitated. Something emanated from the dark recesses; they felt presences other than Allie, Cager, and Edwin—and these spirits weren't so forgiving. These ghosts were angry at Jed and Becky for invading their resting place.

"I can't go any farther," Becky said. "Not now."

Jed put his arm around her, and they retreated. Without a word, they embraced, then lay down on the blankets and made love again, slowly this time, still feeling regret and sweet pain and guilt all mixed together.

***

They awoke to the sound of men's voices outside the mine. As afraid as Becky had been the night before as she was assailed by the memories of the past, it was the sound of one man's voice that made it all real.

She would have recognized Jonathan Meredith's voice anywhere.

She hesitated, and then, before Jed could stop her, she stuck her head out of the entrance. Men were walking toward them, but her eyes settled on one thickset man with a big, black beard. "Stay back!" she cried. "I've got a gun trained on you."

She waved her arm behind her, and Jed put a rifle in her hand. She took a bead on Meredith's chest.

Her finger tightened on the trigger…and she hesitated. All during the brief conversation she and Jed had with Meredith, Becky thought about shooting him; she just couldn't quite bring herself to do it.

Someone else shot first. One of the men below them grabbed his neck and toppled over. Becky couldn't make sense of it. Were they fighting each other? She saw movement in the trees behind the campground. An Indian rose up out of the desert, aimed a rifle at the men below, and fired. The men began running for the mine.

Becky withdrew and looked at Jed. "What do we do?" she asked.

"We have to let them in," Jed said. "It isn't just Meredith out there."

She stood up and walked to the back of the chamber. Jed joined her, and they both pointed their rifles at the entrance, waiting to see who would appear first.

Chapter Thirty-Two

<u>Lost Blue Bucket Mine, Oregon Territory, October 1851</u>

Virginia dove through the entrance and rolled onto the rocky surface of the cave floor, barely missing the campfire at the center of the chamber. Angus and Drake were scrambling deeper into the cave, and Virginia hurried to join them. Only then did she turn around to see what was happening.

They were in the midst of an armed tableau, frozen for the moment, with the two sides pointing guns at each other. Jed and Becky both had rifles aimed at the men across from them, while Meredith and his men had weapons pointed back at them. It was an uneven fight, perhaps, but no one had fired the first shot.

Virginia recognized Becky instantly.

It came as a shock that she was a young woman, not a girl. In Virginia's mind was the image of the Becky Catledge in Ellen Meredith's diaries, a plucky young girl who rode and shot better than most men, who had stared down a grizzly. But of course, that story was years in the past now.

To her surprise, Virginia realized that Becky was actually a couple of years older than her. She had similar coloring, blonde hair and blue eyes, but she was a bigger girl than Virginia, with sturdier arms and legs, her features broader and more open.

Becky's eyes were fixed on Jonathan Meredith, and her finger was tightening on the trigger of her rifle. Virginia stepped into the line of fire.

"Stop, Becky," she said. Becky stared at her curiously and lowered her rifle slightly to one side, at the ready. "My name is Virginia Reed. Your mother sent me to find you."

"My mother sent you? …And my father?"

Virginia turned away, wondering what to say, but Becky caught the shadow flow across her face.

"Damn you, Meredith!" Becky cried. She raised her rifle again, and Meredith, for once, was caught by surprise, his rifle no longer pointing at Becky.

"No!" Virginia cried out, blocking the shot again, raising her hands. "You must not do this, Becky. Jonathan Meredith will see justice, I promise you that."

"You don't know him," Becky said grimly.

Unexpectedly, Angus broke in. "The lass is right, Miss Reed. He's guilty as hell."

"I won't execute a man without a trial," Virginia said.

"You had no problem hanging that fellow who robbed the stagecoach," Drake reminded her.

"That was different," Virginia said. *But was it really?* she wondered. While she hadn't actually seen Meredith kill anyone, there was little doubt that he'd done so. "We caught him in the act. We have no absolute proof of Meredith's guilt."

Angus shook his head sadly. "That's just it, Miss Reed. Men like Meredith get away with it; they cover up their crimes too well to be caught. You know he's guilty. It's a mistake to let him live."

Meredith had recovered his aplomb and was watching and listening with a bemused smile. "You folks seem to forget you're outgunned. But I don't understand why you think I'm such a bad man."

"You admitted to killing Gus Catledge," Angus said, giving Becky a quick, worried glance. The girl blanched but didn't pull the trigger.

"In self-defense," Meredith said. "I'm sorry it happened, but you can't deny a man a chance to defend himself. You folks were my prisoners. Ask yourselves: Why did I let you live? Did you think of that?"

Virginia had thought about it, and she had her suspicions. She'd seen how Meredith had eyed her when he thought she wasn't looking. But she suspected the real reason was that not all his men were ready to kill for him in cold blood. Killing Indians was one thing; killing a woman and unarmed men was another. Samuel, for one, looked like he regretted ever hooking up with this crew. He was sitting with his back to the wall, his head in his hands.

"This is a mistake," Jed said to the others. "Meredith fooled me for a long time, but he's evil. He killed Edwin. And I'm certain he killed Allie and Cager."

"I thought Edwin was with you," Meredith said. "I have no idea what happened to Allie and Cager."

"You're lying," Becky said. "You murdered them."

"Murdered?" Meredith said. "Why would I harm the children? They must have had an accident."

"No," Becky insisted. "It was you."

"How can you believe such a thing?" Meredith asked, sounding aggrieved.

"Because they told me so." Becky motioned to the cave surrounding them.

Dead silence greeted this remark as everyone stared at her. Even Samuel lifted his head, looking at her in shock. But despite the silence, Becky sounded so certain that Virginia sensed they believed her.

"But if they're dead," Samuel asked with a slight fearful shrug. "How could you…?"

"Is it so hard to believe?" Virginia turned to look at the man. "Can't you feel them?"

"Feel what?" Samuel asked, though from his tone and the look on his face, he already knew what she was going to say.

"There are spirits haunting this place," Virginia said. "It is a sacred spot for the Indians."

Meredith barked out a laugh, looking over at his men. "Spirits? Haunting? Are you talking about ghosts?"

Virginia didn't answer.

"I never believed in such things either," Angus said, "until I came face to face with them. Believe me, boys, there are spirits and creatures in the wilds that no civilized man would believe in. Search your hearts. Admit you sense something uncanny about this place."

Becky handed her gun to Virginia, who was so surprised that she took it without question. Becky walked up to Meredith, putting her face inches from his and fixing him with a glare of such intensity that he backed up a step.

"If you won't believe me, then I will show you," she said. She raised her arms. "I summon the spirits of this place. Give me justice!"

Ghostly lights appeared in the darkness at the back of the mine. But this was not light that banished the dark, but which suffused it with dread and fear. These were not the ghosts of three young children, but something ancient, primal. The lights swirled, and then, without warning, surged toward them.

Virginia shuddered as she felt the spirits pass through her, and she stiffened as memories flowed into her. She forced herself to open her eyes.

Ghostly shapes whirled about the heads of the gunmen. Then, as if picking the most vulnerable target, the spectral lights shot into Samuel's head, and he cried out. He scrambled for the entrance and started to climb out of the mine.

"What's wrong with him?" Meredith shouted. "Stop him!"

Clement grabbed the boy and pulled him back.

Samuel fought him. "We're going to be buried alive!"

"There's nothing there," Meredith said. "It's all in your head."

"NO!" Samuel shouted. He shook Clement off and dove for the entrance again. Again, Clement stopped him and dragged him back into the cave. In desperation, Samuel grasped the wooden support beams shoring up the opening. With a thundering roar, the entrance collapsed. The ground shook; dust filled the cavern.

"Damn you!" Clement cried. He grabbed Samuel by the throat, nearly lifting him off his feet, and slapped the younger man across the face, trying to bring him to his senses.

In a flash, Samuel drew his knife and plunged it into Clement's chest.

The bigger man dropped Samuel and looked down at the knife in disbelief. He reached down and pulled it out. Blood followed his hand and sprayed out over the blade and into Samuel's open mouth and wide eyes.

Clement dropped to his knees with a sigh and toppled over.

One by one, the ghosts swirled about Samuel in his torment, ancient spirits who sought vengeance against the living.

"Oh, God!" Samuel shouted. "Get out of my head!" He put both hands over his ears as if he was hearing something or someone no one else could hear. He jerked one way and then the other, and then he rose above the floor of the cave and floated there, screaming.

The ghosts of the vengeful spirits flowed into and around him, one after another, and he kept on screaming. Virginia had a sudden clear vision in her head of a house in flames: a fire that Samuel had set, killing his mother and younger sister.

"Mama!" he cried. "I'm sorry!"

Then, without any hesitation, so quickly that no one could have stopped him, he pulled his pistol from his belt, put the barrel into his mouth, and pulled the trigger. Blood splattered against the walls of the cave. The glittering gold streaks glowed red.

Samuel hung in the air a moment longer with half of his head missing, and then flopped to the floor.

And then the ghosts came for Virginia.

Chapter Thirty-Three

<u>Lost Blue Bucket Mine, Oregon Territory, October 1851</u>

The First People were angry. This had once been their land, but newcomers had forced them into the desert until their final stand had been made in this very cave. Here, the last of the warriors had protected the sacred chamber where their loved ones descended into the underworld after death, free of shame, anger, or guilt.

The warriors had died, still on guard, not even aware that they were no longer living. Millennia passed. New tribes came, like them but not like them. The ghost warriors attacked these strangers, and to their dismay, found that their weapons, their very bodies, passed through the intruders.

But they also discovered that they could find the secret shame of the living, the guilty conscience of any invader, driving them to desperate acts. In time, the new tribes left them alone, and once again, the protectors slept. More millennia passed.

And then they were awakened by violence in the cave above them. They found the bodies of three newcomers stranger than any of those who had come before, two of them children. The warriors took pity upon them and raised them up, but the children were innocent and unaware. These new souls, who possessed no anger, only confusion, disturbed the ancient spectral warriors, who left them alone.

But they sought out the murderer and brought down their anger upon him.

The murderer was empty of all emotion except hate, a hate equal to theirs.

And yet, there was something deep down inside him, so deep down that the murderer wasn't aware it was there. The warriors tried to awaken this secret, but their prey escaped them, hiding in the daylight at the front of the cave.

The dead never left the shadows. They festered in the blackness of the earth and nurtured their malevolence toward the living.

Then something called them forth again, and they surged to the front of the cave, where they found the entrance closed and the latest invaders trapped. Instantly, they found the weakest of the invaders, a man tortured by his conscience.

Now he was dead too. The spectral warriors turned their attention to the others, and with unerring instinct, struck at their very souls.

***

The darkness wavered and then disappeared, replaced by a rough wooden cabin. It was freezing inside the cabin despite the smoky fire blackening the walls, sending smoke into Virginia's eyes. Bayliss stood at the center of the cabin, smiling at her sadly, the young man she could have loved if she had been mature enough to understand his worth. Bayliss, who had given his life for her. Tears sprang to her eyes; it was a familiar pain, one she'd relived many times.

Virginia was staggered by the vision, and yet she accepted it.

It was not her first experience with the "other," with those who belonged to fairy tales, to ancient legends. But never before had she felt such a concentration of that realm, which was neither past nor present but a place between, where souls still lingered, waiting for the moment when they would at long last be released from their earthly bonds.

The fear and anger was overwhelming. Virginia could see in the eyes of her friends, for whom ghosts were a myth, a thing that children were afraid of but that adults had forgotten to fear, the realization that there was a world behind the one they knew. Purgatory was real.

Here resided old souls and new souls, those ancient and those newly dead, congregated in these dark tunnels, drawn by long-ago wrongs, longing for justice. These were souls neither damned nor blessed, but caught in between, trapped in endless torment. Virginia realized that it was up to her to give them release, for she was the Canowiki.

The living were paralyzed by fear of the dead, overwhelmed by guilt and shame for everything they had ever done wrong. But these thoughts and feelings were not new to her. Indeed, she'd suffered them every night of her life, waking up in the small hours, hearing the pleas of those she had not been able to save, the recriminations of those she'd had to kill, the silence of those she had saved.

So this was no different; this was what she expected, and so she continued to be aware of her surroundings, of the real world. Those she had been sent to save were in danger. She fought the fear and dread within her.

As Virginia came back to the present, she saw that all the others were lying on the ground, moaning and thrashing, unaware of their surroundings.

All but one.

Jonathan Meredith was sitting with his back to the wall, staring at her from across the cave, rifle in his lap. Virginia put her hands around the grip of her pistol and made sure Meredith saw her doing it.

It seemed obvious that there was no guilt, no shame in Meredith's mind. The ghosts swirled about his head, but they could find no purchase. Any crime he had committed, he had long ago rationalized away.

***

Jonathan Meredith watched his enemies and his companions writhe on the floor of the cave, crying in pain or in shame, he wasn't sure which. He'd seen people consumed by guilt before and wondered upon it, but never completely understood it. It was weakness, this inability to accept what one has done.

Old wrongs he'd committed came back to him, and though he recognized that the world might see these events as criminal, he saw them as simple necessity. He'd felt sorry for those who had endangered him—whom he had destroyed—for a few days, and then gone on with his life. Only Sarah…

He closed off his mind, putting the memory out of reach like he always did.

And now they were trapped in the Lost Blue Bucket Mine. Everyone knew the location of the gold, everyone who threatened him. He suspected that not all of them were going to survive the coming ordeal—and if he could arrange it, he would try to make sure that no one survived but him. If he could but find a way out of here without the Indians scalping him, all his problems would be solved.

Only one other person in the mine seemed aware of her surroundings. Virginia Reed was staring at him, pistol in hand. *I should shoot her right now.* He'd heard stories about the girl, about how she had managed to survive more than one catastrophe. This might be the last time that he could get the drop on her.

He smiled at her. "We seem to be the only ones who aren't overwhelmed by guilt," he said.

"I accepted my responsibility for the choices I made long ago," she said. "But you…you apparently have no remorse."

"I have done nothing wrong." He shrugged. "I think we're going to have to work together if we want to get out of here."

She stared at him stonily, as if everything within her wanted to say no, but she had others to worry about. She nodded. "We will work together until we get out of here," she said. *But not a moment longer.*

***

Virginia had no illusions that Meredith would abide by the agreement to cooperate. She would have to be constantly vigilant. She had more at stake than Meredith, who cared about no one but himself. Virginia had promised Abigail Catledge that she would find and rescue Becky. Gus Catledge's death only made that promise more binding.

Becky was nearby, and it seemed as if she was half in and half out of consciousness. The girl had risen up a couple of times, crying out, and then fallen back into quiet moaning. Now she rose up again, crying out, "Edwin!"

***

Becky woke up from her dreams of the past. Jed was lying beside her, twitching and moaning. Everyone else in the mine seemed to be incapacitated too, except for Jonathan Meredith and the woman who had introduced herself as Virginia Reed, who were faced off against each other. There was no mistaking the animosity between the two.

"Becky?" she heard. Jed was sitting up, his hands rubbing his face, his eyes frantically searching for her. She stepped toward him, and the relief that bloomed on his face made her forget her vow to kill Meredith, if only for a moment.

"I'm here," she said, kneeling beside him, clutching his head to her chest. "I'm never leaving you again."

She looked over her shoulder. Virginia had turned her attention back to Meredith, and he was returning the gaze. Becky had a sudden sense that the justice for her friends' murderer was in someone else's hands, and for the first time since the trip began, she felt the burden lift. She would take care of Jed. Meredith would meet his fate, of that she was sure.

The spirits who had invaded the chamber began to dissipate, to flow back into the darkness. The vengeful spirits had the living trapped, and Becky sensed they were in no hurry. She felt only sadness now, and when she closed her eyes, it seemed to her that she could see the shimmering shapes of Allie, Cager, and Edwin, looking as they had looked when they were alive, gazing down on her with pity.

"I'm sorry," she said. "I'm sorry I didn't come sooner."

The ghosts didn't answer, but one by one, they blinked away, until only Edwin was left. The look on his face was one of love and forgiveness, and Becky cried out at the overwhelming sense of mortification she felt for having abandoned him.

Then he too was gone, though a small part of his presence lingered, as if to promise he would be back.

Chapter Thirty-Four

The fire was sputtering, sending more smoke than light into the cavern, and the smoke had nowhere to escape.

One of the branches that had supported the entrance was sticking out of the rubble, and Virginia pulled it out, catching her breath as more rocks tumbled down. She threw the wood onto the fire.

Jed and Becky were holding each other and staring at the fire. Drake was just waking up, while Angus was getting to his feet, looking shaky.

"What in God's name was that?" he muttered.

"Spirits of the First People," Virginia said. "Those who were here before even the Indians. They don't like us newcomers."

"I saw children," Drake said. "How is that possible?"

Jonathan Meredith was still sitting with his back to the wall, his gun pointed vaguely in their direction. Virginia shot a glance at Becky, but instead of looking enraged, she looked sad and perhaps relieved, as if a burden she had carried for too long had been lifted.

"I think we have our proof," Virginia said. "I'm betting if we venture further into the tunnels, we'll find their bodies."

"You want justice?" Meredith said. His voice was flat, showing no fear. "We're all dead, can't you see? It will take days to clear the entrance, if it's possible at all."

"No." Becky spoke up. "There is another way out."

"No, there isn't," Meredith said. "I'd know about it."

"How far did you explore?" Virginia asked.

Meredith avoided her eyes. She guessed that he hadn't strayed far from the entrance at all. The piles of packs and bedding in the front chamber implied that he'd brought others here to do the work. She shuddered, wondering why the personal possessions had been left behind.

Now, after the sudden closing off of fresh air, the smoke from the fire was trailing backward into the darkness. She detected a faint odor she recognized; the smell of death. The smell wafted from deeper in the cave, pushed by a slight breeze. She said, "If there is air, there must be another exit."

As if in confirmation, ghost lights appeared at the back of the cave, wavering as if urging them to hurry.

Jed broke away from Becky and walked to a small alcove near where the entrance had been. "We found a pile of torches here," he said. He bent down and picked up a handful of broken branches wrapped in cloth.

"We'd better start now," Virginia said. "It doesn't matter if it is night or day, it only matters that we get out of here."

No one argued with her, though Meredith held back until the last moment before following the rest of them.

Virginia saw that at the rear of the front chamber, the cave split into two tunnels, both of which showed signs of having been widened by tools. The walls glittered with tiny specks of light, and near the center divide, there were piles of ore, with larger chunks of shining metal. It was as if the others didn't notice this, except Drake, who bent down and picked up a large rock. "Is this…?"

"When we get home, I'll pay you more than all the gold you can carry," Virginia said. "Leave it."

The big man dropped the rock reluctantly. Becky and Jed were standing near the left-hand tunnel, as if hesitant to continue. When Virginia reached their side, the smell of death wafted out of the blackness.

"We have to go on," Virginia said. "Be careful."

The bodies of their friends are down there, she thought. *God give them strength.*

They reached a cave-in, where part of the floor had tumbled into a lower chamber. The odor was overwhelming now. Even Angus gagged at the smell. He pulled a handkerchief from his suit and held it to his nose. Drake leaned over and spewed his last meal onto the rocks.

They picked their way slowly downward. There was a rotting body at the bottom, but it was that of an adult man. Whoever it was had been ravaged by creatures, with bones and hair and bits of rotting flesh scattered about the rocks. There was a journal lying amid the carnage, and Virginia picked it up and put it in her pack.

Meredith was following the others a few yards back and, one by one, as they passed the body, they looked back at him. He ignored them.

The cavern was no longer man-made, but was a hole created by the earth splitting along a seam, with straight, almost sharp edges. They worked their way deeper into the darkness.

"We're still going downward," Meredith muttered. "You're only going to bury us deeper."

"What the hell does it matter?" Angus said, almost cheerfully.

They reached the end of the natural cleft. There was a small hole there, barely large enough for someone to crawl through. All of them saw a small ghost light floating there, darting in and out of the hole. They hesitated at the narrow aperture.

A small cave opened out to the left. It only extended a few yards before ending in a wall that was so perfectly flat it could have been carved by hand. There, lying at the base of the wall, were the remains of three bodies, carefully and respectfully arranged. Someone had taken two burned-out torches and fashioned them into a crude cross, which they had propped against the wall.

Becky cried out, falling to her knees, and lowered her head. Jed stood behind her, his hand on her shoulder. Two of the bodies were those of children; one of them was larger and dressed in men's clothing.

"Edwin," Jed breathed. He turned toward Meredith, raising his hand to strike, but the older man had anticipated him and had his gun aimed squarely at his stepson's chest. Drake took two quick steps and brought the handle of his pistol down on the back of Meredith's head.

The man fell forward, the gun discharging harmlessly against the flat wall, the bullet ricocheting back the way they had come.

"You son of a bitch," Drake snarled. "You murder even children?" He reached down and grabbed Meredith's gun, then searched the motionless man, finding a bowie knife in his belt.

Meredith stirred, moaning. Angus leaned down. "You're going to hang from the gallows, mister," he said. "If you live that long."

Meredith shook his head, then spit. "I don't care. None of you matter. The only person I ever cared about was taken from me, but these children laughed and played as if Sarah never existed. I hated them."

Becky had barely seemed to notice the confrontation, but now she rose. Her face was blank, almost serene. She turned to the small hole where the ghostly light still danced, and before anyone could stop her, she slid through.

Virginia almost cried out, and then realized that the girl had done what needed to be done. They were down to their last couple of torches. If they didn't find a way out soon, they'd be lost in darkness forever.

"I'll go first," she said to Angus. "Send Meredith in after me, so I can keep him covered."

Angus nodded, and Virginia bent down. "Give me a torch," she said.

Angus put an unlit torch in her hand. "It's the last one," he said.

She pushed her pack through the hole, and then got on her stomach and followed it.

The stench of death permeated the chamber beyond, seeming to cling to her skin, her eyes, her mouth. She lit the last torch. There was a dead body at the center of a pile of bones, bloated, flesh not yet sloughing away from the skeleton. She caught a glimpse of a scurrying creature in the shadows and turned to see a huge rat as it slipped into a hole that seemed no larger around than the creature's tail. She shuddered.

The light of Edwin's ghost was at the far end of the chamber, illuminating another hole that seemed even smaller than the one she had just crawled through. There was a rustle behind her, and Meredith came through. He crawled on his hands and knees through the bones, saw the rotting body, and got to his feet and stumbled to the back wall, next to Becky, who barely seemed to notice he was there.

"Damn," Virginia heard Drake say as his head appeared, his face flushed, his eyes wide with strain. "This is a tight fit."

The top of his shoulders appeared and then—nothing. He lay there gasping. "I think…I think I'm stuck."

Virginia almost laughed. This chamber of horrors was just too much. Bones and bodies and dreadful spirits, and now a stuck companion. She turned to Becky, who seemed to finally be coming back to the present. Virginia handed over her pistol.

"Keep an eye on Meredith," she said. "Shoot him if he tries anything."

She reached down and tried to find a way to pull Drake through, but she could barely get her slender fingers around his shoulders. Finally, she got them under his armpits and began to pull.

Becky cried out behind her, and Virginia lost her grip at the same moment. She fell backward, landing on her rear. She cried out from the pain, momentarily blinded, stars flashing through her vision. Then she saw Meredith standing over her, pistol in hand.

Virginia got to her feet, gauging the distance between them. Meredith backed up a step. "I won't mind shooting you, Miss Reed," he said.

Virginia calmed herself, deciding she would have to wait for her moment.

Meredith waved his gun toward the back wall, and Virginia followed his instructions, moving to Becky's side.

"Damn you, Meredith," Drake snarled. "You're finished."

Meredith took two quick steps and slammed his boot against the side of Drake's head. The thud seemed to send shock waves all the way across the chamber, and there was a sharp crack. Drake's head lolled unnaturally to one side and stayed there, unmoving.

"Like a cork in a whiskey bottle," Meredith said cheerfully. "That ought to keep the others out long enough."

Long enough for what? Virginia wondered, then saw Meredith's leer.

"Which of you should I kill first?" Meredith said. "Two beautiful women who have been nothing but a pox on my life. I'll be glad to be done with you." He grabbed Becky, who cried out.

Virginia didn't say anything, amazed that the man couldn't sense the growing hatred in the chamber. The ancient spirits were rising out of the bones, coming through the walls, filling every inch with their red and blinding hatred.

The spirits swirled around Meredith's head, but he didn't seem to notice them. Faster and faster they circled, and then, in a flash, they went into the man's eyes, his ears, his mouth, and then into the center of his belly.

Chapter Thirty-Five

<u>Lost Blue Bucket Mine, Oregon Territory, October 1851</u>

"Jonathan!" Meredith awoke to a harsh, shrewish voice he had once obeyed without question. He hadn't thought of her in years.

"Eliza?" he muttered. He felt the girl in his arms squirm a little. He held Becky tighter and jammed the muzzle of the gun to her head. *It is only an illusion,* he thought. *My wife isn't here.*

Eliza's harsh voice overrode his doubts. "What are you doing, Jonathan? Where is Sarah?"

At the sound of his daughter's name, all the anger and hate that had crusted over his memories began to crack. He'd held back these thoughts, these feelings for so long. He'd denied his old life, his old emotions. But Eliza would not allow him that any longer.

"Why did you kill me, Jonathan?" His first wife had been a harridan, a nag, a scold…and yet, she had always known how to get through to him with her sharp voice and her uncanny ability to see his vulnerabilities.

He felt a small stirring of guilt. It was just a small crack in the hardened shell of his defenses, but he sensed the reservoir of shame beneath, a wellspring he hadn't known existed. Not because of Eliza—she had deserved her fate—but because it reminded him of Sarah.

He could never think about Sarah for long before feeling himself soften and lose focus, so he never thought of her; he never spoke her name.

Until now.

"*You* killed Sarah," he said.

"No, Jonathan," Eliza said. "You killed her. It was you who harnessed the horses. It was you who neglected to fix the wheel. I tried to stop, but you had spooked the horses too much. It was you, Jonathan."

"No!" he cried. Without realizing it, he let go of Becky, who dropped to the ground. He didn't see her grab a femur from the pile of bones. He didn't noticed her raising it over her head.

His head exploded with pain at the same time that all the guilt and shame he'd hidden from himself and from the world broke through and filled his body like fire. He dropped to his knees.

He only vaguely noticed when Virginia Reed approached him. He felt his arms being wrenched behind his back and bound, but he didn't care. He only cared for the burning light before his eyes.

"You killed Sarah!" his wife wailed, and then the light exploded, and he was blinded.

Out of the darkness, flash of light rose up from the bones in the shape of his precious Sarah, floating in the middle of the chamber.

"Papa?" The small girl's voice circled the chamber as if it was seeking him. "Where's Mama?"

It isn't real, Jonathan thought. *It is just this place getting to me. Nothing more.*

"Where's Mama, Papa?"

"Shut up," he said aloud.

The Reed girl was looking at him peculiarly. "It isn't real," he said to her—and to himself. "She isn't here."

"It's all real," Virginia Reed said. "I hear her."

"Papa?" The small voice, which had once been so precious to him, began as a mere spark. But with every word, the blaze was growing.

"Sarah," he said. "Sleep in peace, daughter. None of this concerns you."

"Why did you hurt Mama?" the voice continued, soft and yet relentless.

"She was already dying," he said. That was what he'd always told himself, that smothering Eliza was a kindness, that she was so mangled and torn that she never would have survived, that the rage he had felt while holding his hands over his wife's nose and mouth was directed at God, not at her.

Sarah's little broken body had been lying by his side as he killed his wife. His daughter's eyes had been closed. She couldn't have seen what he had done. It was an illusion, created by the ghosts of this place. It was the danger playing tricks on his mind, or perhaps it was the bad air, and he was being smothered and his tormented body was contriving nightmares.

"Why didn't you save me, Papa?" Sarah's voice asked. "Why didn't we stay home? I liked it there."

"I wanted a better life for you, Sarah," he answered. He didn't care anymore that the two women in the chamber were staring at him. "What if something happened to me? I wanted us to be someplace where there were more people, where I could help you. We would have been dirt-poor back home, Sarah. I couldn't have taken care of you."

"Papa?" The little voice still seemed to be seeking him, as if she didn't recognize her own father. His heart shredded, the painful shards spreading through his body. He was not the Papa she had known, kind and attentive and loving. He'd turned away from all that in his anger, determined to take from this world what he wanted, if for no other reason than to keep others from being happy.

"Where are you, Papa? Why did you leave me?"

"I'm here, Sarah. I'm sorry. I didn't leave you!"

"Papa!" The small voice grew in volume, turning into the wail of a banshee. Jonathan cried out and fell to his knees.

***

"What's happening?" Becky whispered.

"The impossible," Virginia said. "It appears that Jonathan Meredith has a conscience after all."

"Sarah was his daughter," Becky said. "But she died on the trail, only a few weeks after leaving Independence. How could she be here?"

"I don't think it matters how or why," Virginia said. "The guilt is in his mind, and this chamber intensifies it."

Becky gulped. She was white and shaking, and without a doubt dealing with her own guilt and shame, just as Virginia's mind was filled with regret and pain over failing Jean Baptiste and Bayliss, just as George Donner now hovered before her, asking why she couldn't have been stronger, why she couldn't have saved them all. No matter that it was Donner who had led them to the slaughter—the guilt she felt was as deep as if she had been the one who had chosen the route, who had entrapped them in the snows.

Meredith was on his knees, gibbering. "Sarah…Sarah…" he repeated over and over again. He fell onto his side and curled up in a ball. "I never meant to hurt you. It wasn't my fault!"

Becky approached carefully and poked him in the side with her foot, as if not quite trusting her eyes. "I think maybe he loved her," she said.

"He loved himself," Virginia said. "His daughter was merely an extension of that."

Becky shook her head in wonderment. "No, you didn't know him. He was different before Sarah died. Not a good man, but…"

"Every evil man has his reasons for the evil he does. He may have loved Sarah, but that is no excuse."

Becky didn't try to defend Meredith further. In the ensuing silence, they heard distant voices. There was a small scraping sound, and they both turned to see Drake's lifeless body moving forward a few inches.

Becky took one of the dead man's arms and Virginia took the other, and between them, they pulled him all the way into the chamber. Angus scrambled through the hole moments later, gun in hand.

He took in the sight of the two women, and then his eyes darted about the chamber, not even seeing Meredith until he heard the man groan.

"Sarah!" Meredith cried out at the top of his voice. Then he curled up even tighter into a ball.

"Will wonders never cease," Angus said. "Who's Sarah?"

"Long story," Virginia said. Angus peered into her face, then decided to accept her explanation, or lack thereof. He leaned through the hole and shouted, "It's safe! Come on through!"

Jed scrambled in and went to Becky's side, taking her in his arms. She seemed to almost collapse at his comforting touch, and put her face against his chest and started crying. Virginia felt like crying too, and it was clear that everyone was feeling the same strong emotions.

"What is this place?" Jed asked.

"It is all our fears and all our shame and every little thing we ever did wrong," Virginia said. "We can deal with it later. Don't think about it now; we're all guilty of something."

"Some more than others," Angus said, looking down at Meredith in horror. "I have to say, I never thought I felt any guilt over the loss of my comrades in arms, but Sergeant Fitzgerald seems to be holding a grudge. Old Carr and young Stilton, whom I barely knew—they're coming at me. How do we get out of this place?"

They all turned to Becky, who pushed herself away from Jed, wiping her eyes. "I don't know. I don't think Allie and Cager and Edwin like this place much."

"Edwin?" Jed called out.

A light appeared at the far end of the chamber. It was flickering, barely there, but gave enough illumination for them to see a small hole in the rocks. Then the light blinked out.

"What do we do with this blighter?" Angus said, walking over to Meredith and toeing him in the stomach, though not as gently as Becky had. "We can't very well carry him out of here."

No one responded at first. All of them knew the answer, but none of them wanted to say it. Instead, they turned to Virginia.

"If the deed must be done," she said, "it must be one of you."

Again, there was silence.

"I say we just leave him here," Jed said. "Let him rot."

"With his hands tied?" Virginia asked. "Kinder to shoot him."

Becky looked down at the shivering man. It was as if Meredith was gone, replaced by this mound of empty flesh. "We will untie him, and we will leave him. If he dares to show his face, we make sure that he is arrested for his crimes. We have enough witnesses, enough evidence to make sure he never does any more harm."

"What if he escapes?" Jed demanded. "What if he goes back East and hurts other people?"

Becky held out the pistol. "You have my blessing to shoot him right here."

Jed glanced away, his countenance darkening, his hand twitching on the gun, and for a moment Virginia thought he'd take up the dare. Then he looked at the ground and sighed. "I can't just kill him, no matter what he did to Edwin."

Angus was standing to one side, a bemused look on his face. "I'll do it for you," he said. "I have a feeling he wouldn't think twice in the same circumstances."

Becky shook her head. "It must be one of us. But I think John Meredith is finished, one way or another. He'll be but a shadow…a ghost of himself."

If we are lucky, a ghost who haunts only himself, Virginia thought. Still, if he escaped and did further harm, it would be on their heads. "Let's go," she said. She motioned toward the exit, and Jed and Becky immediately made for it, wanting nothing more than to escape the bone chamber and its quandaries. Angus motioned for Virginia to go ahead of him, but she shook her head.

"You go on," she said.

He peered at her face as if trying to read her intentions. Then he nodded, squirmed into the narrow hole, and disappeared from view.

Virginia went back to Meredith, who was no longer moving or speaking at all. He was breathing heavily, but seemed unaware of his surroundings or of her.

Virginia pulled out her bowie knife and knelt beside him. She put the blade to Meredith's throat.

It might be a kindness, she thought. Then she heard her father's voice— not that of his ghost, for John Reed was still very much alive, but that of her hero, the man she most admired. "Never take a life unless you must," he'd said to her once, when she had shot a coyote on their property and then just left it on the ground.

"You must leave." Drake's clear voice filled the chamber. She gasped and turned to his body, but he was unmoving. Instead, there was a bright light hovering above the corpse. "Tell Mary…" his voice said. "Tell her I loved…"

And then the light shrank and blinked out.

"I'm sorry, Drake," Virginia said sadly.

She looked down at Meredith, all thoughts of vengeance vanishing. She lowered her knife and quickly cut his bonds away. "Don't ever show your face again," she whispered.

She sheathed her blade and turned away. She went to the hole and looked back. John Meredith moaned, "Sarah, please…"

Virginia began to leave, but at the last second, she turned back and addressed the ghosts of the First People.

"I promise you, no one will ever disturb you again," she said. "You may join your ancestors. You have the word of the Canowiki."

She didn't know if the word meant anything to them, but something must have gotten through. The dread she had felt since entering the bone chamber lifted from her, and for the first time in days, she felt hope as she climbed up toward the light far above.

***

The ghosts did not bother the rats. The creatures felt neither guilt nor shame. They were hungry, but the man quivering on the ground was still alive, even healthy, so it took some time before they approached him. One of them took a quick bite of an exposed finger, and when the prey didn't react, the others crawled over him, each looking for a soft place to begin feeding.

He cried out when they started tearing into him, but he didn't rise; he didn't swat them away. One rat crawled onto his face and began eating the soft lips even as they were moving, making the same motion over and over again, a sound the rat didn't understand.

"Sarah…"

***

Edwin floated, leading the living away from the bone chamber. He especially didn't like it there. The old ghosts were powerful, and when they noticed the ghosts of the children at all, it was to fill them with dread.

At first, he had drifted, aware that there were living people in the upper chambers but content to leave them alone. He didn't remember how he'd gotten here. Then he had woken in darkness to see Allie and Cager standing over him, looking as confused as he felt.

"Edwin?" Cager asked.

It was then that Edwin noticed that Cager's leg was healed. Edwin sat up and kept rising until he was floating above the floor. It scared him. "Where am I?"

"You are dead," Allie said. Her voice was flat, but it sent him flying about the cavern, looking for escape, looking for oblivion. Instead, he found his own broken body, blood welling from a hole in his back, and then he remembered: he'd followed his stepfather to this place, feeling proud that Jonathan was finally including him in his business.

"I found gold," Jonathan had said.

Edwin had thrilled to the idea. He would be so rich that he could find Becky Catledge and propose to her.

Instead, in the darkness, he'd stumbled across the bones of his friends. He had begun to turn to confront his stepfather when he felt something slam into his back, as if the walls of the cavern had fallen in on him.

He'd drifted alone after that. Allie and Cager were always together, speaking some strange language of their own making, but they were rarely conscious of their own existence. The ghosts of the First People slept, stirred only when the living arrived, and then they arose, little more than wisps of vengeance looking for those who still felt fear and pain and guilt.

Now, as he led his brother and Becky to the exit, Edwin floated above Becky, wishing he could touch her, hold her, speak to her. She could sense his thoughts, but she couldn't seem to hear his words. There was daylight above him, and before, he'd been repelled by the sight, as if the living world repulsed him. Now, it seemed to be drawing him.

He heard Allie and Cager behind him, talking in their secret language. And then they were at the threshold, and Edwin felt himself drawn forward as if by a strong, sucking wind. But he held back for one more moment.

He reached out with a ghostly hand and brushed Becky's face, and she put her hand to her cheek in wonder.

Goodbye, Becky. I always loved you.

He let go and felt the blue sky pull him upward, felt his soul melting into eternity, and he smiled.

Epilogue

"Hello, Bidwell," Virginia kept her voice soft. "We have unfinished business."

He turned around, and when he saw who it was, he gave her a slow grin. He started to take off his clothes, and she let him.

Virginia waited in the shadows of the rose bushes and watched Mary leave. Mary was allowed to meet the wives of other prominent men for a meeting of the Ladies Aid Society once a week. It was one of the few times her husband let her go out unaccompanied.

The butler, Mr. Lee, had retired for the day and was inside his cottage. Virginia wished she could confront him, for there was no doubt that he was completely aware of what was happening in the mansion.

She waited until Mary's carriage was out of sight, then slipped through the servant's entrance. It was unlocked. The maid, Jane, was reading on her bed, with the door to her room open. She looked up as Virginia passed and nodded.

Virginia made her way to the library in the dark and took a seat. Oliver Hoskins would come in for a nightcap soon after dinner. According to Jane, he usually drank two or three classes of sherry, sometimes more.

He walked in muttering to himself, lit the lamp, and turned around. When he saw Virginia, his hands went to his waist as if to reach for a weapon, but he was wearing his housecoat, and he was unarmed. For a moment, he seemed to expand, like a wild animal trying to make itself bigger and more intimidating. Then he relaxed and smiled.

"Miss Reed," he said. "You just missed Mary. She won't be back for a few hours."

"I'm not here to see Mary," Virginia said.

"I see," Hoskins said. His brows pinched together, perplexed. "In that case, will you join me for a drink?"

"I won't be staying that long, Mr. Hoskins."

He turned his back on her, as if to signal that he wasn't afraid of her in the slightest. He poured himself a full glass of sherry. Then he turned back around and took a sip. He raised his eyebrows as if signaling for her to continue.

"I thought you should know that there will be no more gold coming from Jonathan Meredith," Virginia said.

He shrugged. "I've met the man, but whatever makes you think we're business associates?"

"At first I thought it was mere coincidence that Mary ended up here. But the more I thought about it, the more mysterious it became. I believe that after you learned of the gold, you tracked down Mary Perkins. Perhaps you didn't intend to marry her at first, just to use her, but somewhere along the line, you realized that nothing short of being her husband would unlock the secret of the Lost Blue Bucket Mine."

"The lost what?"

Virginia ignored the question. "I wondered how Jonathan Meredith rose so far and so fast in Portland society. Gold itself will buy only so much. For him to have succeeded so fast in business, he must have had help. When I finally tracked down Meredith, I noticed that his supplies and equipment all came from your stores."

"Miss Reed, most of the miners in this area buy their supplies from me. That is hardly unusual."

"Perhaps," Virginia said. "But I thought your interest in me and Mary was most unusual. I believe you have known all along about the Lost Blue Bucket Mine, and that you provided the seed money for Meredith's enterprises."

Hoskins shrugged again and drained his sherry glass. He turned to pour himself another. "Even if that is true, there is nothing nefarious in it," he said.

"You had to have known what Meredith was doing to his miners," Virginia said. "All the missing men worked for you."

"How could you possibly know that?"

"I met them," Virginia said. "Or rather, I met their ghosts."

Hoskins laughed, but the ridicule was unconvincing. Until that moment, Virginia hadn't been sure just how much the man knew.

He is the mastermind of the whole plan, she thought.

"I must warn you," Virginia said. "The Lost Blue Bucket Mine is no longer accessible to you."

Hoskins drained his second glass of sherry and poured a third. He walked over toward Virginia, who tensed, all her Canowiki senses at full alert. He sat down in the chair across from her and leaned forward.

"To be honest, I don't know where the mine is," he said. "That was the one secret I could not pry from Meredith. I had him followed, of course, but he was very canny about covering his tracks. You're right that his workers came from my docks. They were supposed to report back to me, but none of them returned, as far as I know. So your precious mine is all yours."

"Not mine," Virginia said. "It belongs to the people who have lived there for thousands of years."

Hoskins snorted, as if to dismiss the entire idea.

"One final matter before I leave you," Virginia said. "Mary is my friend. If you do anything to try to make her reveal the location of the mine…I will make you pay."

"Does she know the location?" Hoskins asked, sitting back in his chair, giving Virginia a speculative look. Only then was she certain that he really didn't know.

"She does not," Virginia said. "It was the children who found the gold. They were the ones who suffered at Meredith's hands. You may think it is simply business, Mr. Hoskins, but their blood is on your hands as well."

"I had nothing to do with it," Hoskins said. "As far as the gold is concerned, I would like to have had more, of course, but…" he shrugged "…for me, the matter is finished."

Virginia rose from her chair, but Hoskins made no effort to join her. She went to the door, and then turned around.

"Mary is frightened of you, Mr. Hoskins. I don't know who or what you are, but I'm warning you now to treat her kindly. If I hear different, I will return and make you sorry you were ever born."

Hoskins didn't even acknowledge her.

Virginia left the library, letting the door slam behind her. A loud crash came from the library, and the hairs on the back of her neck rose. An inhuman howl came from behind the door, and then the mansion shook as if something huge and menacing had stomped down so hard that the entire structure shook.

Whatever was behind the closed doors to the library was no longer human, but something powerful and supernatural.

Go back and confront the beast now, she thought. *Mary will never be safe living under his roof.*

She heard a carriage pulling up in front of the mansion. Mary was returning home early. Virginia hurried down the narrow staircase to the servant's quarters. Jane was waiting by the back door, white faced.

"Keep an eye on Mary," Virginia said. "Let me know the moment that anything happens." She reached into her pocket and pulled out a large gold nugget.

"I will," Jane said. "You don't have to pay me, Miss Reed. I will do it without reward."

"I'd rather you have it," Virginia said, pressing the nugget into her hand. "Be careful, Jane. Whatever you do, don't let Mr. Hoskins or Mr. Lee know what you are doing. Promise?"

Jane stared down at the gold nugget as if mesmerized.

"Jane!" Virginia said sharply. "This is for the two of you if you should ever need to escape this place."

"Yes, Miss Reed, I'll be careful."

Virginia turned to go, still feeling reluctant. *It's a mistake to leave,* she thought. *But I can't just kill Mary's husband because I suspect him of being unnatural.*

She made her way down the long driveway to where Angus was waiting with the horses.

"Are we done, Miss Reed?" he asked, handing her the reins to the Appaloosa.

"For now, Angus," she said. She mounted the horse, and amazingly, her heart lifted. She was going home to dearest Frank at last. She could only hope that nothing would make her leave again.

She felt the Canowiki within her stir but then subside, apparently having decided to let her keep her illusions for now. The joy of going home crowded out all other thoughts and fears. For now, the darkness was lifted.

I'm coming home, Frank.

About the Author

Duncan McGeary is a native Oregonian, who has lived most of his life in Bend, Oregon, on the dry side of the Cascade Mountains. (His stories are often located in this western terrain.) After graduating for the University of Oregon (Go Ducks!) he returned to his hometown, having had his first three fantasy novels published in the early 1980's.

He bought a bookstore, Pegasus Books, in downtown Bend in 1984, got married to Linda, raised two sons, Todd and Toby, and spent the next 30 years trying to keep the store alive.

With the store thriving, he is now devoting his stored up creative energies writing again. Visit his website at www.duncanmcgeary.com.

www.ingramcontent.com/pod-product-compliance
Lightning Source LLC
Chambersburg PA
CBHW032004050726
47590CB00006B/2039